THE FORETELLING OF
GEORGIE SPIDER

THE FORETELLING OF
GEORGIE
SPIDER

AMBELIN
KWAYMULLINA

CANDLEWICK PRESS

Copyright © 2015 by Ambelin Kwaymullina

First U.S. edition 2017

Library of Congress Catalog Card Number pending
ISBN 978-0-7636-9210-0

17 18 19 20 21 22 BVG 10 9 8 7 6 5 4 3 2 1

Printed in Berryville, VA, U.S.A.

This book was typeset in Garamond.

Candlewick Press
99 Dover Street
Somerville, Massachusetts 02144

visit us at www.candlewick.com

For my mother
and the generations of Palyku women
who walked the hard roads
without losing themselves.

And for everyone who dreams
of a future for our species
that is better than our present.

THE END

ASHALA

I floated, adrift in my own consciousness. All alone in the peaceful dark.

Except I wasn't really alone and I wasn't in the dark. Or my body wasn't. I was lying in the tunnel system beneath the caves, and there were lights enough around me, even if I wasn't aware of them. There were people as well, plus all the other life in the Firstwood. Above the room I was in were the caverns where the spiders and moths and rock beetles lived, and outside of that was the forest itself. Towering tuart trees, and peppermints, and rivers and lakes and birds and wolves and . . . everything. Every*one*. Life went on, even after the whole world got turned upside down.

Life went on, even when not everybody lived.

I pushed the faces of the ones I'd lost out of my head. I couldn't focus on them now, not on the two who were gone, and not even on the one who I might still be able to save. I had to drift or this whole thing wasn't going to work. So I did the exercise I'd been taught. First I pictured how I looked right now. A brown-skinned girl, dressed in a khaki shirt and pants that hung loosely on my frame. It hadn't seemed to matter so much to eat regular meals lately, or to brush my hair, which was tangled around my head. There was a needle in one of my arms, attached to a tube that connected to a bag of clear fluid. And there were wires on my forehead, running to a machine that was even more of a mess than my hair. It was a muddled bunch of circuits and connections that looked like a piece of junk, but I'd been promised it would do what it was supposed to do.

I imagined myself rising above it all, releasing my hold on myself until I was drifting in blackness again. It was soothing, except it seemed like I'd been waiting for something to happen for a *really* long time — *No, don't get impatient*. I'd been warned this wasn't going to

2

be exactly like the other times I had shared someone else's memories.

With the help of my best friend, Ember, I'd lived through pieces of another person's life twice before. I'd once thought Em's power to alter or share experiences was her ability, just like Sleepwalking was mine, until I'd found out she was an Artificial Intelligence New Gaia Lifeform — an "aingl." Ember was one of eight synthetic beings created by the legendary scientist Alexander Hoffman, and she didn't use an ability to manipulate memories. She used miniature devices called "nanomites." It was nanomites that were flowing into me now, not that I could see them. They were way too small for that. But the liquid running into my arm through the needle was bursting with the critters. The mites, together with the machine, were going to splice someone else's experiences into my own. In my mind, I'd return to the start and relive every moment of the events that had led up to what people were calling "the Awakening." Only this time around I'd see things through two sets of eyes. My own and Georgie's.

It had begun to dawn on me soon after everything was over that there'd been things people hadn't told me. The more I'd thought about it, the more I realized that there'd been something big going on, something that had

Georgie at its center. Except she wouldn't talk about it. She couldn't seem to find the right words. But she'd said she was willing to share her memories, which was how I'd ended up here. I needed to understand, and not just for myself. Seeing the whole picture of the events of the past two months was the only hope I had left of figuring out how to reach the person I might still be able to save.

There was a flash of green light in the darkness. It was quickly followed by another, only of a different color—the reddy-orange of wolf fur. After that came more red lights, and then more green. *Memories.* I was sure of it. The green were Georgie's, and the red mine, and I knew I'd be seeing her experiences mixed in with my own at critical points. The lights circled above my head, arranging themselves into a pattern. *Green, red, red, green...* But I had no time to absorb more than that, because they all flashed at once. I blinked, momentarily blinded, and found I was floating up to where the lights were.

Panic shot through me. *I can't live through losing them again!* But I could, because I had to. I gritted my teeth and stretched my arms upward, reaching for the tale the memories told.

The story of how the Tribe changed the world, and what it cost us.

The story of how they died.

THE FORETELLING

GEORGIE
TWO MONTHS AGO

My name is Georgie Spider, and this is the real world.

This is the real world. I think. Unless . . . unless it isn't.

It wasn't working. Telling myself in my head that the world was real didn't anchor me in the here and now the way it did when Ash said "This is the real world" out loud. Maybe because she was always so sure, and I never was. *How does she know which world is real?* I'd have to ask her. Then I would know, too. Or had I already asked, and she'd said, "There's only one world, Georgie"? I wasn't certain if that conversation *had* happened or if it was something that *might* happen. Ash's answer made no sense anyway, because every moment was filled with millions of possible futures, and every future was a world of its own. Had I said any of that to Ash? I didn't know, and I might not have explained it right even if I did. It was hard to describe things that other people couldn't see, and Ash wasn't a Foreteller. It was only me who could look into the future.

I was staring at futures now, and they were telling me something. But I didn't know what, even though I'd filled up three other caves and a whole wall of this one with a map of things-that-might-be. I could never properly track futures, because possibilities were always changing and being changed by one another. But I tried my best. I used twigs or stones or other things I found in the forest to represent possibilities, and I tied them together with string or vines to show where each one connected with another, and . . . *The map isn't right.* It had been right a moment ago, but it wasn't anymore. There'd been a change. . . . *There.* I separated two pieces of vine that I'd twisted together last night. That future didn't link to that other one now. It went somewhere else instead. . . . *There.*

I wound the vine around a feather. A crow feather. *Ember Crow.* She spoke from behind me: "This is when."

"When what?"

Em didn't answer, so I turned around. She wasn't there. No one was there. I was getting lost in a potential future. I needed to move away from the map. So I did—no, I didn't—yes, I did. I went to where the cavern opened onto the treetops and the warm sun streamed in. Or to where the rain was falling, pattering down at an angle to splatter against the rocky floor. Except it wasn't raining—it *was* raining—it wasn't.

I was wandering through futures. I had to find a way to make the words "This is the real world" work without Ash here to say them. Someone had told me something I could try. Someone who smiled a lot. Who had that been? Daniel. He wasn't here, either.

Daniel had gone to Gull City with Ember. *He shouldn't be in the city!* Prime Talbot hated people with abilities, and there were enforcers everywhere, and—no, no, no, that wasn't right. Prime Talbot wasn't the boss of the Gull City government anymore. Prime Belle Willis was, and she wanted to get rid of the Citizenship Accords. Then anyone with an ability wouldn't be an Illegal, and anyone without one wouldn't be a Citizen, and anyone with a harmless ability wouldn't be an Exempt. We'd all just be people. I was confusing the Gull City that existed with the one that might exist, if Talbot was still the Prime. There were so many ways in which things *could* happen that it got hard to remember what *had* happened. The past looked just like the future, and the future looked just like the past, and I didn't know what was real. What had Daniel said I could try? The mirror!

I reached into my pants pocket to take out the little mirror Daniel had brought me from his last trip into the city. Then I held it up, tilting it until I saw green eyes and olive skin and black curls. *Me. That's me.* Daniel had said that if I saw my face and heard my voice it would help, because I'd know the world in which I did that was the here and now. Daniel was usually right. So I shouted, "This *is* the real world!"

It worked. The futures faded away. I was standing in a cave, and the sun *was* shining, and there were anxious chittering noises coming from above me. My spiders were worried. I looked up to where gray furry bodies swarmed over the ceiling. "It's all right," I told them. "I'm all right."

One of them leaped down to land on my hair. He was an older spider, big enough to cover the entire top of my head. I reached upward to stroke the fur that covered the armored shell of his body as I walked back to my map. I could look at it now without getting lost, but I still didn't understand it. I'd never made a map like this one before. Usually I followed small groups of possibilities, not every future I could See at once, because more possibilities meant more worlds for me to disappear into. I'd been hiding from Ash just how often I'd started drifting into futures. I'd been hiding it from Daniel as well, which was harder because he was around me more than she was. He was around me more than anybody. I'd asked him why once. He'd said that I'd know when I was ready to. So I must not be ready, because I still didn't know.

Daniel was why I'd started the map. Four months ago, he'd nearly died helping Ash to save Prime Willis from assassins sent by Ember's bad brother Terence, and I hadn't Foreseen it. I'd failed him and everyone else. Especially Ash and Em, because we'd started the Tribe together and we each had different ways that we were supposed to see. Ash felt every moment all the way down to her bones, so she looked into the now. Ember held whole libraries of history in her perfect memory, so she looked back. But me? I looked ahead.

I'd begun the map a couple of weeks after Daniel nearly died, and within a day I'd found the blizzard.

That was what I called it, even though I'd never seen snow. But Ember had told a story once about a blizzard. She'd described how everything got drowned in white, making it impossible to tell where you were or which direction you should go in. Whatever the map was showing me was like that. A storm was stretching out across futures to swallow everything in nothing, and it was growing larger, which meant it was getting nearer.

"What *are* you?" I asked. The blizzard didn't answer. But the spider on my head chirped. He was telling me his name. *Helper.* I'd never heard of a spider called that before. Spiders didn't have forever names like Ash's wolves did. They named themselves after whatever they happened to be doing, so most of the time they were called Weaver or Crawler.

Helper jumped from my hair onto the map. He scurried from one vine to another and chirped again. Then to another, and chirped for a third time.

He was trying to show me something, and the places he was going weren't where the blizzard was. Helper was going to what came before, the thing that caused the blizzard, only I didn't know what that was, either. But he must be helping me, otherwise he wouldn't be called Helper. I looked across futures, focusing on what made the blizzard instead of the blizzard itself. Whatever it was, it was something bad. Something scary and sad and. . . . *No.*

"Be something else!" I whispered. Be *anything* else. But futures didn't change just because I wanted them to.

I knew what would start the storm that would make the whole world lose its way.

Ashala Wolf was going to die.

THE RESCUE

ASHALA

I crouched down in the thick scrub, peering through the trees and out of the Firstwood. Ahead of me was a rolling landscape of yellowy grasses and rocky red hills, dotted with wildflowers of purple and blue and pink. The grasslands were especially pretty in spring, but I didn't have any time to admire them today. Not when a Tribe member had been stolen from me.

From here I could just make out a small figure tethered to the top of a hill. I was too far away for any details beyond that, but I didn't need to see a pair of almond-shaped eyes or pink ribbons wound into braids to know that the captive was Penelope. It wasn't going to be easy to get her back. Our enemies had to be hiding out there somewhere, and they'd strike the second I went for the hill. I wouldn't be hard to spot, either, because the mottled clothes the Tribe wore to blend in with the Firstwood didn't work nearly so well against the grasslands. It was going to be next to impossible to rescue her alone. So it was a good thing I wasn't.

I looked at the Tribe members who were crouched alongside me. The farthest away was freckled Coral, who was twitching in place and pressing her lips together as if she were trying to stop words from escaping. Chirpers always tended to be as fluttery and talkative as the birds they communicated with, and Coral was more restless than most. Then Rosa, my chubby, golden-skinned little Waterbaby. Serious and steady, and the youngest but strongest of the Waterbabies among us. Next to her was dark-eyed Micah, quick to smile and a quick thinker, too. I was confident he wouldn't freeze in a fight, and while there were Leafers with more raw power, Micah had by far the most control. And the final member of my team — a big black Labrador, nosing at my leg.

I petted Nicky's silky ears. "You stay here and help if I need it. Okay?"

He licked my hand. I was pretty sure he *did* understand, but that didn't mean he was going to obey me. He could be making secret plans of his own. *Or just thinking about chasing something.* It was hard to tell, because in some ways, Nicky was a dog the same as any other, and in other ways, he wasn't. Like Ember, Nicky was an artificial life-form, and he had a link to my mind that no one really understood.

I gave him one last pat and looked over at Coral. "Ready?"

"I'm ready, Ash, I'm ready, ready, ready!"

"Then do it."

Coral threw back her head to let out a high-pitched warbling sound. I shot to my feet and ran, bursting out of the trees.

Dozens of birds came with me. Hawks, mudlarks, crows, magpies, yellowcrests, and honeyeaters swooped and dived through sky and grass, hiding me in a storm of wings. For a few minutes it seemed to be enough to hold my enemies off. Then one of the yellowcrests let out a shrill cry of alarm. The other birds joined in and veered away, leaving me exposed.

I was running toward a wall of flames. One of Pen's captors was a Firestarter.

I swerved to the right, trying to dodge past the wall.

It swerved, too, hovering impossibly in the air as it shifted directly into my path. I went left—the wall went left. *This isn't working!*

A massive ball of water barreled over my head to slam into the fire.

I'd never seen Rosa shift so much water before. She must have been throwing everything she had into this fight. Water tried to drown fire, and fire fought back, blazing brighter and hotter. The water began to turn into steam, filling the air with vapor.

I sprinted onward to the hill, arms and legs pumping and grass whipping around me. As I got close, I could see that Pen was tied to a heavy rock. She was shouting something, but it took a few seconds for me to get near enough to hear what she was saying: "Runner!"

Runner? I glanced about frantically. Whe—

Someone slammed into my back, knocking me to the ground. I lurched up and staggered around to face my attacker. There was no one there, not any longer. Then I heard the swishing sound of someone racing through the grass.

The Runner crashed into my side, sending me stumbling before they sped away. I regained my balance and began to turn in an awkward circle, trying to find them—and heard a startled shout from somewhere to my right. A black-haired boy was struggling furiously against . . . grass. Dozens of writhing strands had risen up to snake around his body, trapping the Runner in a prison of vegetation. *Leafer to the rescue. Thank you, Micah.*

I resumed my journey, slower now that I'd been hurt, reaching the hill and beginning to climb. I'd only managed to get about halfway up when there was a thumping sound and the hillside shook, sending me skidding backward. Rocks and pebbles showered down on my bruised body as I dug in my fingers and toes, trying to stop myself from sliding farther. *Thump! Thump! Thump!* There had to be a Pounder smashing their fist against the base of the hill, only I couldn't see them from here. *They're on the other side.* And I couldn't save Pen until I'd dealt with them.

Before I could move, there was a beating of wings from above, and birds came swooping down. Someone yelled, and a second later I saw a girl tearing away across the grasslands, being pursued by a bunch of determined magpies.

I started to scramble up, only to find that Pen was scrambling *down.* "How'd you get free?"

"Some crows pecked off the ropes."

Well done, Coral. "Come on! We're not safe yet."

The two of us hurried down the hill together, slipping on loose rocks to descend ungracefully to the ground. The moment our feet hit the grasslands, a voice called out, "Ashala!"

I looked up to find a familiar black-haired, blue-eyed figure striding toward us. Connor. I ran over to him, stopping when we were about a pace apart, and smiled up into the sculpted features that I could have gazed at forever.

Then I drew back my fist and punched him in the gut.

He gasped and doubled over. I spun to make my escape, but he recovered fast. I'd barely taken a step when a muscular arm wrapped around my neck and another around my waist.

"Now!" he shouted.

A fireball blazed toward my chest. Pen ran up, shouting and beating her small fists against my captor as I struggled to get free. The arm around my neck tightened, and blind panic set in. I couldn't breathe. . . . *I couldn't breathe* . . . and I could feel the heat of those hungry flames. I was going to burn.

Somewhere on the grasslands, three short, sharp blasts rang out. The fireball winked out of existence.

The game was over.

THE TREES

ASHALA

I shrugged off my captor and walked away, trying to pace out my reaction. I was breathing too fast, and my arm was prickly and hot. I rubbed at it, running my hand over the faint ridges of the burn scars that covered all of my right arm and part of my shoulder. Four months ago, I'd had a fireball thrown at me by a Firestarter working for Ember's brother Terence. Not long before that, Terence himself had nearly strangled me to death. Now I was having difficulty convincing myself that I hadn't almost been hurt in the same ways again. I could just about feel his long fingers squeezing my throat and smell my own flesh burning. It was unnerving how vividly the body could remember pain.

"Are you okay, Ash? I can Mend you if you're hurt!"

"I'm fine, Pen," I replied. And I was. My bruises would heal on their own, and the fear would pass. I turned toward her with what I hoped was a reassuring smile. It felt wavery around the edges, but Pen beamed at me, so it must have been good enough. My gaze fell upon Connor, and I scowled. "Will you put your own face back on, please?"

His entire body rippled, transforming into someone else—broad shouldered, brown haired, and with the shadow of a beard on his face. Wearing a jacket that hadn't been there before, too. When Jules Impersonated somebody, he mirrored them right down to their clothes.

"How'd you know I wasn't him?" Jules demanded.

"I *always* know. I've told you a thousand times before, Connor and I are linked." There'd been a bond between Connor and me ever since Ember had helped us share each other's memories, and apparently it was enough that Jules could never trick either one of us by pretending to be the other. That didn't stop Jules from trying. He seemed to take it as some kind of personal slight on his ability that he couldn't fool us.

Pen looked up at him. "Jules? Do you want me to Mend you?"

"You're hurt?" I took an anxious step toward him. "I didn't hit you too hard, did I?"

Jules let out a shout of laughter. "No offense to your fists of steel there, darling, but I've been beaten up by people who really meant it. No, you didn't hit me too hard." He gazed down at his leg. "But I think that furry slug drew blood."

"Furry slug?" I cast a suspicious glance around. "Pen? Is Mr. Snuffles here?"

Penelope put her nose in the air and reached over to clasp hold of Jules so she could Mend him. I spotted movement in the grass and went over to find a pug. Mr. Snuffles looked up at me and sat, wagging his curly tail and puffing out his chest. He seemed very proud of himself. Biting Jules had obviously been the highlight of his day.

"Pen, I thought we agreed battle games were too dangerous for pugs."

"He wanted to help."

Yeah, that's what she'd said the last time. I shaded my eyes with my hand to survey the grasslands, checking on the rest of the participants in the game. Micah,

Coral, and Rosa were approaching us, together with Nicky, who was bounding along in front. I couldn't spot Connor, who'd been overseeing the whole thing, ready to use his air-controlling ability to intervene if the "battle" went too far. I couldn't find any of our opponents, either—we'd been fighting members of the Saur Tribe, the children who'd been adopted by the huge lizards that lived on the grasslands. Something had to be holding them up. *Eggs?* New baby saurs were coming into the world, and the Saur Tribe was obsessed with being present at every hatching—it was possible Connor was flying them to where the eggs were.

Pen finished her Mending. She released Jules and came over to pick up Mr. Snuffles, hugging him against her so his fat paws hung over her arms. "He was *so* brave, Ash. Aren't you going to thank him for defending you?"

Mender and dog stared at me with identical expectant expressions. I sighed and patted Mr. Snuffles's head.

"Oh, sure," Jules said. "Give the little chomper positive reinforcement for trying to chew my foot off." Then he nodded at something behind me and drawled, "You lost."

Three indignant voices spoke as one, "You cheated!"

I swung around to find that Micah, Rosa, and Coral

21

were there. And Nicky, who ran over to lick my hand before tearing off after a flock of butterflies.

Coral glared at Jules. "The game was supposed to be over when Pen was off the hill!"

Jules shrugged. "There're no rules in a proper fight, Feathers. No one else is gonna fight fair, and if any of you expect them to, you're all going to d—"

"You can't predict what's going to happen in a real fight," I interrupted hastily. "I didn't think Jules would be here, either, but that doesn't mean he was cheating. He was trying to teach you something." *We're all trying to teach you something.* It was time for the part that I hated, the part where I had to make them see this wasn't a game at all.

"Micah? If this had been a real fight, what would you have done differently?"

He frowned, considering the question seriously, which was how Micah considered every question. "I wasn't even watching when Jules grabbed you, because I thought the game was over. But I shouldn't have stopped paying attention, should I?"

"You got it, kid," Jules said. "You're always in a fight until you're sure there's no one left to fight. Better to be paranoid and safe than careless and . . . ah, not safe."

"Well, *I* wouldn't have done anything differently,"

Coral announced. "Me and my birds did great!"

That was the answer I'd expected from her. Coral was one of the Tribe members who was having trouble grasping exactly what it was we were facing.

"Coral, we could be fighting Illegals like us—" I stopped. Because the Illegals who worked for Terence, the ones Jules had named "minions," *weren't* like us. They had abilities and they were teenagers, but that was where the similarities ended. Terence had his minions so twisted up that they believed the only way for them to become part of the Balance—the inherent harmony between all life—was to do what Terence asked of them. It was all so pointless because it wasn't even true that having an ability made people unnatural. That was just something that some Citizens said.

I bent down so my face was on the same level as Coral's. "If it had been a bad Firestarter out there today, they wouldn't have just made fire float in the air. They would have burned the birds to get to me."

Her skin went white beneath her freckles. "They wouldn't. Not *birds.*"

"Yes, birds," Jules said impatiently. "Minions don't care about birds."

Coral looked like she might throw up. "Then . . . then . . . if minions come here, I'm going to tell the birds to fly away really fast and really far, so no one will ever catch them!"

That was a familiar reaction. Every animal-speaker said pretty much the same thing. Every Tribe member, if it came to that. We couldn't all speak the language of another species, but part of our connection with the forest was having a bond with the animals, and none of us could bear to think of them being hurt.

"Ash?" Rosa's face was creased with worry. "What should I have done differently?"

I straightened. "You did good to stop the fire. That's a huge danger for us, because everything around here would burn easily."

Jules shifted. He was bursting to speak, and I knew what he wanted to say. He would have had the same idea that occurred to me when I'd seen how good Rosa was at controlling water. It wasn't a nice idea, but I said it anyway. "You know the way you held the water around the fire? You could also hold it around someone's head."

Pen let out an outraged gasp. "Rosa could *drown* someone if she kept the water there for long enough. Killing is wrong!"

I sighed. "Yes. Killing is wrong. Except—um, I mean, that is—"

"Except," Jules interrupted, "if it's a choice between you dying and the person attacking you dying? You want it to be the other guy."

I nodded. Because that was what it came down to in the end. And the Tribe had to know it.

"The minions won't hesitate to kill us," I told them. "So if you're fighting for your life, or someone else's life, then you do whatever you have to. Doesn't mean you have to like it. Doesn't mean you won't feel bad about it afterward. But we fight back. We defend ourselves and one another and the Firstwood however we can and with whatever we've got. And if that means killing . . ." I took a breath, forcing out the words. "Then that means killing."

None of them spoke. I scanned their faces. They'd understood, and they'd had enough. The four of them were tired out from the fight and from this conversation. "Okay. Well done, all of you. Now get back to the Firstwood, and remember you're excused from your usual duties for today and tomorrow."

They turned toward the forest, walking with weary footsteps in the direction of the trees. I watched as they disappeared into the distance, growing smaller as they got farther away. *Small enough to fit in my hand.* For a second I had an insane desire to reach out, as if I could nestle them in my palm and protect them from every bad thing in the world.

From beside me, Jules spoke, "That dog's still not helping you, huh?"

He meant Nicky, and I shook my head. I'd been trying for months to get Nicky to switch on my ability, just like he'd done once before when I'd been in terrible danger, but so far I'd had no success. "Either he doesn't understand what he's supposed to do, or he understands too much. I think he knows I'm not actually in any danger in these games and I don't need to Sleepwalk."

"But you can't be sure what he knows. Which means chances are you won't be swooping in with your all-powerful ability to save us."

"It's not *quite* all-powerful." Although it was powerful enough. When I Sleepwalked I saw the world as a vivid dream that I could control, and whatever impossible thing I did in my dream happened in the world. Problem was, I generally had to be asleep to do it. "But no, I'm not sure what Nicky will do in a real fight."

Jules swiveled to face me, and I realized with a shock that he was angry. I hadn't heard it in his voice, but I could see it in his face now as he said, "Then you've got to stop telling those kids it's wrong to kill."

"I also tell them to kill if they have to, in case you haven't noticed."

"It's not enough! You know what you should be saying? That the only right thing is to live, and whatever they have to do to make that happen is right as well." His gaze turned inward, and he suddenly looked older, in a grim, worn-down kind of way. "Survival isn't about rules, wolfgirl. It's vicious and it's ugly, and if the Tribe can't learn to be like that, the minions are going to beat us."

I sighed. "No, Jules. Us becoming vicious and ugly is *how* the minions beat us."

"What?"

"The minions would throw animals into danger, and kill little kids, and use their abilities to torture people—nothing's off-limits! And, yeah, if we were prepared to do those things, maybe we'd beat them. Although I doubt it, because they'll always be better at it than us. But," I concluded, "even if we did win, it wouldn't matter. Because we wouldn't be Tribe anymore."

"You can't care about that!" he spluttered.

"I *have* to care about that."

"No, you really don't. And you know when we won't be Tribe anymore? When we're all dead. So if you want to survive this—if you want the Tribe to survive

27

this . . ." His mouth twisted into a hard, bitter curve. "Everyone had better be prepared to do whatever it takes, and become whoever they have to be."

He stalked away, leaving me staring glumly after him. *Should I follow?* But he was the one who'd walked off, and it didn't seem like he wanted to talk—or fight—anymore. I wished Em were here, because she'd know the right words to say to him. Although probably any words would be right, so long as they came from her.

There was a flash of movement in the distance. I shifted to see Connor emerging from around the side of one of the hills, along with a spiky-haired boy dressed in a yellowy color that blended in with the grass. It could be hard to tell one member of the Saur Tribe from another from far away, since they all wore yellow clothes and had hair as black as saur scales. But there was no mistaking the distinctive sense of barely contained energy this boy was radiating. *Jaz.*

I hurried to meet them.

"What kept you two?" I asked as I drew near.

"Coral's magpies got a little overenthusiastic," Connor answered. "Jasmine had some injuries—only minor, though. She's fine. The others took her back to the saurs."

"Why didn't you bring her to Pen?"

Jaz sniffed. "We're saur, Ash."

Which was his way of saying his Tribe was tougher than magpies, and injuries, and my Tribe, and pretty much everything else on the face of the earth. Jaz nodded after Jules's retreating figure. "You two have a fight?"

"No — well, yes — how'd you know that, anyway?"

He folded his arms, studying me out of tawny eyes that I still hadn't gotten used to. Four months ago, Jaz had absorbed the death inferno of another Firestarter, and while it didn't seem to have hurt him, his eyes had gone from black to a startling shade of gold. "Jules told you to stop saying killing is wrong, didn't he?"

"Yeah. Have you two been talking?"

"Sometimes. He belongs here, you know."

"Of course he belongs —"

"No," Jaz interrupted. "I mean he belongs *here*. On the grasslands."

Connor shook his head. "He's part of our Tribe, Jaz, not yours."

Jaz sniffed. "That's only 'cause he's with Ember. Jules is saur."

I didn't know what he meant, and it must have showed on my face, because Jaz added, "It's like this,

Ash. You killed someone once, and you had to do it, else that guard would have killed you instead. But it still bothered you."

That was putting it mildly. It had taken me a long time to come to terms with what I'd had to do to save myself. "Of course it bothered me. You can't take a life without . . ." My voice trailed off. Jaz was giving me a look that indicated I was missing something obvious.

"I killed that minion Firestarter before he could set fire to the grasslands," he said. "You know how many times I've thought about him since?" His gaze sharpened, becoming very saur. "Not once."

Oh. And I understood, or at least I did if I looked at it in the way a wolf would. My wolves were predators, just like the lizards, and that didn't mean they held life lightly. But they didn't regret the life that ended so that they might live. "I get it, Jaz. And I can see why you'd believe Jules was saur. But I don't think he is. Not in his heart."

Jaz opened his mouth to say something else, but no words came out. Instead his eyes went unfocused in a way that was immediately recognizable. Like all saurs, Jaz could talk with his mind. After a second, he said, "I've got to go, Ash. Eggs, you know."

"I know!" I darted forward to hug him, just as there was a trilling sound in the distance and a saur came skittering in our direction. *Hatches-with-Stars*. The smallest and fastest of the saurs, and the only one with blue scales instead of black. Jaz broke free of me and sprinted across to her, swinging onto her back, and the two of them raced away.

I let out a sigh as I watched him disappear into the grasses and the hills. "Do you think we're getting this right? What we're doing with the Tribe, I mean?"

"Yes," Connor answered. "Don't you?"

"Yes — no — I hope so! Jules certainly doesn't think so." And Jules knew the minions best, because he'd been Terence's unwilling spy for years before Ember had freed him from dependency on the toxin Terence used to control him. I stared after Jaz. "Maybe we should be more saur? Just a little bit?"

"We are not saur. We are trees."

That last word seemed to rustle like the wind through leaves, and I spun to look at Connor. He was staring at the Firstwood, and his eyes had gone very dark, the purple-blue of a forest lake. There was something between Connor and the forest that even I didn't understand. He was the only one in the Tribe who didn't have an animal, and it seemed to be because his bond was with the Firstwood itself. "We hold on to the earth," he said softly. "We reach to the sky. And we are . . . shelter."

Yes. That was right. We were right. I knew it, because I felt it. "Then we just have to make sure the Tribe understands."

Connor's gaze flicked back to me. He knew what I wasn't saying, and he didn't say it, either. The reason it was so important that the Tribe understood who they were was because they'd have to know it without us. Bad things were coming our way, and Connor and I would always be where the fighting was fiercest. We stood between the trees, and the Tribe, and danger.

We probably wouldn't make it to the end.

But there was no point in thinking about that. We knew it, we'd known it for a while, and we couldn't change it. Instead I reached out to clasp his hands in mine and said, "Feel what I feel."

Connor and I had been practicing sharing emotions for weeks, in case it was ever useful in a fight, and found it had an unexpected result. We could make everything else recede, creating a space that consisted only of each other. I sent everything I was feeling radiating out to him — the sunshine on my skin. The scent of the wildflowers in the air. And that I loved him and always would.

My feelings mingled with his and were returned to me magnified. The world and our worries loosed their hold until all that contained us was each other. I'd flown with Connor a hundred times. I felt like I was flying now.

I pressed my lips to his and soared.

THE CHOICES

GEORGIE

The wind was howling, and everything had turned to white. I was drowning, but not in water. Emptiness was stealing my breath.

Someone grabbed hold of my shoulders. "Georgie! *Georgie!*"

The world came into focus, and so did the person standing in front of me. A person with brown skin, green eyes, and sun-streaked dark hair that fell over his face. I reached up to brush it back.

"Your hands are like ice!" Daniel exclaimed. He

stripped off his jacket, draping it over my shoulders. "Why are you so cold?"

"Everything went away. It was cold."

From my map, Helper chittered crossly at me. He wasn't happy about me being lost twice in one day. If it had been one day. Had it been one day?

Daniel took hold of my arm, steering me over to the opening in the cave wall and letting me go once I was standing in the sunlight.

"Look at me, Georgie!"

I gazed doubtfully up at him. He seemed real. But everything always did. "Aren't you and Ember in Gull City?"

"I got home just now. Ember, too."

I glanced around the cave, looking for Em, and Daniel added, "She went to find Connor and Jules and Ash. This is real, I promise."

Yes, it was, because it wasn't cold here. We weren't in the world where Ash was dead. Not yet.

My name is Georgie Spider. This is the real world. Daniel is worried about me. I didn't want him to be worried. "We should go help Em find the others. They might still be on the grasslands." That was where they'd been this morning.

But Daniel shook his head. "She can find them on

her own. I want you to talk to me about that map. And don't try telling me again that it's just an ordinary map, except bigger. I know that isn't true."

"How do you know?"

He smiled at me. "Because I know you, Georgie." Then his smile went away. "Can you tell me what's going on?"

I wasn't sure if I could. I hadn't seen a future where I did, so I didn't know what happened if I told. I liked to know before I spoke. But I had to tell someone. This was too scary a thing to know all by myself.

"Ash is going to die."

He went still. Then he said, *"When?"*

"All the whens. Every future I can See, and that's not even the worst thing."

"What could be worse than Ash dying?"

"Everybody dying." But that wasn't right. "Or maybe they don't die, not on the outside. Something happens to them on the inside, though. If Ash dies, there's this storm, and it's going to cut people off from everything and everyone. That will make them cold, and they'll get colder and colder until they can't feel anything at all."

"That's why you were cold? You were looking at the storm?"

I nodded, and Daniel's gaze drifted over to the map. "Every future . . ." He frowned. "You've been following multiple futures at once. Georgie, that's dangerous for you!"

"I had to See."

"You have to stop."

I shook my head.

Daniel sighed. "Then don't work on the map alone."

"I have to do it alone. I'm the only Foreteller."

"I mean I'll stay with you. Make sure you don't get lost. Let me help, Georgie."

There was an excited chirping from the map and from the ceiling above me. The spiders thought two helpers were better than one, and they liked Daniel. I liked Daniel. He was the only person in the Tribe who always looked at me as if I made sense. But I didn't know if there was anything he could do now, because I didn't know if there was anything *I* could do. "I can't find a way to save her. I can't find a future where she lives."

"Then we'll have to make one."

He didn't understand. I couldn't do that. Sometimes I could do something or say something that pushed things in the direction of one future or another, but that was if the future was already there. It wasn't the same if the futures didn't exist to begin with. "We can't. *I* can't."

"I think you can." He sounded very sure of that, and Daniel was usually right. Maybe I could make a future? I wandered back to the map, but it looked the same as before. Ash ended and then everything else did.

"We could warn Ash," Daniel suggested. "Tell her to be more careful."

"No! We can't tell her anything about this."

"Why not?"

My gaze roamed over the vines strung across the wall, reading the connections. "Ash doesn't run from danger. She wouldn't behave any different if she knew."

"Not even when the world depends on her being alive?"

"I could tell her that, but she wouldn't really believe it, because she wouldn't believe she's that important. Besides, keeping her safe means other people being in danger. Ash wouldn't be able to stop herself from trying to protect the people who were trying to protect her."

Daniel nodded. "Okay. Well, what about if we keep her away from any danger without her knowing? Georgie, her death—is it something to do with Gull

City? Because big things are happening there. I promised Em I'd let her tell you about it, but if it would help you to know now . . ."

"It doesn't matter. I mean, it does matter, but it's just another future. The danger is *everywhere*. It's impossible to keep Ash away from it!"

Helper suddenly chittered and leaped across the map, scuttling into one of the gaps. He chittered again, but I didn't understand what he was trying to tell me.

"You're off the map!" I said. "There aren't any futures where you are."

"Maybe that's it," Daniel said. "If you can't find a future where she lives, maybe you need to look where the futures aren't."

Look at where the futures weren't? I'd never done that before. I moved closer to the cave wall, gazing into the spaces between the connections. I still couldn't See anything. But that wasn't the only way to know what was ahead. When Ash and I had first come to the forest, we'd been able to smell eucalyptus long before we'd been near enough to see the trees. I leaned into a gap in the map and closed my eyes, breathing in the space that was filled with what I couldn't See.

My eyes flew open. "Choices!" I spun around. "It's

39

choices, Daniel! *That's* what changes things."

He was smiling at me again. "Whose choices?"

That was a good question. It deserved a good answer. I turned back to my futures to find one.

There were no gaps in the map anymore. New possibilities were glimmering everywhere now that I understood how what-was-to-be could be changed. "I don't know yet. More than one person. More than two, even." I was going to need more vine. I opened my mouth to ask Daniel to get some. But I didn't say the words. The possibilities were telling me something else. "The others are having a meeting. In the Overhang."

"I know," Daniel replied. "It's about what's happening in the city. But we don't have to go if you need to be here."

I did need to be here. Only I needed to be there as well, and I could be here later, but I had to be there now. "I think we have to go."

Daniel held out his arm to me, and I clasped hold of it, and we walked out of the cave together. Helper chirped a happy good-bye at me as I left, and I chirped back at him, because I was happy, too. I was happy even though the new possibilities in my map were shining less brightly than any futures I'd ever Seen.

It meant they weren't very likely to happen. It meant
Ash was still probably going to die. But before I hadn't
Seen a way and now I did.

*My name is Georgie Spider and I am going to save
Ashala Wolf.*

THE NEWS

ASHALA

I leaned back, resting my weight on my palms and stretching out my legs. I was sitting atop a flat orangey-colored boulder, staring up at the underside of yet another boulder that arched overhead. Connor was lounging at my side, and I reached out to twine my fingers in his hair. He looked across and smiled the smile that made me forget to breathe.

Ember said, "Georgie's *always* late!"

I sucked in oxygen, letting my hand fall away from Connor and looking over to where Jules and Em were sitting on the other side of the rock. Em was drumming her fingers against the granite — whatever her news was must have been something big, because she was bursting to tell it. But there was no point in getting impatient; Georgie and Daniel would get here when they got here. Georgie had told me once that she didn't know why people always worried about being places "on time" when time itself was always moving. "I'm sure they'll be here soon."

Em scowled in the direction of the caves, as if Georgie and Daniel were going to sense they were being glared at and come running. Then Jules leaned over to murmur something in her ear, and she tossed back her red curls and laughed. Jules could always make her laugh, and he was obviously in a much better mood now that she was home. He didn't even seem to be mad at me anymore, although I knew that didn't mean he wasn't. He'd just set it aside for the moment. Jules was good at that. He didn't really hold on to anything. *Except for Em.*

There was a stirring in the trees, and I pointed. "Here they are now."

I gave Daniel a little wave, pleased to see him back in the Firstwood. Georgie was pleased, too; she was hanging on to his arm, chattering away and apparently totally present in the here and now. Maybe she'd finally given up on that enormous web I'd been trying to pry her away from. *Or maybe it's just Daniel.* There was a deep calm to Daniel that was endlessly reassuring; even in the worst of moments, nothing ever seemed quite so difficult or so desperate when he was around.

They settled onto the rock with the rest of us, and Ember said, "What I've got to tell everyone? It's about the Council of Primes meeting."

"Have they canceled it?" I asked hopefully. None of us were happy about the Primes of the seven cities gathering together in Gull City for their Council meeting. It was an obvious target for Terence, who'd attacked Prime Willis with minions once before in an effort to convince the world that Illegals were violent criminals.

Em shook her head. "It hasn't been canceled and we don't want it to be, because Belle Willis has gotten the other Primes to agree to vote on something significant at the Council. It's a bit complicated, but if they vote yes . . ." She looked around at everyone, focusing her mismatched eyes — one brown and one blue — on each of our faces. "They're going to start letting people out of detention."

Connor drew in a sharp breath. I sat up, not sure I'd heard Em right. "*Out* of detention? You mean, end the Citizenship Accords?"

She laughed. "I'm afraid the news isn't quite that good, Ash! They're voting on whether they should Reassess people already in detention, to see if any of them should get an Exemption."

I must have been missing something, because I didn't see why that was such a big deal. "But everyone who's in detention has the kind of ability that could be used to hurt someone. They're not eligible for an Exemption! How is Reassessing them going to change that?"

"They're going to be Assessed under different criteria. The government will take into account the way people have behaved while they've been detained."

I had no idea what that meant. But Connor did. "You mean whether the detainees have followed the rules?" he asked drily. "Did exactly what they were told, didn't talk back to the guards, that sort of thing?"

Ember nodded, and Jules let out a cynical bark of laughter. "That sounds about right. Citizens walk around free unless they do something bad. But Illegals? We get locked up until we prove we're good."

"That's terrible!" I spluttered. "They're treating Illegals like . . . like . . ."

Ember finished the sentence for me. "Like we're tiny children who have to show we've done our chores before we get a treat. *I* know. But this was the only way Willis could get the Primes to vote on change. And she's going to use it to do something for us." She beamed at me, her round face glowing in anticipation, and I realized that what she'd said so far wasn't the news she'd been waiting to share, or at least not all of it. "She's going to give the entire Tribe Exemptions."

I gaped at her. *Exemptions.* Not an end to the Citizenship Accords, but an end to them applying to us. It wasn't the same as Citizenship, because an Exemption could always be revoked. But it was more than I'd ever thought we'd have. A smile spread over my face, so big it hurt my cheeks to smile it. "That means . . . we could go into the towns and the city, and ride the Rail, and no one could arrest us!"

"And," Georgie said excitedly, "the best part is, Daniel could visit his grandma. And Keiko could visit her mom, and Micah his mom and dad, and Anika her uncle, and Lia her sister!"

She'd listed every Tribe member with a relative who'd helped them escape, and she was absolutely right. What was most important was that anyone with a family who cared about them would be able to visit without worrying about either getting detained themselves or having their family arrested for harboring an Illegal. "That *is* the best part, Georgie!"

"I wouldn't start celebrating yet," Jules said. "'Cause I can't see the other Primes voting yes on any of this."

Georgie's face fell. Daniel cast an annoyed glance at Jules and said, "Willis isn't going to tell them about giving Exemptions to the Tribe. She's just going to apply the new Exemption criteria to runaways as well as detainees. And as for the rest — Willis thinks there's a chance." Georgie brightened, and Daniel's attention shifted to me. "But, Ash, she wants you to come to the city. To meet with some of the Primes. Talk to them about abilities."

"*Me?* Why?"

"Because," Ember said, "you are a symbol. Of Illegals everywhere."

"But there're heaps of other runaways besides me! Not to mention everyone in detention."

"Perhaps, but yours is the name everyone knows. Ashala Wolf. Leader of the Tribe."

I shifted uncomfortably. I didn't like people knowing my name. It made me and the Tribe a target. "Of course I'll go if it'll help, but — we don't have those Exemptions yet, you know. No one had better try arresting us!"

"Willis said she'll make sure that doesn't happen."

Jules rolled his eyes. "Willis might not even be able to take care of herself. Terence isn't gonna like the Primes voting on letting people out of detention. If he wasn't planning something before, he'll be thinking about it now."

"It's just possible," Ember said thoughtfully, "that he might *not* try something. Terence has got to be responsible for the rumors that Prime Talbot will return to Gull City. If he's really planning a comeback, he won't want to risk getting caught targeting the other Primes. He'll need their support."

Terence had been the Prime of Gull City for years before he faked his own death, and the stories that he'd return to save the city from some kind of Illegal threat just wouldn't go away. "Yeah, but Em—Terence isn't exactly rational. He might not do the logical thing."

"There's also Neville Rose," Daniel said quietly. "We don't know what he's advising Terence to do."

"Something bad," I said. It would always be something bad. "But clever." Neville Rose was an evil man, but not a stupid or reckless one. On the contrary, there was something chillingly thoughtful about the way he inflicted pain. And the last time I'd seen him, he'd made a promise. *I'll be seeing you, Ashala Wolf.* . . . I shuddered and turned my thoughts away from him.

"The two of them might not even be working together anymore," Jules pointed out. "Terence never did get along with anyone who wasn't under his total control, and from what you've all said about Rose, he isn't a shut-up-and-take-orders kind of guy."

"He's not," Connor agreed. "But Terence must want—or need—Neville for something. He went to a great deal of trouble to rescue him."

No one said anything to that, but everyone looked grim. Neville had been rescued before he could be punished for crimes that included experimenting on detainees. I'd been his victim, too, although I'd put myself in Detention Center 3 on purpose to save the detainees there. That didn't mean being Neville's prisoner had been an easy thing to live through. The experience had cost me, and Neville's escape had almost cost us a lot more.

Georgie reached across to put her hand on Daniel's. She hadn't forgotten he'd almost died after Neville had stabbed him. None of us had. I lifted my chin. "You know what? It doesn't matter what Terence has planned, or Neville. The Tribe is never going to be safe as long as there're people out there who hate abilities, and laws that make it okay to hate. And this vote is bigger than the one change." I looked at Em. "Isn't it?"

"It has larger implications," she agreed. "As change gathers momentum, people will *stop* arguing over whether there should be alterations to the accords and *start* arguing about what exactly the changes should be or how fast they should happen. If we can get to that point, the end of the Citizenship Accords becomes . . . inevitable."

I was pleased with myself for spotting what the vote might really mean. It was Ember who had taught me to think like that, putting little pieces together into a bigger picture, but she was still way better at it than I was. She was better at it than anyone.

"Also," Georgie said, "it's the same whether you go or don't."

I tried to unravel what that meant. "Are you saying I won't make a difference?"

"No, Ash! You always make a difference. You *are* the difference."

I waited for her to explain more, but her gaze had drifted off across the forest. Georgie had moved on to something else inside her head, and I wasn't going to get any more out of her right now.

Daniel cleared his throat. "So who goes?"

That was an easy list to make. I counted off on my fingers. "Connor." If there was trouble, we'd need Connor's ability to fight, and he wasn't going to let me walk into this alone anyway. "Jules." There was absolutely no end to the ways being able to Impersonate someone in authority might be useful in the city. "Ember." She was the smartest, besides being our early-warning system for Terence. Em could sense when another member of her family was approaching. "And me."

"What about Pen?" Jules asked. "It wouldn't hurt to have a Mender around."

"We *will* have a Mender around," I answered. "Dr. Wentworth won't be far from Prime Willis." Rae Wentworth was the best Mender I'd ever seen, and she was Belle Willis's personal physician. "We don't need Pen, too."

"We should take Nicky," Connor said. "If there's even a chance he can activate your ability, we might need him."

I sucked in a breath, considering that. I didn't want Nicky anywhere near where other aingls might be, because Nicky had once been Ember's brother Dominic. In his first life he'd died centuries ago, torn apart by people who were scared of him for no better reason than that he was different. They'd used an ability to do it, too — that was the source of Terence's hatred of abilities. Ember had gotten hold of the few circuits that were left of Dominic about a year back and rebuilt him as Nicky. She said that this was a good second life for her gentle brother, who'd only ever wanted to love and be loved, but she wasn't sure how the rest of her family would react. Some of them might try to turn him back into the Dominic they remembered. But Em would warn us if one of her family was near — we'd have plenty of time to get Nicky away.

"Okay. Nicky as well." I looked over at Georgie and Daniel. "That'll leave you two in charge of the Tribe while we're gone. Are you okay with that?"

I expected either or both of them to say yes right away — Georgie because she never left the Firstwood anyway, and Daniel because he could always be relied on to do whatever was needed. Instead, Daniel looked to Georgie as if he was waiting for her to decide. But Georgie was still staring into the trees.

Daniel nudged her. She blinked, glancing around like she was surprised to find us all here. "Oh! Yes. We'll stay. Are you finished talking now?"

I bit back a smile. "Yeah, we're done."

"Good. I have to go map." She rose and took off into the forest, Daniel trailing after her. *She hasn't given up on the map, then.* But at least she had Daniel with her now, and she was obviously willing to let him stay with her when she mapped. She hadn't been very keen on me hanging around. Not that she'd come right out and told me to go, but she knew I was scared of spiders, and I wasn't convinced that one of them falling on my head had been an accident.

I stood, holding my hand out to Em. "Come on," I said as I pulled her up. "You have to tell the Tribe that they might be getting Exemptions."

"They'll be all over the forest at this time of day, Ash! I can tell them tonight, when they're all together for dinner."

"Why should we wait? We can find them. We'll start at the food garden. Some of the Leafers at least will be there."

Jules leaned back against the rock with an exaggerated yawn. "You two do that. I don't feel like wandering around the forest."

"Besides," Connor added, "someone needs to update Jaz on everything that's happening. We'll go tell him."

Em frowned. "Can't you just mindspeak Jaz?"

I gave her a friendly shove toward the edge of the rock. "He's out of range. Too far into the grasslands. Eggs, you know!"

My gaze met Jules's as Ember climbed down into the forest. He knew why I wanted to take Em to the Tribe, and I didn't even need to look at Connor to know he did as well. Jules understood Ember. Connor understood me. And they were giving this day to the both of us.

"How do you think I should tell them?" Ember asked as we made our way through the towering tuarts. "I mean, should I explain about Reassessments first, or should I *start* with the Exemptions and then explain, or—"

"Whichever way you pick is fine, Em," I answered. She went quiet, rehearsing words in her head, and we walked on in silence.

Em had been right when she said the Tribe would be all over the forest. That was the whole point. She was going to get to tell this news many times over, which meant she'd have lots of happy moments, all wrapped up in the one day. Ember needed happiness to counterbalance the weight of the sadness she carried inside her. *And the guilt.* She'd never forgiven herself for inventing the Citizenship Accords. She'd done it after Dominic had died, when the aingls had been crazy with grief and terrified that people with abilities were coming for them. Now it made her sad, and Ember could be sad in a way that was deep and bleak and endless. But Ember, with her perfect recall, would forever keep every moment of this day. And if I didn't make it through this, she'd hold on to it for both of us.

I trailed my hand along the trees and tried to record the world the way she did, drinking in every detail. The roughness of the bark beneath my fingers. The lemony scent of the tuarts in bloom.

And two friends, walking in the sunshine of a spring afternoon.

THE LAKE

ASHALA

The sun was sparkling across the surface of the lake in places and casting sharp shadows in others, making it a jagged patchwork of light and shade. I'd been coming here every afternoon for the past few days because I'd be leaving for the city in about a week, and before I went I wanted to see my grandpa. Except so far he wasn't coming out.

My many-times great-grandfather was an ancient earth spirit, a giant Serpent who lived in the water. He'd made my people back in the old world when "race" had meant something. Then, after the old world had ended in the Reckoning, he'd made the trees and all the other life around here.

I strode to the water's edge. "Grandpa?"

No answer. But everything surrounding me was just a little too quiet. That was good, because the spookier this place felt, the more likely it was that Grandpa was around. He wasn't always, because he went traveling sometimes. I wasn't even sure how a giant Serpent managed to get around without causing a panic, but ancient spirits probably had their own ways of doing things.

I walked into the shallows. It was cold, so I stopped, hoping I wouldn't need to go any farther. "Grandpa? Are you here? Come out!"

Still nothing. I heaved a sigh and went striding toward the depths — and stumbled when the pressure of the water on my legs vanished.

The lake was gone. My pants were wet up to my knees, but there was no other sign that there'd ever been water here. For a second I stared stupidly down at the dry earth. Then I looked up and around, my breath coming quick and fast. *Everything* was gone. No trees. No animals. No anything. Just a bleak landscape of dirt and sky, both so gray they seemed to blur into each other.

I rubbed at my eyes. *I'm hallucinating, I'm Sleepwalking, I'm . . . something!* I tried to imagine the Firstwood coming back, re-creating every detail of the forest in my mind. If I *was* somehow Sleepwalking and this was a dream, I should have been able to control what happened. But the trees didn't return. I was alone. My breath came faster still. *Don't panic. Try to think logically about this.* But there *was* no logic to this! Then I heard a sound coming from somewhere in the distance. A keening noise that went up and down, like a song.

Grandpa sometimes sang.

I turned in the direction of the noise to see a far-off rise in the earth. Grandpa could be behind it. Cupping my hands to my mouth, I shouted, "Grandpa!"

No answer, but the singing continued. He might not have heard me. Either that or it wasn't Grandpa. *Probably best not to call out again until I'm sure.* I started to run, pelting along through the eerie, empty landscape. I ran for what seemed like hours, the song getting louder as I approached the rise. Only it wasn't really a song. It seemed more like . . . some kind of call? Perhaps the creature behind the rise was shouting out for its family the same way I had been for Grandpa. Or perhaps it *was* Grandpa, calling out for me. Whatever the sound was, it was beautiful, because it was the only proof I had that I wasn't the only living thing in the world.

Then it stopped, and I was surrounded by silence.

For a second, I stopped, too. Then I charged forward, faster than before, terrified that whoever had been singing was gone. I reached the rise and scrambled frantically upward to peer over the top.

Grandpa was on the other side, his big shining blue body piled into a heap of coils and his head tipped up to the sky. I sagged in relief. Everything was going to be all right. Grandpa would get me home. He was facing away from me, and I opened my mouth to let him know I was here. But before I could get a word out, the air was filled with a high-pitched warble, only it wasn't coming from Grandpa. It wasn't coming from any direction in particular as far as I could tell. It was just everywhere. Then there was another sound, only this time more of a low rumble. And a third sound, and a fourth, and dozens more after that, until the whole world was filled with voices. Somehow they all blended together, becoming a melody that swelled into something vast and powerful that sent tears leaking from my eyes and laughter bubbling up in my throat. It was wonderful. Terrible. *Painful.* I curled up on the sand, digging my fingers into my palms as I tried to cope with a song that seemed to be turning me inside out.

Finally the song ended. I uncurled cautiously. My entire body was tender. I sat up, wincing, and looked over the rise again.

Grandpa had twisted around and was looking back at me. **Hello, Granddaughter.**

"You knew I was here the whole time, didn't you?"

I know many things.

In other words, yes. I shifted so that I was perched on the top of the rise, staring down at him. "What is this place? And what was that song?"

This place is the end of the world. And the beginning.

"How can it be the end *and* the beginning?"

This is the time between the world that was and the one that will be.

"The world that was? You mean the old world?" I gazed around at the dead landscape. "Have I traveled back in time? Or is this some kind of dream?"

Yes.

Grandpa did like being tricky. I tried another question. "And the song? What was that about?"

You.

"*Me?*"

And others like you.

"You mean people with abilities?" I stared at him

in disbelief. I knew my grandpa could do amazing things—I mean, he'd once brought Connor back from the dead—but this was the first I'd heard of this. "Grandpa, you're not saying . . . you *can't* have created abilities?"

I am not saying that I can't have created abilities.

The colors in his eyes were whirling. He thought he was hilarious. "You know what I mean!" I shook my head. "Me, the Tribe—abilities everywhere—all because of you?"

It was not only me.

"Those other voices? Were they other ancient spirits?" I looked around, like they'd suddenly appear, which for all I knew they could. "Why can't I see them?"

They are not here. The whirling stopped. **I called and they answered from elsewhere. Elsewhen.**

That would have totally confused me once. But I'd spent some time with two different ancient spirits now—Grandpa and the cat spirit named Starbeauty who lived in Spinifex City—and I'd gotten much better at understanding them. Time didn't seem to work the same for spirits as it did for us. Or maybe time worked the same for everyone, and spirits understood it better.

"They were singing from a different time."

Yes.

He sounded terribly sad.

"Some of those spirits don't exist anymore, do they?"

Grandpa didn't reply, but he went slithering around the rise, coiling until his huge head was resting at my side. I reached out to put my hand on his scales. "I'm really sorry."

It did not turn out as we had meant.

"Because they died?"

All things die, and all things live. It did not turn out as we had meant because you were supposed to provide the things that were needed for humans to be. Water. Food. Warmth.

"I don't see how . . ." But I did see. Waterbabies could make water out of nothing, Leafers could make anything grow, and Firestarters created fire. And abilities had only started appearing toward the end of the Reckoning, at a time when being able to make fire or water or food could have made all the difference. "We were supposed to make sure that humanity survived?"

Without cost. He let out a breath in a sigh that sent wind rushing across the gray landscape. **Humans did not see the connections between themselves**

and the earth in the world that was. There was a cost.

And I got it. "You were trying to make humans the resources instead of the earth! So we wouldn't use everything up. That was clever, Grandpa." Except that it hadn't turned out as he had meant. Because thanks to Alexander Hoffman's solar generators and recycling technology, humans hadn't needed abilities to survive. Then someone with an ability had killed one of the aingls, and the Citizenship Accords had been created, and it had all gone wrong.

"They're talking about making more Exemptions," I told him. I was never sure how much he knew about what was happening in the world. "The Tribe might even get some. Maybe things could be as they were meant to be after all."

No.

My heart leaped into my throat. "The Tribe won't get their Exemptions?"

He tilted his head to one side. **The world will not become as it was meant to be unless you become as you were meant to be.**

"I don't know what that is!"

He twisted until I was staring right into his swirling eyes. **Do you dream because you are a Sleepwalker,**

Granddaughter? Or are you a Sleepwalker because you dream? And will you dream of what was meant?

That made even less sense than what he'd said before. I was still trying to figure it out when a voice behind me shouted, "Ash!"

I spun. But there was nobody there, just the endless grayness, so I turned back to Grandpa.

He was gone.

"Grandpa? Grandpa! Where are you? Don't you dare leave me here!"

Someone put a hand on my arm from behind. I swiveled, flinging it off — and found myself staring into a familiar pair of pale-green eyes. *"Georgie?"*

She let her hand fall. "Hey, Ash."

I looked around. There was no grayness anymore. I was standing in the lake, surrounded by tuarts. Everything was back, or I was.

"Georgie, I didn't just . . . appear out of nowhere, did I?"

"No. Can you do that?"

"No, I don't think I can." I'd never left the Firstwood. It had all been inside my mind. I shook my head wonderingly. "I was here, and not."

Georgie took hold of my arm again and said very seriously, "Ash. This is the real world."

For a second I stared at her. Then I realized. *Here, and not.* Georgie knew exactly what that was like, and which words I spoke to draw her home. I smothered a laugh. "Thanks, Georgie. I'm okay now."

I splashed out of the lake with her following. When I reached the shore I dropped to the ground, resting my arms across my knees and staring out at the water. Georgie sat at my side. I wasn't looking directly at her, but I could sense her looking at me, so I turned to face her.

"Did you want me for something?" I asked. "Is that why you came to find me?"

She shook her head. "I came because when you're standing in the water, this is where I am."

That was Georgie-logic, and I accepted it. She kept staring at me, an anxious expression in her eyes. "Were you in a future, Ash?"

"No. Yes." Wow, I was sounding exactly like Georgie herself. "I was in the past, I think. Or I was seeing something that happened in the past. But if things had gone how they were supposed to, the future would've been different." And I could see that future, too, at least inside my own head. A world where abilities were respected instead of feared, one where all the people and all the earth really *did* exist in harmony. A true

65

Balance. I did dream of what was meant. I always had.

"Ash? Are you okay?"

I wiped at my eyes and nodded. "Yeah."

"Are you sure?"

"I'm fine, Georgie. I just saw something that upset me. In the future. Or the past. Or wherever."

She put her arm around my shoulders. "Do you know how the world turns, Ash?"

"On its axis," I replied promptly. Ember had taught me that.

Georgie shook her head. "No. It turns on choices."

Choices. Like Grandpa and the ancient spirits choosing to make abilities. Or the aingls making the Citizenship Accords and the whole world choosing to keep them going. Or the way each of us made real the possibility of who we were. *Do you dream because you are a Sleepwalker . . . or are you a Sleepwalker because you dream? . . .* Something about that struck me as hopeful, because if bad choices and bad ideas could make the world, then good ones could, too.

"I guess the world kind of does turn on choices, Georgie!"

She hugged me and stood up. "Are you going to be okay here on your own? Because I have to go now. But I can stay if you need me."

I shook my head. "I'm fine. Unless you're heading back to that map. Because if you are, then I *desperately* need you, and you can stay here and get some fresh air and sunlight."

She grinned. "I'm going to meet Daniel."

"Go on, then, Georgie."

She went skipping away into the forest, leaving me to stare out at the water and think about what was meant to be.

THE FIRST

GEORGIE

I wandered between the trees and over the earth and in the dappled light that came shining through the leaves. Today was a good day. I had helped Ash. I had told her what was real. But even better was that I had finally found the first person whose choices mattered. I'd sent Daniel to get Jules before I'd gone to see Ash, and now Jules would be waiting for me.

There was a sound ahead, like rushing water, only it was rushing air. I stopped moving and waited for Daniel to materialize in front of me. He was so fast that no one could see him when he Ran.

When he appeared, I asked, "Couldn't you find Jules?"

"He's in the caves. I've told him you want to talk to him about a future. But Georgie, are you sure we should tell him everything?"

I felt sick to my stomach. Daniel never asked if I was sure. "I don't think I'm wrong. . . ."

He shook his head. "No—sorry. *Sorry.* I didn't mean that you were wrong. It's just that Jules has made no secret of the fact that he doesn't like the way we do things here, and he's with the Tribe because he's with Ember. Not because he follows Ash."

The queasiness vanished. It wasn't me Daniel doubted. "You don't trust him."

"I *want* to trust him. He's Tribe. But I don't know about him yet." His mouth flattened out, the way it did when he was thinking about something that upset him. "And it's not as if we haven't been wrong about someone before."

He meant Briony, who'd betrayed the Tribe to Neville Rose and died trying to escape him when he'd betrayed her in turn. "You're worried because I didn't See what Bry was going to do."

"I'm worried because none of us did, and somebody

should have realized how untrustworthy she was. *I should have seen it.*"

He thought that because he was a hawk. Daniel's eyesight was as sharp as that of the birds he was bonded with. He noticed tiny details about people.

"I don't think Jules is like Briony," I said. "But I didn't think *Bry* was like Bry, either. Until she was."

"Me, too. Which is what makes me wonder whether we need to tell Jules everything. Because if he can't be trusted, it'd be better that he knew less about us instead of more."

I hadn't thought about not telling Jules everything before. Now I wasn't sure what to do. I stared into futures, trying to find an answer. It was more difficult to do when I couldn't turn them into a map, so I closed my eyes, shutting out the forest so that all I could See were the possibilities in my head. *What do I do?* The futures told me.

I opened my eyes again. "We have to tell him. If he's going to make the right choices, he needs to know everything we do. You see, it's—"

Daniel held up a hand. "You don't need to explain. If you say we tell him, then we do."

He thought I was right. He didn't doubt me. Now we

had to go tell Jules, and I wanted to be there and not here. "Let's Run, Daniel!"

I put my arms around his neck and he lifted me up. Then he Ran and everything turned into a blur. It looked this way for me but not for Daniel. Everything slowed down for him. He'd told me he thought he saw the world the way I did when he Ran, because everything moved so slowly he could see all the ways things might happen. I said maybe that meant I saw the world the way he did when he *didn't* Run, with everything blurred so you couldn't tell what was to come. Only I didn't understand how he could make any decisions when he didn't know what was coming. I didn't understand how anyone could.

When the world returned, we were in my cave. Jules was pressed against the far wall, staring across the room in wide-eyed terror at where Helper was crouched in the center of the map with his fur standing on end and his front legs raised.

"Helper!" I ran over to him. "Are you all right?"

"Is *he* all right?" Jules spluttered. "That thing could have killed me!"

Daniel frowned at him. "You touched the map, didn't you? Even though I told you not to."

71

"I was only looking! I mean, I might've shifted a bit of vine to get a better view. . . . How was I supposed to know it was his nest?"

I brushed down Helper's fur. "It's okay now," I said to him. "Jules won't do that again. You're a good boy for looking after the map."

Jules took a cautious step away from the wall. "What is it with everyone praising animals for attacking me?"

"He didn't attack you," I replied indignantly. "If he'd bitten you, you'd be dead. Even if he'd only spat a little bit of venom at you, your skin would be burned. Also it would have started to rot by now."

Jules swallowed. "Listen, why don't you tell me what this is all about? Because I've got things to do. Somewhere else. Far, *far* away from here."

"Something bad is going to happen," I said. "And I think you can help stop it."

"Oh, yeah? Stop what, exactly?"

"Ash is going to die."

Jules went pale. "That *is* bad. Ember would never get over it."

"Nor would Ash," Daniel pointed out.

Jules shrugged. "You've got your priorities; I've got mine. Anyway, I didn't even think wolfgirl could die!

Doesn't she have some kind of guardian Serpent that can bring people back from the dead?"

"You mean her grandpa?" I asked.

"If that's what she calls him."

"That's who he is."

He looked doubtful. Ash had said not everyone found it easy to understand about ancient earth spirits.

"The Serpent *and* Ash brought Connor back," I said. "She was Sleepwalking and he used her ability. I don't know if it could work that way for her."

Daniel added, "Georgie is seeing Ash die across different futures. So it doesn't seem as if the Serpent can—or will—intervene this time."

Jules rubbed at his jaw. "Okay. No help from the giant snake. What about if we keep her away from the ci—" He stopped talking, staring at me. "No. That's what you meant before, isn't it? Back when we were all sitting in the Overhang, and you said it didn't matter if she stays or goes?"

I nodded. "Keeping her here isn't the way to stop it. You're the one who can stop it. You're the first."

"The first what?"

"The first person whose choices will matter."

"What does that even mean?"

Perhaps I hadn't explained it right. I looked at Daniel.

"From what Georgie can tell," he said, "there are certain people whose choices will be critical to whether Ash lives or dies."

"And I'm the first, huh? Who are the others?"

"I don't know yet," I answered. "I only just found you."

"All right . . . then what do I choose?"

"I don't know that, either. I can't know that. There are too many possibilities and too many choices."

He threw up his hands. "Then what am I supposed to do? You do realize you've only got about a week before she leaves the Firstwood? It'd be good to have some kind of plan by then, don't you think?"

"It isn't so much about having a plan," Daniel said. "Not when there're so many possibilities in play. It's about making the right choices when the time comes to make them. And we might not be able to tell you what to choose, but I think I can tell you *how* to choose."

He sounded stern. I'd never heard Daniel sound like that before. I hadn't even known Daniel *could* sound like that. He never spoke that way to me.

"Knowing Ash is in danger will change how you act," Daniel continued. "So I think part of it is making the choices that you might not have made if you didn't know about the danger. And the rest? Be Tribe, Jules. Because we don't give in and we don't give up, especially when one of us is in trouble."

"You think I'll give up?"

Daniel gave him a hawk stare that said, *I notice everything about you.* "Why don't you tell me?"

Jules muttered under his breath. "Just because I don't worship at the feet of the great Ashala Wolf . . ." Then he waved at the map. "This danger you're seeing. Is it Ash who gets in trouble? Or is it flyboy?"

I didn't know who flyboy was. But Daniel said, "He means Connor."

Jules nodded. "I was with Connor in Spinifex City before he went to rescue Ash from Terence. If she was dead, he wasn't coming back. And it's the same for her, isn't it? Neither one of them outlives the other for long."

I swung around to stare at the possibilities spread out across the wall. "You're right. Connor dying or Ash dying—it's the same. They're so . . . um, so . . ."

"Tangled up together," Jules said. "Have you told them yet? About the danger?"

"We can't. If Ash knows, she dies trying to stop other people from helping her. And if Connor knows . . ."
I studied possibilities. "He gets himself killed trying

to stop people from protecting *him*. Or they each die trying to save the other." I sighed. "They're no good at saving their own lives. Because neither of them think they should have lived."

I turned back to Jules. He seemed confused. Something I'd said hadn't made sense. I went over the words in my head, trying to work out what it was that hadn't been clear.

Then Daniel said, "Before they came to the Firstwood, Ash lost her little sister and Connor lost his mother. Neither of them were there when it happened, and both think that if they had been they could've saved them. That they *should* have died saving them instead of being the ones who survived."

The confusion went away from Jules's face. He understood now. "Have you told anyone else about all this?"

"No," I said. "The more people who know, the more chance there is of Ash finding out, and if she finds out, she dies, because she won't let us protect her. Anyway, it's only the people whose choices matter who can stop this. So you can't tell anyone."

"Hey, I don't want to share," Jules replied. "I just want to make sure you're not telling Red."

"Because it would make her sad?"

76

"Because it would make her more than sad. Red thinks she broke the world and wolfgirl is going to fix it, and if you take the hope of that away . . . Red won't cope, especially if there's nothing she can do to help. And if she does come up in your web as someone whose choices matter, you come and find me first, understand? You come and get me before you tell her."

"I will. Promise."

He let out a breath. "Okay. Well, unless there's something else you can tell me, I better go start thinking about how I'm going to save the world."

"There's nothing else," I said. "I'll come find you if there is."

Jules walked out, but in a strange kind of way, looking at me instead of where he was going. Then I realized he was looking at Helper. Jules didn't take his eyes off the spider until he'd made it out of the cave, and his footsteps hurried away very quickly once he was outside.

Helper chirped a gleeful question at me.

"You didn't *exactly* drive him off," I told him. "But he was very afraid of you."

"Has anything changed?" Daniel asked. "Now that Jules knows?"

I wasn't sure. I stepped closer to my futures, moving

77

across the wall as I reached out to trail my hand along the connections. The futures were speaking. I could hear snatches of conversations, like voices from a faraway cave. Jules's voice: *I told her what she's signing up for. She still wants to come.* Then chatter too faint to make out, followed by the voice of a man I didn't know: *Must I save humanity again? It really is becoming rather tiresome.*

I stopped when I reached the edge of the wall and pulled my hand away. "There's a change." I frowned. That wasn't right. "There's the *possibility* of a change. I think we have to wait for things to . . . become."

I yawned, rubbing at my eyes. I'd been mapping and mapping, and I was tired. "I should look for the other people. Whose choices matter."

"You need to rest."

Helper chittered. He thought I needed rest as well, and it wasn't good to map when I was this worn out. It became too hard to See. I could make mistakes, and mistakes were bad. Mistakes might get Ash killed. "I suppose I could sleep for a little while."

I went to the bedroll I kept in the corner and lay down, cushioning my head on the pillow. Daniel sat beside me. My eyes were heavy, so I let them close. "You have to wake me up if Jules comes back," I said.

"In case he has any more questions. Or if Ash wants to know something."

"You don't need to worry about anyone or anything," Daniel said. "Go to sleep, Georgie."

So I did.

THE STATION

ASHALA

Gull City had changed.

I was trying not to stare as if I'd never seen the place before, because acting like a tourist wouldn't fit with the Gull City–blue shirt and pants I was wearing. I was supposed to look as though I lived here, and I had, once. But this just wasn't the city I'd grown up in. There were hardly any enforcers on the streets, and the ones that were around didn't seem to be conducting any spot Citizenship checks. There *had* been a lot of enforcers at the gates, but they'd been on the lookout for Terence and Neville—part of the security Willis had put in place at the entrances to the city. And almost every second person I saw was wearing a pin with a red question mark on it. "The Question" was a tool of the reform movement, and it was this: *Does a person with an ability belong to the Balance?* The more people who answered yes, the more difficult it was to justify how we were treated under the Citizenship Accords. Judging by all the pins, there seemed to be a *lot* of people answering yes. Change was in the air. I breathed it in and smiled.

Connor was walking at my side and Ember ahead, with Nicky beside her. The four of us were going to meet Jules, who should have been on the morning train. Like Em, he had a genuine Citizenship tattoo, so he could ride the Rail without worrying about random checks. That meant he could get here in about a day and not the ten days it had taken Connor, Nicky, and me to travel cross-country. We'd arrived an hour ago, to find that Jules hadn't traveled with Em as he'd been supposed to because he was sick. Jules suffered from bouts of extreme weakness, an aftereffect of the toxin Terence had once infected him with. If he wasn't on today's train it meant he was too weak to come and we'd have to do this without him.

We turned a corner onto the entrance to the station and merged with the crowds going inside. I hadn't been in this place since I was a kid, but it was about as big as I remembered. Trains rolled in and out of a huge white structure with a high roof that curved overhead. Some of the older parts of the city were constructed from salvaged old-world materials, but the station had been built after the recyclers were working properly. It was made of composite, white and shiny and embedded with sparkling flecks of color that were all that remained of whatever had been recycled to make it. *Old things make new things.* Old worlds made new ones. Today it didn't seem so impossible that this world could take what it had and make something else. Something better.

The three of us, and Nicky, made our way to the platform, positioning ourselves among everyone else who was waiting for the train. The big clock on the wall was telling me it was 10:50; we had ten minutes until it arrived. That seemed like a long time to be standing here with all these Citizens. Not to mention the enforcers — like the gates, this entrance was being watched. But no one was paying any attention to us, and there was no reason why they should. We were just three more people in blue with a dog, among all the others who'd brought the family canine to greet people getting off the train. Ember said Willis had offered us an enforcer escort, but Em wasn't comfortable with our movements being tracked and neither was I. Better to go as unnoticed as possible and look after ourselves rather than relying on the government to do it. And I definitely didn't want anyone finding out that we had our own base in the city, in the form of the storage unit owned by Daniel's grandma.

The minutes on the clock ticked slowly by until the train finally came rolling in, shuddering to a stop. I stood on tiptoes as the doors slid open and passengers began to pour out, searching for a familiar face. *If Jules is wearing his face.* Maybe I should wait for him to find us. Then the crowd parted, and there he was. I lifted my hand to wave — and froze.

Tripping along at Jules's side was a girl with pink ribbons in her hair.

"*Penelope?*" I gasped. "Em, what—"

"I didn't know anything about this!"

Pen let go of Jules and came running up. "Don't be mad, Ash, please? I wanted to come."

"I'm not mad at you," I told her, glaring at Jules over the top of her head.

He shrugged. "Told you I thought we could use a Mender."

83

"And I said it wasn't necessary! Or was this about you? Because if you were too sick to come without Penelope, you should have stayed home."

"I'm not sick, wolfgirl. Just needed an excuse to catch a different train, since I knew Red would never go for bringing Pen with us."

Ember drew in a shocked, hurt breath. "You lied to me?"

Pen opened her mouth to speak, obviously wanting to rush to Jules's defense. He frowned at her and shook his head. At least he had enough decency not to hide behind her, but as for the rest . . . I didn't know whether I was more angry *at* him or disappointed *in* him. *Or maybe I wouldn't be so angry if I wasn't so disappointed.*

This wasn't the place to talk about it. "Come on. We need to get out of here."

We started walking. After a moment, Jules said, "Something wrong, wolfgirl? 'Cause you keep looking around as if you're expecting to see someone looking back."

I was and I hadn't even realized it. "Don't like the crowds, is all."

"Is it, though?" He scratched at his jaw. "Why don't I mingle with the masses, see if anyone's got their eye on us?"

Connor frowned. "You think we're being watched?"

"I think Ash has good instincts. Can't hurt to make sure we're not being followed." He vanished into the throng of people, and Pen reached for my hand, clinging on tightly. Then she reached for Connor's as well.

"It'll be okay," I whispered as we started to move toward the exit.

She smiled up at me. "I know it will, Ash. Because I'm here."

She thought she was safe from anything as long as she was with us. I had to get her out of the station and away from so many Citizens. I quickened my pace, and Em hissed, "Don't walk fast. We need to give Jules a chance to figure out if anyone's watching."

I slowed down again, shooting a concerned glance at Em. Her voice had sounded empty. *I can't believe Jules did this to her.* I couldn't believe he'd done it to us. When we got out of here, I was going to—

A thunderous noise ripped through the station and shattered my thoughts into pieces. *BOOM!*

I was going . . . I was going to . . . Why was I lying on the ground? I'd been standing upright a second ago. Now I was facedown on the composite floor. My eyes stung, and I could taste the acrid tang of smoke. But I couldn't hear a thing, not over the ringing in my ears.

A small hand gripped my shoulder. Warmth seemed to flow into me, and the ringing noise started to fade. My eyes cleared, too, although the air itself was hazy. I could see . . . rubble. Blood. Bodies. *Explosion?*

The ringing went away completely. With it gone, I could hear sobbing. Shouting. Screaming. I lurched up, searching for the others. Pen was beside me, and Nicky next to her. Connor was standing protectively over us. Ember was at his side, twisting back and forth as she scanned the area. And Jules . . .

Jules wasn't here. "Where's Jules?"

"I don't know!" Em answered. "Ash, I can't see him!"

I started looking, forcing myself to stare into the nightmare around us, gazing at the faces of the dead. *Not Jules . . . not Jules . . .* I couldn't always tell, because sometimes there wasn't a whole body. Only pieces. I swallowed, willing myself not to throw up. Debris was scattered everywhere except where we were; we'd been lucky — oh. No, we hadn't. *Connor.* But Connor hadn't been with Jules to save him. Not only that, but we'd been moving away from the platform, and that had put us a good distance from the blast. If Jules had gone toward it, he would have been at the heart of the explosion.

If Jules had gone toward it, he was probably dead.

I cast a desperate glance toward the worst of the rubble and the smoke and the blood. There were some enforcers there already, trying to free people from the debris, and some Menders as well. More would come—more *were* coming, rushing in through the entrance—but there was no way they were getting everyone out in time.

I pointed to the rubble and spoke to Connor. "Jules could be in there. And there were kids and dogs on the platform—if you were careful, no one would even know you were using an ability."

Penelope snapped, "No!" I blinked down at her, and she glared up at both of us. "You can't go into danger. You both have to stay safe. Jules would want you to stay safe!"

There was a hysterical edge to her voice. Pen was frightened and she thought we could protect her. I opened my mouth to say something soothing. Before I could get a word out, a shout cut through the chaos. "Ashala Wolf!"

I spun in the direction of the sound. A lanky enforcer was pointing right at me. Lanky—and young. *Minion.*

"That's the leader of the Tribe!" he yelled. "She's responsible for this!"

People were turning our way. Enforcers and Menders and ordinary Citizens, their faces twisted with suspicion and fear. The enforcers began to stalk toward us, hands falling to the swords at their hips. *Rhondarite* swords, and contact with the stuff blocked abilities. My thoughts raced in panicked circles as I tried to decide what to do. We couldn't let the enforcers get near us. But if we used an ability to protect ourselves, we'd be terrifying everyone here, and no one would ever believe that we hadn't caused the explosion.

Then a husky, powerful voice rolled through the station, "Leave her alone!"

My jaw dropped. I *knew* that voice. A stout blond woman came striding through the haze to march up to my side. Prime Belle Willis put her hand on my shoulder. "Ashala Wolf is *not* responsible for this." She jabbed a finger at the minion. "That boy is the one who caused the explosion. He is an impostor who works for former Prime Talbot. Arrest him at once!"

The enforcers shifted toward the minion. Willis leaned in to whisper, "Get ready to bolt. Because I really don't know how long anyone's gonna buy this."

Not Willis. *Jules.*

Ember sucked in a sharp breath. "You're alive."

Jules, who was usually so good at staying in character, threw her an entirely un-Willis-like crooked grin. "I'm hard to kill. And believe me, many have tried."

The enforcers began to advance on the minion, who took a step back. He was in the same situation we'd been in a moment ago. He didn't want to use an ability, not when he was trying to throw all suspicion onto us. But he didn't want to get caught, either.

The minion ran, pelting out of the station and into the city. Enforcers tore after him, and Jules said, "Now's our chance! Let's go."

"You go," Connor told him. "I'm staying. I'll meet you at the unit."

"What do you mean, you're staying?" Jules hissed.

Connor shrugged. "Kids and dogs."

Jules was obviously confused, so I added, "The Tribe doesn't leave children or animals in trouble." To Connor, I said, "Stay safe."

"You, too."

He swiveled to stride toward the wreckage. Jules looked between Connor and me and made a growling sound that was strange to hear coming from Willis's mouth. "I'll go with flyboy. You all get out of here."

He hurried after Connor, and the rest of us began to make our way to the exit. Ember walked on one side of me, Pen on the other, and Nicky trotted ahead. *If he could activate my ability I could save everyone.* Well, a lot of people, at least. Only he didn't seem interested. *Maybe I'm not in enough danger today.* The last time Nicky had made my ability work, I really had been about to die. Today Connor had saved me from the explosion, and he would've gotten me and the others away from the enforcers, too. *Either that or getting my ability to work that first time was some kind of fluke.*

Pen pressed against me. "People are looking, Ash."

She was right. There were glances being directed at us. Too many glances.

Ember shook her head. "I don't want anyone following us. I'll make a distraction and you sneak off, okay? See you at the unit."

She walked away and I surveyed the station, planning how to get out. There was a train stopped nearby. *If we duck around it . . .* My gaze followed my escape route, only to meet that of a fair-haired boy in the distance. An injured boy, holding a hand to his head. He mouthed something at me. Asking for help? Then he did it again. But this time he clapped his hands together, and I understood the word he was mouthing, a second too late: *Boom.*

BOOM!

• • •

Blackness.

More blackness. Which was strange because I was awake. I should have been able to see something. Maybe I wasn't awake? But I was almost sure I was, and I was almost sure I hadn't been before. Perhaps there was something wrong with my eyes. Also my arms and my legs, because I couldn't move them. No, that was because things were pressing on me. Hard, sharp—metallite? The train. I was beneath the train. It didn't seem to hurt that much. Vaguely I realized that might not be a good sign. *Connor will get me out.* Only maybe I'd been here for a while, and Connor hadn't gotten me out. *How big was the explosion? Could he be dead?* I'd know if he was dead. He was probably just being careful. There were probably layers of wreckage, and he was moving them one at a time, or something—or he was hurt, too—*I've got to get out of here!*

I pushed my legs against the wreckage. That *did* hurt, sending agony shooting through my body. I lay still, gasping, waiting for the pain to ease.

Someone said, "Don't move, Ash."

"Pen? Where are you?"

"Here." There was faint pressure on my hand. *Oh.* She was holding my hand. For some reason I hadn't noticed that before.

"Pen? Are you okay?"

"I'm fine. Menders are hard to hurt."

They were, too, in the same way that Firestarters didn't burn and Waterbabies couldn't drown. A Mender could absorb a lot of damage before it seriously harmed them, depending on the strength of their ability. *And Pen is strong.* Not as strong as Dr. Wentworth, who'd once survived having her skull caved in with a rock, but still . . .

"Ash?"

"Yeah?"

"How do you feel?"

"Fine." Better than fine. Warm, pleasant energy was running through my body. Pen was Mending me. "You should look after yourself, Pen! Hey, where's Nicky? If he can activate my ability we can Sleepwalk out of here!"

"I don't know where he is."

He'd been right at my side, and he was almost indestructible. I hoped he wasn't trapped. Or hurt. Like Ember, Nicky experienced pain the same as organic beings; he just healed quicker. But even if he had been hurt, he was probably better by now, and he didn't need to be close to me to make my ability work. The last time he'd done it, he'd been on the grasslands and I'd been in the detention center. I tried calling out in my head, *Nicky? I need to Sleepwalk!*

There was no response, which wasn't surprising, since I felt exhausted. My ability required energy. Lots of energy. It simply wouldn't work when I was too tired. Why was I so tired? I hadn't been before.

"Ash? Talk to me. I don't want you to pass out again. Tell me about when I came to the Firstwood."

"You already know about that. You were there."

"Tell me anyway. Please, Ash."

Pen was scared. I should keep her distracted until Connor came to save us. . . . If Connor came to save us . . . *Connor is coming to save us.*

"I remember you were a scrap of a kid. All skin and bone because you hadn't eaten in days. Mr. Snuffles had more weight on him than you did, because you'd been giving most of what food you'd been able to find to him."

"He was only a puppy. He needed food."

"That's what you said then. You said—" I broke off as I caught a movement out of the corner of my eye, a quick flash of reddy-brown fur and yellow eyes. *Pack Leader?*

"Ash?"

I blinked. Nothing was moving now. "Sorry, Pen. I thought I saw a wolf. Crazy, right?" I sniffed. "Hey, do you smell that?"

"Smell what?"

"Eucalyptus."

Pen was quiet for a moment. "No, Ash. I don't smell that."

"You must, it's so strong—hey, there's a light! Can you see the light? Connor must be here!"

There was an even longer silence. Then Pen said, in a voice that sounded strange, "No, I can't see the light. Ash, you have to keep talking to me, okay? You can't stop, not for a second." Her grip on my hand tightened, and even more warmth flooded through my system. Pen spoke again. "You asked me why I'd run away, remember? Because Menders hardly ever run, seeing as they get Exemptions. What did I say?"

"It was because of Mr. Snuffles. It was all because of Mr. Snuffles."

"What about him? Tell me!"

"You healed him. He'd been in a fight with another dog, and you healed him. And they would've given you an Exemption, but they wouldn't have let you keep Mr. Snuffles. Because Menders are only allowed to Mend if they already have an Exemption. You didn't. They would've rehoused Mr. Snuffles with another family. Stupid laws! So you ran away."

"Yes, I did. Can you still see that light?"

"Um — no. Sorry, Pen. It's gone. Maybe it'll come back."

"I think it might be good that it's gone, Ash." She sounded exhausted, and heat was still flowing steadily through me.

"I think you should stop Mending now."

"I'm all right, Ash. Do you remember, when I came to the Firstwood, I was worried you wouldn't take Mr. Snuffles?"

"I remember, silly girl. You thought maybe the Tribe wasn't for dogs. As if we would've turned him away."

"You said he'd have a home forever. That we both would." She coughed. It had a wet sound to it that I didn't like.

"Pen, I think you need to Mend yourself." I tried to move my hand away from hers. I couldn't; my arm was trapped under wreckage and my hand was stuck. "I want you to let me go."

"You have to listen to me, Ash. You have to do something for me."

"Anything."

"You have to make a world where dogs don't get taken away from people who love them. I always think about all the kids who get taken to detention. Some of them must have dogs, and the government won't let them have them in detention. That's wrong, Ash."

"I know."

"And you have to look after Mr. Snuffles. He gets cold, you know. Sometimes he needs extra blankets."

Now I was seriously worried. "I won't need to look after him, because you will, and you'll help me make a good world for dogs, too. Let me go and Mend yourself! That's an order."

When she didn't answer I tried to pull my hand away again. I didn't have enough range of movement, and she just tightened her grip. I tried to persuade her instead. "Pen, I feel fine, and it's not like you'll need much Mending; you said yourself Menders are hard to hurt. . . ."

"We are. But that doesn't mean we can never be hurt." She coughed again, the wet sound more pronounced—and bubbling. *Blood.*

"Penelope Mudlark, let me go!"

"It won't do any good. I only had enough for one." Another cough, and she added, sounding surprised, "You know what, Ash? I *can* smell eucalyptus."

I couldn't anymore. "What do you mean, enough for one?"

"We're hurt, Ash. We're really, really hurt. And I couldn't save both of us."

96

I thrashed against the wreckage. It shifted, creaking and groaning as if it might be about to fall, and I went still. "Pen, you have to try to save yourself. You just have to hold on for a while. Once Connor gets us out there'll be other Menders and they'll be able to help you. Please, Pen, please try, please."

There was no answer. "Pen? *Pen!*"

Silence, and the hand on mine had grown limp. I twisted my fingers so I was clinging on to her, pinching at her skin, trying to make her respond.

I was still holding on and begging for her to speak when Connor pulled the train off us. I started screaming when he tried to make me let go. Then someone put a hand on my head.

Heat stormed through my body, and the world went black again.

THE RECOVERY

ASHALA

I was somewhere between being asleep and awake, and I didn't want to wake up all the way, even though there was a reason I should. But I couldn't remember what it was. That didn't mean it wasn't an important reason. It felt important. It *felt* like I needed to wake up. I tried to open my eyes and found that my eyelids were too heavy to move. I tried again, and this time my eyes blinked open onto light.

I was lying on my side in a bed, staring out through a window at leaves and sunshine. *Forest? Garden?* I didn't know, because I couldn't see enough of outside to be sure. Where was I?

"Ashala?"

Connor. I turned my head to find he was sitting beside the bed. His eyes were sunken and his marble features seemed brittle, as if he'd crumble to the touch.

I tried to get up. He leaned over to press me gently back down. "Lie still. You need to rest."

"What happened to you? Are you sick?"

He choked back a laugh that had a ragged edge to it. "Nothing happened to me, Ashala. Not compared with what happened to you."

"Then . . . what happened to me?"

"You don't remember?"

"We were going somewhere, weren't we? Is this where we were going?"

My gaze roamed around the room. I was in a sparkling composite space that held a bedside table, a bookcase scattered with books, and a set of drawers with a huge vase of colorful flowers on top. There was a big painting on the wall opposite me that showed a tall golden-haired man standing atop a mountain and staring off into the distance. *Alexander Hoffman.* I knew from Ember that he didn't really look like that; people had painted him how they'd imagined him to be.

I sniffed, noticing a strange scent in the air. *Honeysuckle.* Which wasn't strange at all; there was some honeysuckle in the vase. It felt wrong to me, though. Surely there'd been another scent around before, something sharper and more soothing.

"Ashala? What's the last thing you remember?"

Eucalyptus. "I was in the Firstwood! Where are we now?"

"The Prime's Residence."

"In *Gull City*?" I stared at him. "How did we get here so fast? Wasn't I just in the forest with Penel—"

Everything came flooding back.

I lurched upward with a gasp. "Pen! The train! She was trapped with me under the train!" I grabbed hold of Connor's shirt. "You have to get her out."

"I did get her out."

"Where is she?"

He didn't answer. But I knew by the sudden flare of pain in his eyes what his answer was going to be. So I said something first. "No."

"Ashala—"

"No! You got her out, you said you got her out. . . ."

"Not in time. She's gone, Ashala."

A part of my mind was still wailing, *No, no, no . . .* The other part remembered that Pen hadn't been the only person I cared about at the station. "What about the others? Ember? Nicky? Jules?"

"Everyone's okay."

He'd hesitated before he spoke. "Connor, if one of them is . . . is hurt, you have to tell me!" Except Ember and Nicky couldn't be hurt, at least not permanently; they both seemed so fragile to me at times that it was hard to remember that. "Jules?"

"He's fine, I promise. Nicky did himself some damage, but he's better now."

"What kind of damage?"

"Tore up his paws, first digging himself out and then trying to dig you out. If it wasn't for him, we wouldn't have even known where to look. There was wreckage everywhere."

"And you? You weren't hurt? Don't lie to me!"

He sighed. "I was knocked unconscious by the blast. Wentworth Mended me — I wasn't even out for very long!" His mouth twisted. "Only it was long enough. It's why I wasn't in time."

He thought he'd been the one who'd failed. He didn't realize it had been me. "*I'm* why you weren't in time. Pen only had enough power to Mend one of us, and she . . . she chose me." Tears began to leak out of my eyes, and more followed, until they were gushing

101

down my face in waves. I clung to Connor, howling my grief until finally I ran out of tears, if not out of sadness.

"I want to see Pen," I whispered.

"You can't."

"Don't you dare tell me I'm not strong enough!" I pulled away from him. "I want to see her, and I want to see her now."

"That's not why you can't see her. We buried her."

"Already?"

"It's been three days since the explosion."

"I've been unconscious for three *days*?"

The brittleness of his features grew more pronounced. "You were . . . crushed." The way he spoke that last word told me all I'd ever want to know about how I'd looked when he got me out from under the train. "It took Wentworth herself to save you. She'd come running to the station as soon as she heard about the first explosion."

The hand on my head and the heat storming through my body. That had been Dr. Wentworth. All the help Pen and I had needed had been there. They just hadn't been able to get to us. *If Connor hadn't been unconscious . . . or maybe if I hadn't sent him to help the others . . . If I hadn't been wounded so badly, or if Pen hadn't.*

If Nicky had been able to help me Sleepwalk. But I knew now why he hadn't. I'd been injured too badly to use my ability. *Maybe if we'd had that enforcer escort.* But no, that wouldn't have made a bit of difference, except to make us easier for the minions to spot in the crowd.

"I could take you to the cemetery," Connor offered. "To visit her."

"I wanted to see her face. The cemetery . . ." I shook my head. "She isn't there. Pen and I—when we were under the train, we could smell eucalyptus. First me, then her. I think I was dying, and she kept me alive, but after that she was dying. It's why she could smell the forest." If I'd had any tears left, I would have cried them. All that was in me now was an aching emptiness. "She was going home."

He pulled me to him, and I rested my head on his chest, closing my eyes to shut out the world. Nothing would make me feel better. But there was some comfort in the steady rise and fall of his breathing and the shelter of his arms. *I will stay like this. I will stay like this forever.*

Connor shifted. I made a protesting noise, and he said, "I have to get Wentworth. She wanted to check you over when you woke."

I spoke against his chest. "'M fine."

"One of the others can sit with you, if you like—Ember and Nicky are outside. Jules, too."

A flame of anger flickered, and then another, building to a steady fire. "I don't want to see Jules."

"I think you should."

"If it wasn't for him, Pen wouldn't have been here!"

"I know."

I straightened, eyeing him with a frown. "You don't seem very angry about it."

"I am. Or I was." His gaze slid away from mine, and he added in a low voice, "Jules shouldn't have brought Penelope here. And I'd trade my life for hers in a second if I could, or for any of the Tribe, you know that." He looked back at me. "But I cannot be angry with him, because I am glad you are alive."

And it was wrong to be glad when my life had come at the cost of one of the Tribe. I knew because I felt it, too. "I'm glad to *be* alive," I confessed. "Not that—if I could go back, if I could make her save herself instead of me, I would—"

"I know." The ghost of a smile pulled at his lips. "I had this moment, when we found out the Tribe might be getting Exemptions. For an instant, I thought that you and I might live through this after all, and I *wish* I'd never thought it! Because before that I'd accepted that we probably didn't have long, and now . . ." He leaned back, running a hand through his hair. "I have grown greedy and selfish. It doesn't seem like enough time."

"For me, either," I admitted. "And it isn't enough. Not for you or me. Not for Pen. Things shouldn't be like this. The world shouldn't be like this." *It's not what was meant.* We exchanged weary glances, acknowledging a hard truth neither of us could change. But at least it was a truth we knew together.

Connor rose to his feet and bent to press a kiss to the top of my head, holding on to me for a moment. Then he let me go and said, "Talk to Jules, Ashala. Whatever he's done, he's Tribe and he needs you. Besides, there's another reason I'm having trouble being angry with him."

"What?"

"You'll know it when you see him."

I sighed. "Fine. Send him in."

He went out, and I heard the murmur of voices. After a few minutes Jules came in, along with Nicky, who took a flying leap to land on the bed. He flattened himself down, tail wagging furiously. I patted his head, and he licked my hand before flopping at my feet, heaving a contented sigh to be back in his usual spot. In the Firstwood, he liked to lie on the end of my bedroll. I knew he'd sleep for hours now.

Jules closed the door and walked farther into the room. I understood immediately what Connor had meant about having another reason not to be mad. Jules was a wreck. His eyes were bloodshot and he'd lost a noticeable amount of weight. I'd wanted to yell at him. Now I didn't have the heart.

Instead I said, "You should never have brought Penelope to the city. And I think you know that."

He shrugged. "She chose to come."

"It wasn't her choice to make! And it wasn't yours, either."

His eyes suddenly blazed. "It *was* my choice. It was my choice, and I made it, and the consequences of it — that's on me. I did this and I know it. She died because of me."

"No, Jules, she died because a minion blew up a train. And because she was brave, and special, and . . ." My throat was closing over.

Jules shoved his hands in his pockets and stared at the floor. "Are you going to throw me out?"

"You just got here."

His gaze flicked back to me. "Not out of the room, wolfgirl. Out of the Tribe."

106

"What? No!"

"Red wouldn't come with me if you did, you know. She won't leave you. Anyway, she's not even talking to me at the moment."

"This isn't about Ember. This is about you."

He eyed me warily, and I continued. "Jules, I've only been prepared to throw one person out of the Tribe, and that was Briony, who was feeding information to the government. She would have destroyed us. I think you were trying to help, in your way. But we have rules, and those rules are important. They're how we care for each other, and looking after each other is the heart of who we are."

"And if I don't follow the rules I'm out?"

He didn't get it. I wanted to tell him he was family, only I knew it wouldn't mean anything to him. He'd never had a family before us, so he didn't know what it was to belong. Then I realized he did. Because Jules was connected to the forest the same way the rest of the Tribe was—through an animal. Through a snowy lemon-crested cockatoo, to be exact.

I knew who Jules was. I just wasn't sure he did.

"You call me wolfgirl all the time. And I *am* a wolf. But you're a yellowcrest."

"So?"

"So when yellowcrests feed on the ground, one of them always stays in a tree to keep watch so it can warn the others if there's danger. Wolves are hunters. But yellowcrests — yellowcrests are guardians."

He was giving me a look that suggested he thought I'd gone crazy. "You can't possibly believe that means I'm some kind of guardian!"

"That's exactly what I believe. I think you've been trying to warn me that there's danger and we need to fly away. And you're worried I haven't listened, only I *have*. I understand exactly how much trouble we're in, except I can't fly away from myself. I have to do what I think is right for the Tribe. And I need to know I can rely on you."

He was quiet for a moment. Then he met my gaze squarely and said, "You can trust me to protect the heart of the Tribe."

He was telling the truth. In fact, I didn't think I'd ever seen him so sincere, at least not over something that wasn't to do with Ember. He'd understood. "Okay."

Jules leaned forward, resting his hands on the bed end. "How're you feeling, anyway? Well enough to travel?"

"I suppose, but we're not going anywhere yet. I've still got to meet the Primes."

He straightened, surprise flickering across his face. "Connor didn't tell you?"

"Tell me what?"

"Um. Maybe we should wait—"

"Tell me what, Jules?"

Jules sighed. "The Council meeting has been canceled. The three Primes who weren't here already turned back to their cities when they heard about the explosion. And the Primes who are here aren't planning to be for long."

"They're not going to vote on Exemptions?"

He laughed, but there was no humor in it. "No, darling, they're not voting on Exemptions. We'll be lucky if they don't make the Citizenship Accords worse. Illegals blew up a train, you know."

"Minions blew up a train!"

"Doesn't matter. All Illegals are the same to Citizens. Well, to most Citizens, anyway. They don't trust us, and they can't tell us apart. Even after what flyboy did."

I frowned, and Jules said, "He didn't tell you that, either, huh? After he got you out, he helped free everybody else who was trapped." He shook his head. "I don't know, maybe if he could've got to everybody in time—but people still died. Including some kids."

I rubbed at my arms, which were covered in goose

pimples even though the room was warm. I was cold from the inside out. "You're saying Illegals are being blamed for the explosions. All Illegals."

"Yep."

I sensed there was something he still wasn't saying, and it wasn't hard to guess what, not when a minion had pointed me out at the station. "The *Tribe* is being blamed?"

"There're rumors. Which is why we gotta get out of here just as soon as you can put one foot in front of the other. People are scared of us, and scared makes people vicious and stupid."

I couldn't believe how fast and how badly everything had gone wrong. We'd been set up, and it had worked spectacularly well. "They planned this. Terence. Neville. Both of them."

"Yeah. Which means they had to know we were coming to the city. Someone in the government's been leaking information. Willis says it could only have been one of eight people, 'cause that's how many knew you were meeting with the Primes. She's got them under house arrest until she figures out which one was responsible."

Too late. Willis was plugging leaks in a boat that had already sunk. The vote was canceled and the chance for change was gone. I put my head in my hands. Things were even worse than I'd thought. I didn't know how I was going to get Pen her world that was safe for kids and dogs now.

I heard the door open and looked up to find Dr. Wentworth had arrived. Her hair was longer than when I'd last seen her, falling to her shoulders in dark waves. Otherwise she was the same, tall and brown skinned and radiating concern. Connor came in behind her, and then Em, who looked about as worn out as Connor and a whole lot paler. I smiled at her and she smiled back, but it wasn't the smile that usually lit up her features. Or maybe it was, and there was just too much sadness in her face for one smile to take it away.

Wentworth strode over, reaching down to take my hand in hers. After a second she said, "You're doing much better, Ashala, although you do need more time to fully recover. I wouldn't advise traveling yet."

"I'm not going anywhere," I told her. "I want to see the Primes."

Connor and Ember exchanged uneasy glances.

"I know the Council meeting's canceled," I added impatiently. "I want to see them anyway."

Em glared at Jules. "You told her?"

"I didn't know that she didn't know!"

"She *just* woke up. If you'd thought for even a second, you would have realized it wasn't a good idea to hit her with everything at once!"

I blinked at the icy edge to her tone. I'd never heard her speak to Jules like that. Jules didn't say anything, but his mouth tightened in anger. No, not anger. *Pain.*

I was going to have to talk to Em before this tore them apart, but now wasn't the time. "Dr. Wentworth? Can you arrange a meeting?"

"Prime Willis can," she replied. "But Ashala—I'm not quite sure what you hope to achieve by it."

"I might not achieve anything," I admitted. "Only there're going to be people out there who'll want to make the Citizenship Accords tougher. That means it's going to matter what the Primes think of us, and Prime Willis thought I could make a difference to that before."

She sighed. "I'll do what I can. Right now you *must* sleep. This will take a while to organize anyway, and the Primes aren't leaving until the day after tomorrow." She strode to the door and held it open, gesturing to the others. "One of you can sit with her. The rest have to go."

It was obvious who stayed. There was only one person I hadn't seen alone yet. Jules and Connor knew

112

it, too. They followed Wentworth out and shut the door behind them.

Em hurried to my side, settling onto the chair. "You have to lie down, Ash. And close your eyes. Do you need another pillow or anything?"

"I've got enough pillows." I sank into the bed, bending my legs to avoid Nicky, who was starting to snore. But I didn't close my eyes yet.

"I forgave Jules, you know," I told her.

"You did? But he lied to you! He betrayed us. And Penelope—"

"I know," I interrupted. "He was wrong. He understands he was wrong." I reached for her hand. "He lied to you as well, and you can be as mad at him about that as you like. Except you have to be mad for you and not for me."

She didn't say anything; she just put her other hand over mine. Carefully, as though she was worried I'd break. Which was strange, because I was worried she would.

"You haven't sensed Terence, Em?"

She shook her head. "No. And I walked the boundaries of the city. If he was within a day of here, I would know."

"What do you think he's got planned next?"

"You're supposed to be sleeping."

"I will. In a moment." I yawned. "I just need to know. What do you think?"

"I think that maybe the kind of thing that happened at the station *is* what he's got planned next. Stupid, senseless violence, perpetrated by Illegals. A few more attacks like that, and people will look at us all as if we're killers." She bowed her head and whispered, "I'm sorry, Ash."

And there it was. I'd known she'd been blaming herself. It was the source of the sadness in her face, and why I'd pushed her to talk about Terence. "You're not your brother, and you're not responsible for the things he does. You have to know that, Em, because I need you to be strong. So you can help me. And Pen."

She looked up. "Pen?"

"I promised her something, right before . . . before the end. I promised her a better world. It was the only thing she wanted, and I can't do it by myself." My throat was closing over again, only not because of tears. It was fear that was choking me. I hadn't realized how scared I was of failing until I'd admitted out loud that this was one promise I might not be able to keep. "All this guilt over things that aren't your fault makes you weak, and you can't help me if you're weak."

114

Ember lifted her chin, and the sadness retreated. Banished to where it couldn't destroy her, for now. "You can rely on me."

"I know."

"And," she added, "it wasn't your fault, either. If I can't blame *my*self, then you don't get to blame yourself. Deal?"

That was the problem with best friends; they knew you as well as you knew them.

"Deal." Which was another promise I wasn't sure I could keep. I closed my eyes, because there was nothing more to say, and anyway it was too hard to keep them open any longer. But I kept hold of Em's hand and she kept hold of mine. As I dozed off, it occurred to me that we were both doing it for the same reason.

We each wanted the other to know that she wasn't alone.

THE SONG

GEORGIE

Penelope was dead.

She had died three days ago. That was when Mr. Snuffles had thrown back his head and howled and howled. He'd done it for hours, and when he couldn't howl anymore he'd whimpered. Then he'd lain on the ground and gone very quiet.

The whole Tribe knew that the only thing that would make Mr. Snuffles act like that was if something bad had happened to Pen. Everyone was worried. I didn't tell them not to be. I couldn't tell them that, because

I'd Seen a future change, and the change was so big I knew it was a death. But the only thing we could do for Penelope now was to take care of her dog. So that's what I told them to do, and that's what we did.

For three days the Tribe had taken turns sitting with Mr. Snuffles. We wrapped him in a blanket and brought him water. We couldn't hunt for him, because we didn't hunt the forest animals, but the other Tribe dogs shared their food with him.

On the first day he ate a little.

On the second he didn't eat anything at all.

The third day was today, and he'd stopped drinking. I didn't need a map to tell his future. Mr. Snuffles was going to die if I couldn't think of a way to save him. I'd thought all morning without finding an answer. Then I'd thought about what Ash would try if she were here. That was when I'd known what needed to be done. I'd picked up Mr. Snuffles and started walking. Daniel had walked, too, coming with us into the forest.

"I can take him for a while," Daniel said. "He must be getting heavy."

"He's not heavy." That was a lie. My arms were aching even though Mr. Snuffles was thinner than he'd been three days ago. But it was right that I should carry his weight.

We went on, past tree after tree until we came to the one I wanted. It was old and gnarled, and one of its roots arched over a hole that went down into the earth. This was where Ash's Pack lived.

"Hello?" I called. "Wolves? Are you there?"

For a while only silence came from the hole. Then there was a stirring and a scuffling, and a wolf crawled out. I usually wasn't any better at telling Ash's wolves apart than Ash was at telling my spiders apart, but I knew this one because he was much bigger than any of the others.

"Hello, Pack Leader," I said. The wolf flicked his ears in my direction, watching me out of yellow eyes. I wasn't sure if he understood me. I didn't speak wolf, only spider. But Ash had been able to talk to my spiders once, when I needed help. I was hoping I'd be able to do the same with her wolves.

I put Mr. Snuffles down in front of Pack Leader and stepped back.

"That's Mr. Snuffles," I said. "He's sad. He's so sad he's dying."

The wolf stared down at the pug. Mr. Snuffles just lay there, all floppy and miserable. Pack Leader looked back at me, tilting his head to one side.

"If you're asking what you can do, I don't know," I told him. "If you're asking why you should help, Mr. Snuffles is part of our pack, and Ash is part of *your* pack, so he belongs to you, too, in a way. Also, it's important to Ash that he lives. Because if she comes back and he's dead, she'll be the one who's sad. She'll be so sad that she'll never really get over it."

Pack Leader watched me for a second longer. Then he bent over Mr. Snuffles and made a soft whuffing sound. Mr. Snuffles looked up, and Pack Leader rested his long wolfy nose against Mr. Snuffles's flat puggy one. After a moment, Mr. Snuffles rolled to his feet. Pack Leader turned his head toward the den and yipped.

More wolves emerged, one after the other, until there were twelve of them altogether. They sniffed at Mr. Snuffles, who sniffed at them in return and made happy snorting noises. Then Pack Leader loped off into the trees. The wolves ran after him. So did Mr. Snuffles, and he had his curly tail wagging and his head in the air.

He was going to live. My legs went weak with relief, and I hung on to Daniel's arm to keep my balance. He put one of his hands over mine and said, "It wasn't your fault. Pen volunteered to go, and she knew it could be dangerous."

That didn't mean it wasn't my fault. Didn't Daniel see how one thing had created the next thing? I'd told Jules his choices mattered, and Jules had said he wanted to take Pen to the city. Then I'd looked in my map and discovered that Pen was the second person whose choices were important, so I'd talked to Pen, too. Now Pen was dead.

"If I hadn't Seen what I Saw, and told Jules, he wouldn't have led me to Pen. If I hadn't told Pen what I Saw, she wouldn't have gone to the city. If she hadn't gone to the city, she'd still be alive."

"None of that makes it your fault."

He still didn't understand. "Pen's choices didn't matter before I talked to Jules. But once he said he was taking her with him, they *did* matter. I am a person who changes things."

"We're all people who change things."

"I am the person who changes things and people die."

He shook his head. "You are the person who changes things and people live."

That was true also. "Sometimes I wish I wasn't the person who changed things at all."

"Don't say that!"

"Why not?"

He shifted until he was standing in front of me. "Because extraordinary people shouldn't wish to be ordinary."

I glanced up at him. "Maybe I'm not extraordinary."

"You are."

I'd never heard anyone sound more certain about anything. Not even Ash, when she said the world was real. It must be right. I didn't want it to be right. "I don't want to look anymore, Daniel! I don't want to See any more bad things and I don't want any more bad things to happen because of me."

"It isn't because of you." He reached out to push my curls back from my face, cupping my jaw in his hand. "None of this is because of you." Then his attention was caught by something behind me, and his gaze flicked upward. "Georgie," he whispered. "Look up."

I did. The trees were packed with mudlarks. I'd never seen so many together at once, and every one of them was fluffing out its black and white feathers and watching us out of beady black eyes. One began to sing. Another answered, and another, and another, until we were surrounded by warbling melodies.

Mudlarks were Penelope's animal, and I didn't speak mudlark any more than I spoke wolf. Only today I did. They were telling me that there was always danger. Storms came, and tree cats, and lizards to steal eggs. What mattered was that while you were here, you sang. Penelope's life had been a song, one that Mended lives. One that saved a life. But mudlarks always sang in duets. Someone had to answer her. *I* had to answer her. *Extraordinary people shouldn't wish to be ordinary.* They shouldn't wish for anyone else to be ordinary, either. Pen hadn't been, and I couldn't treat her as if she were ordinary now by making this about my choices when it had been about hers.

I sang out to the birds, "I understand."

The mudlarks let out a few last trilling notes and departed in a flurry of wings. They left behind silence and feathers that drifted downward to fall onto Daniel and me, clinging to our hair and clothes.

Daniel took an especially pretty feather out of the air and tucked it behind my ear. I found one for him and tucked it behind his.

We smiled at each other, and I said, "Extraordinary people need to map."

THE PRIMES

ASHALA

I was going to meet the Primes. At — of all things! — an afternoon tea.

I'd rested all yesterday and through the night, and now I was going to be a surprise guest. Belle Willis hadn't told the other Primes I was coming to their farewell get-together because she'd been worried some of them might refuse to turn up if she did. I only hoped they'd be willing to listen once I was in the room. But judging by the suspicious gazes directed at Connor, Ember, Jules, and me as we walked through the Residence, people really were afraid. Some of the enforcers lining the hallways had even put their hands on the weapons at their hips as we passed by, and not all of them were carrying rhondarite swords. A few had streakers, and a hit from an energy weapon could kill us quick. It was so unfair, especially when the presence of our escort must have made it obvious we were supposed to be here. Belle Willis's husband, Henry, was bouncing along ahead of us, a portly, dark-skinned man who radiated happiness and goodwill. I'd never met him before today, but he might just have been the most cheerful person on the entire planet. Not even the hostility coming from the enforcers diminished the optimism that clung to him like a fluffy cloud.

We rounded a corner, turning onto yet another hallway. It was quiet here. We'd given Nicky the job of looking after Wentworth because if there was any trouble, her life was more important than anyone's, since she was the one who could keep everyone alive. But there'd been no trouble so far, and it seemed like the biggest thing going on around here today was this afternoon tea. And we had to be getting near to it, because we'd been walking for ages. Ember must have been thinking that, too, because she leaned in to whisper, "Do you remember everything I told you? About the Primes?"

"Yes," I answered, and waited. She was going to ask if I was sure.

A few seconds of silence, then, "Are you sure?"

I whispered back. "Prime Peter Grant is the 'popularist,' and Prime Ian McAllister is the 'true believer.'" Or that was what Ember called them. Grant had only narrowly won the Mangrove City Prime election, and his opinions shifted depending on whatever he thought would help him get reelected. Prime McAllister only cared about the Balance, and while he'd once thought abilities were a threat to it, rumor had it that he wasn't so sure anymore. "And," I concluded, "Prime Isabella Lopez is — well, the boss of Spinifex City. Which means she's all about the taffa."

Taffa beans could be brewed into a tea that resulted in vivid dreams. Spinifex City people believed that those dreams were glimpses into the past or the future or worlds beyond this one. The entire city was so obsessed with taffa that nothing else really mattered there, including abilities. In fact, there were plenty of Illegals working for Ember's brother Leo, who ran the taffa trade. Whether Lopez supported me today or not wasn't going to have anything to do with Illegals being a threat or unnatural or anything like that. All she'd be concerned about was the potential impact of any upheaval in the world on taffa production.

Henry turned another corner. We followed, and found ourselves in a short hallway this time, one that led to a large door. A crowd of enforcers were standing in front of it; that had to be where the Primes were. Henry stopped a few meters away from them and swung around to face me. "You can go in, Ashala. Belle is expecting you." He cast a glance at the distinctly unfriendly-looking enforcers and stepped closer to add in a low voice, "Don't let anyone or anything shake your confidence. What you have to say is important." He beamed. "And I know you'll do wonderfully well!"

I wasn't so sure about that, but I smiled as much of a smile as I had in me—which wasn't much with the wound of Pen's death still so raw and aching. Then I looked from Connor to Em and finally to Jules. I didn't say anything and neither did they. None of us needed words to know that, whatever happened, we were in this together and always would be. Even Jules, my yellowcrest, who wanted us all to fly away home.

Henry gestured to the enforcers, and one of them leaned across to open the door. The rest shuffled aside to allow me to pass. I drew in a steadying breath and strode into a large bright space. We were on the second story, high enough so that the big windows in the wall opposite gave a view across rolling gardens to the cliff edge and the sea. The Primes were sitting in the center of the room, gathered around a low table that sat on top of a checkered blue-and-white rug. Three of them were staring at me in surprise, and since they were each dressed in the color of their cities, it was easy to identify who was who. The thin blond man in Mangrove City brown had to be Prime Grant. The giant with the bristling black beard in Fern City green was Prime McAllister. That left Prime Lopez, round and golden skinned and reclining in a pool of Spinifex City–yellow robes and long dark hair.

Willis patted the empty chair beside hers. "Ashala! I'm so happy you could come. Please join us."

I shut the door, walking across to settle into the chair. Then I smiled across the table at the other Primes, hoping to make a good first impression. Lopez smiled back. McAllister looked thoughtful. And Grant . . . *Okay, this guy is afraid of me.* He'd gone all shaky and pale.

"Ashala *Wolf*?" He gasped. "This girl is a killer! I insist she be removed from here at once!"

Lopez waved a chubby hand in his direction. "Oh,

do stop being so dramatic, Peter. Belle's already said that it was Terence who was behind the attack on the station."

Willis nodded. "I can personally vouch for Ashala's innocence, and she's here now at my invitation. I thought the least we could do is meet with her, since she came so far to see us."

Grant looked at Prime McAllister. "Ian? Surely you won't stand for this!"

McAllister rumbled, "If Belle says the girl didn't do it, then I believe her. Besides, I've got a question I'd like the answer to." He edged forward, studying me out of fierce gray eyes. "I accept you didn't personally cause that explosion. But that doesn't change the fact that abilities were used to cause pain and terror and death. So what I'd like to know is this: do you consider yourself to be part of the Balance?"

Of course I do, you—Yeah, that wasn't the right answer. Instead I said simply, "Yes."

"Why?"

Because I am as human as you. Except that wasn't right, either, because this wasn't about how I felt about myself. It was about how he felt about me and about anyone with an ability. Ember had said once that a belief that any person was less than human was evidence of the inhumanity of those who held the belief, not those who were subjected to it. And after the way I'd seen people react to us today—even after Connor had saved all those lives—I knew that for as long as we had to prove we deserved to be treated the same as everyone else, we never would be.

So I tried something else. "I was once held prisoner by Chief Administrator Neville Rose, back when he ran Detention Center Three. Everyone knows the kinds of things he did. Running a secret rhondarite mine and hoarding energy weapons and experimenting on detainees." *And on me.* I stared right at McAllister, holding his gaze with mine. "He used his power to cause pain and terror and death. And just because it wasn't you who did any of those things doesn't change the fact that it was a Citizen who was responsible."

Grant let out a short humorless laugh. "Hear that? She just compared Ian to a criminal."

"And," Willis put in, "Ian just compared Ashala to a killer."

I shook my head. "That's not what I meant! What I'm saying is, it's ridiculous to try to make the comparison. What should matter is who each of us is, and whether we care about people and the animals and the earth. And the people who don't, the ones who want to cause imbalance — they don't need an ability to do it."

There was a small silence. Finally, McAllister said, "That's . . . an interesting perspective."

Interesting was good. I hoped. And from the way his bushy eyebrows had drawn together in thought, it seemed like he was genuinely considering what I'd said. That didn't get me anywhere with the other two, but then, I doubted anything would change Grant's mind. The station attack had clearly scared him, and if he wasn't prepared to believe Prime Willis when she told him I hadn't done it, there wasn't much chance of him listening to me. As for Lopez — she was watching McAllister and Grant with catlike amusement, enjoying seeing McAllister challenged and Grant at odds with the other Primes. None of this mattered to her in the way I needed it to matter, and I wasn't sure there was a way to solve that.

I was trying to think of something I could say that would persuade her to get involved, when the door swung open. A short beige-robed administrator entered, pushing a trolley that held a teapot, cups, plates, and a bunch of miniature cakes. Afternoon tea had arrived, and as the trolley rolled past me to Willis, I caught a whiff of a cinnamony scent. I frowned. I knew that smell. It wasn't tea in that pot.

Willis murmured her thanks to the administrator, and he left, closing the door behind him. Lopez straightened, gazing at the trolley with more interest than she'd shown in anything else so far today. She'd caught the scent of cinnamon, too. "Is that *taffa*?"

Surprisingly, it was Grant who answered. "Yes."

Everyone looked at him. "It was a gift from an old friend," he explained. "Some rare beans, I understand, I really don't know anything about taffa, but I thought everyone might like to share it with me. I took the liberty of asking your kitchen staff to serve it for us, Belle. I do hope you don't mind."

"Perfectly all right, Peter," Willis replied. "I'm sure we'll all enjoy it." She poured out the taffa, handing everyone a cup of the rich dark liquid and a cake. I accepted both, because I didn't want to offend anyone by refusing, but there was no way I was drinking that taffa. The last time I'd had the stuff it'd given me a horribly vivid nightmare about Neville Rose standing on a hill of bodies. I knew it wasn't taffa alone that caused the dreams — it was the ancient cat spirit Starbeauty who was truly responsible, and she was a long way away in Spinifex City — but I wasn't taking any chances. With my ability, the last thing I needed was any added complications with my dreams.

Lopez took a sip and blinked in surprise. "This *is* a rare blend!"

"There you are, then," Grant said. "The taffa has Isabella's seal of approval. Enjoy, everybody!"

He seemed to have cheered up. *Probably looking forward to getting out of here as soon as the taffa's drunk and the cakes are eaten.* The Primes sipped their taffa, and I pretended to while I tried to come up with a way to get rid of the stuff. There was a large potted plant by one of the windows — maybe I could pour it into there? I was planning a casual stroll across the room when a sudden sense of alarm jolted through me. *Connor?*

There were shouts from outside, and the sizzling sound of streaker fire.

I slammed down my cup and leaped to my feet, sprinting for the door. Before I could get there, a wave of electricity came surging in from underneath and shot upward, covering the door and spreading out to form a hissing, crackling barrier across the walls. A spark flew out to hit my wrist, and I staggered back as pain seared up my arm, leaving it tingling and numb. We were trapped, and the only Illegal I'd ever seen who could do something like this was the minion who'd nearly killed the Prime five months ago. She was supposed to be locked up! *Terence is here. The minions are here.*

Behind me, somebody made a choking noise. Probably Willis; her thoughts must be going in the same direction as mine. But the noise didn't stop, and it was followed by the sound of cups crashing to the floor.

I spun around. *All* the Primes were choking, gulping for air and clutching their throats. My gaze fell on my taffa cup, the only one that was still full. I hadn't drunk, and I was fine. They had, and they weren't.

Poison!

I dashed to Willis, reaching her just as she tumbled out of her chair. She gazed up at me out of terrified eyes, silently begging me to help, but I didn't know what to do. I cast a frantic glance toward the windows. The electricity was covering them, too. There was no way out. And it sounded like Willis's breathing was getting worse, although it was hard to be sure, because it was difficult to hear anything over the panicked thumping of my heart. The Primes were dying, and I had nothing I could use to save them.

Except for my ability.

Nicky, help!

Nothing happened. Either he couldn't sense me or he didn't care about saving the Primes. I closed my eyes, pouring out my terror and desperation as I tried to make him understand. *If the Primes die alone with me I'll be blamed, and the whole world will come after the Tribe. Do you get it, Nicky? If I can't save them, I die, too!*

Still nothing.

Then I fell asleep.

I must have fallen asleep, because I was dreaming, and it was a strange dream. I was sitting on grass that grew in odd blue and white patches, and around me were bright angry lights that hissed with menace. The lights would hurt me if they could. I hunched my shoulders, trying to make myself a smaller target — and saw the bird.

She was flopping on the ground, blue wings fluttering helplessly as she struggled against the taffa vine that was choking her. I lunged forward and grabbed the vine with both my hands, pulling it in two directions so it came away from her neck. But my left arm was oddly weak, and the vine fought back, wrenching itself out of my grasp. I gritted my teeth and took hold of it again, focusing on sending strength flowing into my arm. The weakness faded, and I pulled. The vine tried to slide away, and I held on tighter. *I am stronger than this vine.* I was stronger than anything in my own dream. Power surged through my body, and I gave the vine one last yank.

The vine came free. I fell back and the bird squawked and rose to her feet, fluffing out her feathers. She was okay. I sagged in relief. Then she squawked again, and I could hear the panic in it—no. That sound was coming from *behind* me.

I turned to find there were three more birds—one green, one yellow, one brown—and all of them were being choked. Now I could see that a vine rose up from the grass in a central stalk before splitting into four strands that flowed outward to grasp the birds by their vulnerable necks. I lurched up and nearly fell. My legs were weak and unsteady. Tired. I was so tired, as if the effort of saving one bird had been almost too much. *I'm stronger than tired. I'm stronger than anything.* Only I wasn't, because I'd been . . . injured? I couldn't remember, and it didn't matter anyway because it didn't change what I had to do. Animals were in trouble and I had to help them.

I staggered to the central vine. It was about as tall as me, and I hugged my arms around it, pulling backward as I tried to uproot the deadly thing. It bent, but not much. I pulled again, bracing my feet against the grass. *This is my dream and I am strong. . . . I don't feel strong. . . . I AM strong!*

I threw back my head, snarling my defiance, and *pulled*.

The vine uprooted. It went flying out of the grass, and I flew with it, soaring backward through the air and landing—

—in an armchair?

I gazed around in bewilderment. How had I gotten here? There was no grass, no lights, no taffa vine, and no birds. Just a checkered carpet, fallen cups, electricity on the walls, and the Primes. Grant and Lopez were sitting on the floor next to each other, and Lopez was trembling like a leaf in the wind. Grant was hugging his knees to his chest, rocking back and forth as he muttered to himself. McAllister was in a chair, staring at me with his mouth hanging open. And beside me, Willis was taking one long breath after another, as if she needed to reassure herself that she could still breathe.

The birds—no, the Primes—were shaken and scared and in shock. But they were alive.

THE ACCORDS

ASHALA

My stomach roiled. I put my head in my hands and focused on not throwing up. Sleepwalking always made me sick. Exhausted, too. So much so that holding myself upright in the chair was a mammoth effort. My body craved sleep, but this wasn't over. We were still trapped, and I could still hear streaker fire from outside. I tried to reach out to Connor. All I could sense was my own weariness. *I'd know if he were . . . hurt.* Surely I'd know. Except where *was* he? And where were Jules and Em? They'd been right on the other side of the door, and I knew they'd be trying to reach me. So why hadn't they?

"Ashala?"

I lifted my head to look at Willis.

"Thank you," she said. "It's not enough, but — thank you. And I hate to ask anything else, only can you get us out of this room?"

"Sorry. My ability's all used up. Won't work again for ages now." And to myself, I said, *Connor and Ember and Jules are helping people who've gotten injured.* Or waiting for the best chance to strike. Or something, and I couldn't think about it anymore because I wouldn't be able to function if I did.

McAllister rubbed at his throat. "What I just saw . . . that was you, using your ability?"

His voice was trembling. *Wonderful.* I knew how I looked when I Sleepwalked — moving through the world with my eyes all white, reacting to things no one else could see. Most people found it scary, and McAllister was obviously no exception. "There was some kind of poison in the taffa," I explained wearily. "I had no other way to save you."

From the expression on his face I'd frightened him off abilities for good. But I had much bigger problems than that right now. I forced myself up and staggered to the window, trying to make out what was happening without getting too close to the electricity. I couldn't see much through the sparks, just the green blur of the garden, the blue blur of the ocean beyond, and flashes that probably meant weapons fire. A *lot* of weapons fire. There was the scent of smoke in the air, too. Something was burning. Part of the Residence? The gardens? The city? Whatever was happening, it was bigger than poisoning the Primes.

"Can you see anything?" Willis asked.

"Not much. A lot of streaker fire. And something burning, I think."

Lopez gasped. "What did you say?"

"I said—" I began, and stopped. Lopez wasn't talking to me. She was glaring at Prime Grant.

"Nothing! It was nothing," he babbled. "I don't even know what I'm saying!"

"Liar!" Lopez snapped. She rose to her feet, pointing an accusing finger at Grant. "He just said, 'It was only meant to make us sleep.'"

There was a shocked silence. Then Willis breathed, "Peter, you *knew*. You knew the taffa was poisoned!"

"No! I didn't. I thought . . ." His voice trailed off, and she finished the sentence.

"You thought it would only make us sleep. How

long have you been working with Terence?"

He lifted his chin. "I'm not. I—I haven't done anything, and besides, none of you have any right to judge me!"

McAllister surged out of his chair and reached down to grab hold of the front of Grant's shirt, hauling the smaller man upward. He held him so that Grant's feet dangled above the floor, and snarled into his face, "Tell. The. Truth!"

Prime Grant started talking, the words tripping over one another in his hurry to get them out. "I'm s-sorry, I'm so sorry! Terence said Belle had lost her way and she was being manipulated by rogue Illegals, and, and, when she asked us to meet with the Tribe before the Council meeting I knew it must be true!"

McAllister set him down and took a disgusted step back. "Terence *blew up* the station. It never occurred to you that he was the one who'd lost his way?"

Grant's gaze slid to me. "I thought she was responsible for the station. I was trying to save my city — all the cities — from an Illegal threat —"

"That Terence invented!" Willis interrupted. "Those Illegals you're so afraid of are the ones he controls, you —" She stopped and sucked in a breath. When she spoke again the anger hadn't quite left her voice, but it had retreated to lurk beneath the surface. "Recriminations won't help any of us now. What did you think would happen while we were 'asleep'?"

"Terence was going to take you away to get you some help. He promised you wouldn't be hurt!"

Prime McAllister let out an incredulous bark of laughter. "And you believed him?"

"Naturally he did," Lopez drawled. "We all know that Peter is adept at believing what he wants to believe, especially when there's something in it for him. I suppose Terence told you that you'd be the hero who helped to save Gull City from the big bad Illegals, didn't he, Peter?"

"That wasn't why I did it." But he couldn't meet their eyes. He was foolish and weak. *And this is one of the people who run the world.* This was the man who lived while my brave Penelope was dead. I felt sick for an entirely different reason than before. Sick and angry, because it was so unfair that this was the life I'd been able to save, this man who . . .

I gasped. *This man who knew we were coming to the city.* Terence's information hadn't come from inside the Gull City government. "It was you."

The Primes looked at me, and Grant shrank away. Which was sensible, because I wanted to take him apart with my bare hands. "You told Terence the Tribe was going to be here! *You're responsible for the station.*"

"No, no, I didn't." I could hear the false note in his voice. There was a roaring in my ears and a bitter taste in my mouth. I took a step toward him, so furious I was shaking with it.

Another step — and Willis was in my way. She spoke too softly for the others to hear. "I have an idea, but you need to back off."

I glared at her, and she added, "Ashala — don't let her death be for nothing."

I'd once said something similar to her, over another death. Jeremy Duoro, Willis's adviser and friend, who'd been killed saving my life from a minion Firestarter. I didn't *want* to back off. But her friend had died for me, and I'd promised her it would mean something. I had to let her try whatever it was she wanted to try. I nodded and shifted back to the window. I needed the length of the room between me and Grant; I didn't trust myself any closer.

Willis swung around to the other Primes. When she spoke she was putting her powerful voice to good use, sending her words rolling out over her audience. "There's a battle going on outside. I think Terence is trying to take the city, and if he's prepared to go this far, *none* of your cities are safe." She paused, letting that sink in. The Primes exchanged uneasy glances, and Willis continued, "But we are not helpless. There are four of us here, and that's enough for a Council meeting, which means there's something we can do to defend ourselves. We can vote."

"Vote on what?" Lopez demanded.

"On expanded Exemptions, as we were going to before."

This was her idea? Wild hope welled up, and I shoved it back down. It wouldn't work. It *couldn't* work. She needed four Primes out of the total seven to change the Exemption criteria, which meant everyone in this room had to vote with her. Grant wouldn't and maybe not McAllister, either, not after I'd scared him with Sleepwalking. Except . . . *Belle Willis isn't an idiot.*

She would never have begun this if she didn't think she had a shot.

"Think about it," Willis said in a quieter, more persuasive tone. "The only reason we are alive is because Ashala was here, and Terence didn't know she would be, because I didn't tell anyone she was coming. She's what he didn't plan for, and she's all that protected us." She gestured to the walls. "This electricity? It's the work of *one* of Terence's people, and he's got a lot more.

How do you expect to defend yourselves and your cities unless you've got people with abilities to help you?"

"There're plenty of Exempts already," Lopez pointed out.

McAllister shook his head. "By definition anyone with an Exemption has an ability that can't be used to hurt someone." He cast a sidelong glance at Lopez. "At least, that's how it's supposed to work."

So the other Primes knew or suspected that things were different in Spinifex City. Lopez met McAllister's gaze with a blank I-have-no-idea-what-you-mean expression. She was good at it, too; I expect she'd had a lot of practice.

Wait . . . wait . . . No one's said no! On the contrary, Lopez and McAllister seemed to be considering the idea. Grant was hunched in on himself, his gaze darting between the other Primes. *Weak and stupid.* That worked for us now in the way it had worked against us before, and Willis realized it. Grant could be bullied or convinced. I might just be able to keep my promise to Pen after all.

The corners of my mouth started to lift up into a smile. I tried to straighten them out again.

Then McAllister said, "No." And I didn't have to try. He looked straight across the room at me and continued, "I won't vote on expanded Exemptions. But I *will* vote on ending the Citizenship Accords altogether."

I swayed, so stunned I felt dizzy. I'd heard him wrong. I must have heard him wrong. Except the other Primes were looking at him as if they thought they'd heard him wrong, too.

"Since when are you a reformer, Ian?" Lopez demanded.

"Since today," he replied. "Because I was dying, and for what seems like the first time in my life, I saw things clearly. I *felt* how wrong that poison was. How . . . imbalanced." He nodded at me. "Then you were there and you made things right again, and if that poison was imbalance, then you were its opposite. I no longer believe abilities to be unnatural. And if they aren't . . ." He shrugged his big shoulders. "I can't justify the continuation of a set of accords that treat people with abilities any differently than everybody else."

The expression on his face was the same as the one I'd seen before, the one I'd misinterpreted as fear. I didn't make that mistake this time. It was awe. *The true believer.* I hadn't scared him after all. I'd convinced him.

"Well," Willis said, sounding a bit giddy, "you all

know I've got no problem with ending the accords. Isabella?"

Lopez glanced from McAllister to Willis. "We can't just open the gates to detention centers! That would be doing no favors to Illegals or anyone else. Many of them would have nowhere to go."

"Staged implementation of the change," Willis suggested. "Provided all detainees are released within six months."

Lopez sighed. "I can live with that."

"I can't!" That was Grant. The others turned their attention to him, and he took a quick step back. "I won't be a part of this — and, and you can't make me."

I locked my body into place, forcing myself not to go snarling toward him. *Let Willis do this. Trust her to do this.*

"No one's going to make you do anything," Willis told him soothingly, and I wondered if Grant heard the false note in *her* voice. "But Terence did try to kill you, too, Peter. In fact, if we make it out of here he'll probably want you dead more than any of us, since you're the one who can link him to the poison."

Lopez chimed in, "I don't expect that you'll last more than a few weeks without someone with an ability to protect you." She looked him up and down and gave a contemptuous sniff. "Perhaps fewer."

Grant swallowed. "I suppose I might be willing to consider expanded Exemptions."

"I've already said I won't," McAllister rumbled. "Come on, Peter—vote with us, man. Do it and we'll lie for you."

That got Grant's attention. He shifted toward Prime McAllister and asked in a hopeful tone, "Lie for me?"

"We'll say you had no idea anything was wrong with the taffa. You escaped certain death at the hands of that madman Terence Talbot right along with the rest of us." McAllister glanced around at the others. "Any objections?"

Yes! I object! I want the whole world to know what a traitor and a coward this man is. I shut my teeth on the words before they could escape me. Exposing Grant wouldn't get me the world that was safe for kids and dogs. Keeping the secret might.

Willis and Lopez shook their heads. McAllister raised a bushy eyebrow at me, and I said, "I won't say a word."

Grant brightened. "Well, in that case—I mean, given my responsibility to my people, and the danger Terence poses to the Balance, I suppose I could vote with you."

Lopez rolled her eyes. "You really are a—"

"Let's vote, then," Willis interrupted. "I hereby call to order this meeting of the Council of Primes. Four Primes in attendance. Are we all agreed this is a duly constituted meeting?"

Everyone nodded, and she continued, "The motion under consideration is the repeal of the Citizenship Accords. All in favor?"

Everyone raised their hands.

"Four in favor," Willis said. "None against. Motion carried."

Everyone lowered their hands. I didn't understand. Wasn't someone going to say or do something else? Willis noticed my confusion and said gently, "The Citizenship Accords are repealed, Ashala."

Just like that? I couldn't absorb it; I needed Georgie here to tell me this world was real. It was too sudden, too fast. *Too easy.* I couldn't believe it had been *that* easy to get rid of the accords all this time and nobody ever had. Or, no, not that easy. It was just that it wasn't the actual vote that was the difficult part. The struggle had come before. The struggle had cost lives.

Willis knew it, too; I saw it in the mix of triumph and sadness in her face. She was thinking of Jeremy. And the person I wanted to see most in this moment was someone I was never going to see again. I spoke to her in my head anyway. *The Citizenship Accords are finished, Pen. What you did wasn't for nothing.* Then I smiled, because she'd want me to, a big, bright, happy smile.

I smiled right up until there was stirring in the air behind me, and McAllister yelled a warning. Someone clasped something cold and hard around my neck. Rhondarite!

I jerked away, only I wasn't fast enough. I was wearing a collar, and behind me was the Blinker, the minion whose ability let him disappear from one place and reappear in another. He grinned and vanished. So did the electricity. I had a second to catch a clear view through the window. All I could see was hazy smoke; there was definitely a fire somewhere. Then the door swung open. A dark-skinned, short-haired girl entered the room, dressed in enforcer black—but she was no enforcer.

The Electrifier held up her hands, sending sparks into the air, and gestured toward the far wall. "Primes—pick up the chairs, move them over there, and sit down." Her gaze focused on me, and her expression hardened. "You stay right where you are."

Grant grabbed a chair, scurried across the room, and sat, all straight and still as if he were a little kid in school waiting for the teacher to pat him on the head.

The other Primes hesitated, casting concerned glances in my direction. They didn't want to leave me alone.

"Now!" the Electrifier snarled. She flicked her fingers, sending electricity sizzling through the air above our heads. The Primes ducked and so did I. Those sparks were close enough to feel the heat, and I doubted we'd get more than one warning.

"Go," I told them. "I'm okay." The rhondarite was annoying, but it wasn't like I would've been able to Sleepwalk anyway after exhausting my ability. The Primes still hesitated, and I added, "She'll only hurt me if you don't. *Go!*"

That got them moving. I kept my gaze on the Electrifier as the Primes shuffled toward the chairs, reading the hatred in her face. I hadn't been lying when I'd said she'd hurt me. The last time she'd attacked Prime Willis it had been Connor and I who had defeated her, and minions didn't forget failures. Back then, I'd used my ability to overcome hers. I had no chance against her now.

The Primes finished shifting the chairs and sat reluctantly. The Electrifier called out to someone over her shoulder, "It's all clear. Come in."

I expected to see Terence, with his mousy hair

and washed-out blue eyes. The man who entered the room had white hair and brown eyes that peered from behind a pair of wire-rimmed glasses. He was wearing beige administrator robes and a general air of kindly benevolence, and it was hard to imagine a more harmless-looking old man.

Which only went to show that sometimes you couldn't trust what you saw.

Neville Rose closed the door behind him and smiled at me. It was his nice smile, the one that made him seem like everyone's favorite grandfather. A liar's smile.

"Ashala. I did tell you I'd be seeing you again."

I kept my expression blank, not wanting to give him the satisfaction of a response. He couldn't know just by looking at me that my whole body had gone cold with dread, and I was sure the trembling in my legs wasn't bad enough to be visible from a distance. I didn't want to be afraid of this man. But I was.

Neville watched me for a moment longer, then turned his attention to the Primes. "Allow me to introduce myself to those of you who don't know me. My name is Neville Rose."

"We know who you are," McAllister replied. "A criminal, and Terence's lackey. Where's Terence?"

"Oh, I'm afraid Prime Talbot couldn't possibly enter the city until it was secure." He gestured toward me. "There are dangerous Illegals here, you know."

"Terence is not the Prime!" Willis snapped. "And the only dangerous Illegals are the ones working for him."

Neville put a fatherly hand on the Electrifier's shoulder. "Jenny here — and others like her — have volunteered to protect Prime Talbot, but they have no doubt about their place in this world. You know you're unnatural, don't you, child?"

The Electrifier recited the same nonsense I'd heard from the minions before: "Obedience is service, and service is redemption."

Neville beamed. "Exactly so."

"You're sick," Willis told him. "And so is Terence."

Don't respond, I thought at her. *Don't react. He's enjoying it too much.* I needn't have worried, because Neville had moved on to other prey.

"Peter," he said, heaving a disappointed sigh. "I'm afraid Terence won't be very happy with you."

"You didn't tell me the taffa was poisoned! I could have died!"

"You didn't *drink* it? Weren't you warned not to?"

Grant licked his lips, looking uncertain. "Nobody told me not to drink it."

The color drained out of Neville's face in an excellent imitation of genuine shock. "A terrible mistake. I'm so sorry. Come over here to me, and we'll get a Mender to take a look at you."

Grant stood up and took a few happy steps forward before he suddenly stopped, a panicked expression crossing his face. "The others — they repealed the Citizenship Accords. I didn't want to — they made me do it!"

"You worm!" Lopez hissed.

"Repealed the accords?" Neville chuckled. "You *have* all been busy, haven't you?"

He wasn't angry. Worse than that, he was barely bothering with his usual kindly-grandpa routine. I could think of only one reason why he wouldn't care about the accords being gone or about revealing his true face.

None of us were getting out of this room alive.

"Don't worry about the accords, Peter," Neville said. "We'll get it sorted out."

Reassured, Grant started walking again, looking back to cast a triumphant glance at the other Primes.

Which was when Neville pulled out a streaker and shot him.

Prime Peter Grant stayed on his feet for another second. Then he crumpled to the ground, very surprised and very dead. The suddenness of it was shocking, and yet I wasn't shocked. I hadn't expected Neville to kill so soon or so fast, but I had expected him to kill. Grant was just . . . *first*. And if I couldn't find a way to get the others out of here, it would soon be all of us.

The Primes surged up, shouting at Neville. He leaned down to say something to the Electrifier. She raised her hands, and a crackling wall of energy formed in a circle around the Primes, trapping them in place. Neville put the streaker into his pocket and strolled across the room to me. Slowly, so that I'd have to watch him approach.

I forced my shoulders to relax into a slouch and did my absolute best to look bored.

He stopped about a meter away. "Make the smallest movement toward me and she will hurt them."

I glanced over at the Primes. They were looking in our direction, but they wouldn't have been able to hear from this distance, not over the crackle of the sparks.

"So what? You're going to kill them anyway."

He chuckled. "Clever girl. But I doubt you want to hasten their deaths. Especially when you're still clinging to the hope of rescue."

I was, and I didn't like how confident he was that it wasn't coming. And while I could still hear the sizzle of streakers from outside the window, there was no shouting or weapons fire coming from the doorway side of the room. Only an empty, frightening quiet.

I affected a yawn. "I don't need anyone to rescue me from you. You're not that tough."

"Defiant as always. I knew you would be. You don't surprise me, Ashala. And I don't surprise you. You've no idea how refreshing that is." He nodded at the Primes. "Even they were surprised when I killed Grant. Who will I kill next, do you think?"

Whatever name I gave him *would* be the one he killed next. "Dunno. But," I added, preempting what I knew he was about to say, "I'll be last. So I can watch all the others die."

"That's where you're wrong. I'm not going to kill you. Although you will certainly watch a great many people die in the years to come."

Years? I didn't understand what he meant and I wasn't going to ask. He waited for a second, just to see if I would ask, and then kept talking. "It's occurred to me that it would be a terrible shame if there was never anyone who truly understood my many . . . accomplishments. No witness, as it were, to the wonders of which I am capable. Which is why I am not going to kill you." He smiled, and this time it was his other smile, the one that belonged to a monster who knew exactly how monstrous he was, and rejoiced in it. "You are my audience, Ashala Wolf."

I wanted to throw up. Instead I bared my teeth like any cornered wolf would, and Neville's eyes lit up. This would be no fun at all for him if I broke too easily. I could see the future as if I were Georgie, and I knew he was going to destroy me and take his time doing it. *Years.*

Someone knocked at the door.

Neville frowned and strode over to pull it open, speaking in a sharp tone to someone outside. Another voice murmured in reply. He looked back at me, and the glee I'd seen in his face a second ago was nothing compared to what was there now. *He's got something and it's going to hurt.*

I braced myself for whatever was coming as Neville stepped away from the door, gesturing to someone outside. I still couldn't prevent a whimper from escaping my throat as an enforcer dragged a canine body into the room. *Nicky*. He was utterly limp and covered in so much blood it left a heavy red trail along the white composite floor. *He can't be dead*. But he wasn't moving, and it seemed like he'd taken a lot of damage. Maybe enough that he was hurt too badly to heal himself? *Nicky? Can you hear me? Please wake up!*

He didn't so much as twitch. Neville nudged him with his boot. "Your dog, I think, Ashala." He looked out through the door at something I couldn't see. "Or does the animal belong to him?"

Another enforcer entered, pushing someone in front of her. Someone who had a rhondarite collar on his neck and a head wound that gushed blood down one side of a sculpted face.

Connor.

THE ADMINISTRATOR

ASHALA

I was silent, trying to sense Connor, trying to reach him. The side of his face that wasn't bleeding was bruised, and there was more blood on his clothes than could be accounted for by the head wound. He was badly hurt, blinking woozily and not focusing on anything. I wasn't sure he knew where he was. I wasn't sure he knew who he was.

Neville closed the door behind the departing enforcers and shoved a hand down on Connor's shoulder, forcing him to his knees. I was dimly aware of the Primes shouting, which was about all they could do in their prison of sparks. Neville ignored them. They weren't a part of this. It was about him and me.

"This is becoming quite the reunion, isn't it?" he said. "The three of us together again."

Of course he'd recognized Connor. Back when Neville had taken me prisoner, Connor had been passing as a Citizen and working as an enforcer in Detention Center 3. He was the reason I'd made it out alive. But he couldn't help me now and I couldn't help him.

The Primes were still shouting. Neville wasn't. He wasn't saying anything. I dragged my gaze from Connor's face to his and realized he was waiting for me to speak. I knew what he wanted me to say, and it was futile, but I said it anyway. "Let him live and I'll do anything you want."

"I know," he replied in a sympathetic tone. A pretend voice. "But your problem is, Ashala, that there are so many people for whom you'll do anything. And—did I tell you?—Prime Talbot is appointing me Chief Overseer of the Gull City detention centers."

In other words, he'd have no shortage of victims to torment me with; he didn't need Connor. A strange calm settled over me. *Stupid Neville.* He was ruining his own plan and he didn't even know it. He'd never be able to make me watch people die over and over. Not when he was starting with the one death I wouldn't survive.

My heart rate accelerated to an impossible, painful speed, pounding so hard and so fast it seemed like it would burst. Which it would, and I could use my heartbeats to measure out how long I had before it did. *One.* Neville began to raise the streaker, pointing it at the back of Connor's head. *Two.* I stared at Connor, willing him to recognize me and know I was here, that he hadn't been alone at the end. *Three.*

Nicky came to life.

He leaped for the Electrifier, clamping his powerful jaws around her arm and shoulder and dragging her to the floor. She screamed, and the sparks around the Primes vanished as she poured electricity into Nicky. In almost the same moment, Neville's arm jerked upward and he fired a useless shot at the ceiling.

I lunged for Connor. Only before I could reach him, the windows flew open and I was tumbling backward through the air, out of the room and into the smoke-filled sky. I couldn't see Connor. I couldn't see anyone past the smoke stinging my eyes, or hear anything over the wind that was rushing past my ears. Then I was out of the haze and hurtling through salty air, down a cliff to the roaring sea below. I twisted, trying to work out what was happening. I was moving way too fast. All I could make out were the blurs of other people zooming through the sky like I was. *Connor must be here; no one else could be doing this!* Only how could he use his ability when he'd been wearing a collar?

I soared around the cliff and through the sea spray and up again into the sky. On and on I flew, until suddenly I was careening downward toward — I didn't know, something green. I flung up my arms to shield my face as I plunged through leaves before landing in dirt, getting a mouthful of it.

I spat it out and sat up. I was in a clearing, surrounded by the peeling brown bark and drooping branches of gungurru trees. *The forest outside the city.* There were a bunch of people here, including Wentworth, who was helping the Primes to their feet. But none of the people seemed to be a threat, so I didn't care about them. Ember was standing nearby, wearing red Mender robes for no reason I understood, and Nicky was at her feet. He was rolling on his back, leaving bloody smears across the leaf litter.

I scrambled up with a shout of alarm.

"He's okay!" Em said quickly. "None of that blood

is his; we put it on him to make him seem hurt." She nodded at something over my shoulder. "Turn around, Ash."

I swiveled, and there was Connor. He was standing a few paces behind me with his bleeding head and the collar around his throat. Except right next to him was *another* Connor, this one dressed in enforcer black and unhurt as far as I could tell.

The wounded Connor shimmered, his injuries vanishing as he shifted into a familiar brown-haired figure. And Jules said, "I *knew* I could fool you!"

I gaped at him. Then I ran to Connor and flung my arms around his neck, drinking in the scent of his skin and the feel of his body and the fact that he was safe, safe, safe!

He spoke against my ear. "Did Neville hurt you?"

Not in the way you mean. "I'm okay."

His hold on me tightened. "You will be." And I knew he'd heard—or felt—the words that I hadn't said as well as the ones that I had.

"Are *you* okay?" I demanded. "I can sense—I don't know, something."

"Exhaustion. I pushed my ability to its limits. You've pushed yours, too."

It figured that he'd picked up on my tiredness if

162

I could pick up on his. He was fine. I was fine. And everyone else . . .

I let him go, turning to the others. Nicky was sniffing in the undergrowth. Em was watching me and Connor with a grin, and so was Jules. Like the others, Jules had changed clothes since I'd seen him last—into an enforcer uniform—but the details of why didn't matter right now. What mattered was that no one was hurt. *They're here. They're alive. They're safe.*

My knees buckled. Connor tried to catch me, but he was shaky himself, and the two of us ended up collapsing into the dirt. We both started laughing out of sheer joy and relief at being alive, and once we'd started it was hard to stop.

For some reason Jules and Em weren't smiling anymore. Jules was looking at us with concern, and Em waved to Wentworth, who came hurrying over.

"We're all right," I told Wentworth between giggles. "Anyway, you can't really Mend me right now!" The collar around my neck wouldn't stop her ability, since it wasn't touching her skin, but it would interfere with how well Mending worked on me.

"I can get rid of the collar." She dropped to the ground at my side, leaning forward to press the numbered keys in the collar lock. It clicked open, and

Wentworth pulled it from my neck, tossing it away.

I was so surprised I stopped laughing. "How'd you know the code?"

"Your friends can explain in a moment." She grasped hold of my hand and reached across to put her other hand on Connor's arm. "Hush now, and let me work."

Heat came trickling into my body, flowing along my veins, and soothed away the aches and terrors of the day. That was nice. Being here was nice. I leaned against Connor's shoulder, suddenly feeling the need to be still and quiet for a while. He did, too — he rested his head against mine, and he wasn't laughing anymore, either.

I gazed out at the space around us. People were scattered through the clearing, filling it with colors — beige-robed administrators, red-robed Menders, enforcers in black uniforms, and ordinary Citizens, most of whom were in Gull City blue. But there was some Spinifex City yellow and Fern City green mixed in there as well, probably the staff the other Primes had brought with them. The Primes themselves were standing in the center of it all, crowded together and having an animated conversation with Willis's husband. At the edge of the clearing was a distinctive rock formation, a mammoth curved hunk of orange granite that looked like a giant turtle shell half-buried in the dirt. *Turtle Rock*. I knew where we were—about half an hour outside the city, and the highway was . . . *that way*. Now that I was looking, I could see a bunch of parked cars and trucks through the trees.

The warmth flowing into my body abruptly stopped. I felt better. Sleepy, but calmer and stronger and not . . . well, borderline hysterical.

Wentworth straightened. "You two have overtaxed your strength. Rest, if you can."

She strode off to help another Mender who was working on a wounded enforcer. I sat up, my gaze falling on the open collar on the ground. "Okay, so how did she unlock that thing? She couldn't possibly have guessed all nine numbers!"

"Master code," Connor replied. "It unlocks all Gull City collars."

"There's a *master code*? Since when?"

"Apparently it was one of Jeremy Duoro's ideas," he said, stifling a yawn. He was feeling the aftereffects of the Mending, too. "To provide a simple way to let everyone go if the accords ever changed. Or to give them a way to free a bunch of Illegals at once if a madman like Neville ever got hold of another detention center."

165

I had no idea when he'd found all that out, and I wasn't going to ask. Because it had just dawned on me that he didn't know about the accords. None of them did, and they couldn't go for one more second without knowing it. I lurched to my feet, pulling Connor with me. We should all be standing for this. "Gather 'round, everyone. I've got news."

Nicky ignored me; the forest smells were far more interesting than I was. Em and Jules came over, although I noticed they were keeping a wary distance between them — they came nearer to me, but not each other. *I'll get to that later.* For now . . .

I drew in a deep breath and said, "The Citizenship Accords are gone."

Jules frowned. "What do you mean, gone?"

"I mean gone! Finished. Ended. The Primes voted, and the accords are done."

Em grabbed hold of my arm. "Ash — when? *How?*"

I explained, all the way from the poison to Grant's betrayal and the vote.

When I finished, Connor and Jules were grinning. But Ember turned away. After a second I heard a sniffle.

"You're not crying, Em?"

"No! You know I never cry!"

Her voice broke on the last word, and I moved across to hug her. For a while she cried into my shoulder. Then she wiped at her face and whispered, "I knew you could do it. I always knew."

"*We* did it. We all did it." I stood back to stare into her mismatched eyes, and saw what I'd hoped to see. The weight of the guilt that she carried with her was easing. *Gone. Finished. Ended.* I hoped.

Jules cleared his throat. "Hate to spoil the mood, but our newfound status ain't gonna mean much if we're still standing around here once Neville takes the city."

My heart sank. "You think he's going to take the city?"

"If what happened at the Residence is any indication, probably," Jules answered. "Enforcers just drew their weapons and started killing other enforcers."

"I've never heard of an ability that could make people do that!"

"It wasn't an ability," Connor said. "They're loyal to Terence. As it turns out, a lot of the enforcers working for Willis are loyal to Terence. And after the attack on the station, there were enforcers posted absolutely everywhere. Especially around key government facilities, and around the Prime."

Putting them in the perfect position to take things over from the inside. "This was their plan all along."

A new voice snarled, "Yes."

Belle Willis was striding over to us. "Henry tells me that everything is in chaos. It's a coup." She looked in the direction of the city, and her expression hardened. "My chief of staff is still in there, and she's organizing a counterattack. She'll either stop them—or make it cost them as dearly as possible to win."

She wanted to be there. I knew, because it's what I would have wanted. "If you go back you'll be a target for every minion and every bad enforcer that spots you," I said. "It'd be next to impossible to keep you safe, and a lot of people would die trying."

"I know." She sighed. "That's why I'm leaving. The other Primes have offered to take me with them to one of their cities. But if I do that and the worst happens here, there'll be no center of government for Gull City other than the one Terence runs. It would be better for me to go . . . somewhere else. Somewhere defensible, and large enough to hold a government-in-exile." Her gaze met mine. "Close to allies."

It wasn't hard to figure out where she was talking about. Belle Willis was coming to my part of the world. "You mean Detention Center Three."

She nodded. "If the city falls, danger will follow me."

"Danger will come whether you're there or not." There was no way Neville or Terence was going to just leave the Tribe alone. Except I couldn't have Willis expecting support I wasn't going to be able to give. "We'll help however we can. But we can't be your army. Our priority is the forest." I hoped it wouldn't come down to having to abandon one to save the other. But if it did, I'd choose the Tribe and the trees every time.

"Understood," Willis said. "And you should know, Ashala — I'm sending Henry to Detention Center Two to authorize the release of the detainees. If Terence does take the city, I'm not giving him any more victims than I have to."

That was a good idea. No, that was a *great* idea. Just not quite great enough. "What about Detention Center One?"

"Unfortunately I can only free one center. And there are no children in Detention Center One."

Detention Center 1 was for adults, and Detention Center 2 was for families and kids. But I didn't see why she'd had to choose. "Couldn't you send someone else to the other center?"

"I can't send just anyone. It has to be someone who'll

be believed when they say the Citizenship Accords have ended. Someone the Chief Administrator of the center knows could only have come from me." She waved her arm at the clearing. "There are no senior members of my government here. All I have is Henry, and he can't be in two places at once."

I grinned. "Yes, he can."

Jules had realized what I was thinking and didn't like it. "Bad idea, wolfgirl!"

I tried to think of an argument that would convince him to wear Henry's face. "We need those detainees, Jules. Having more people with abilities on our side could make all the difference, especially if Terence takes the city."

"What makes you think any of 'em are gonna join this fight, even if you get them out? They'll have no reason to trust the government. *Any* government."

"Yeah, but they might trust me. Leader of the Tribe and all that."

"Besides," Connor put in, "it's possible they won't take much convincing once they're told who it is they're fighting against. Neville Rose ran Detention Center One for almost five years. He'll have plenty of enemies among the detainees."

Willis frowned. "My concern is that he might have

friends among the guards. I've replaced the Chief Administrator and all of the senior enforcers, but I'd only just started on the junior staff. My priority was making changes to the center with the children. I haven't had time to put in an entirely new staff in Detention Center One the way I have in Detention Center Two."

That made this a risk, even though not everyone who ever worked for Neville was one of his supporters. Wentworth certainly wasn't, and he'd been her boss until she'd seen what he was and helped to defeat him. "We'll be careful," I said. "But we are going to do this."

Willis was hesitating. I could see the same concern in her face that had been there before, when we'd been in the room with Neville. She was reacting to me as if I were someone she should protect. A kid. She was years too late to protect me or any of the Tribe; we'd already figured out how to protect ourselves. We'd had to, and we weren't going back to putting our lives in the hands of adults now.

I took a step closer to her. "I'm *going,* Prime Willis, and I'm telling you that as the leader of the Tribe. And you need to respect that, because if you can't, this alliance will never work—and Neville and Terence will defeat us both."

She gave a reluctant nod. "What can I do to help?"

"We'll need a vehicle," Connor told her. I hadn't thought of that, but he was right—the center was hours and hours away from here, and Connor had probably tired out his ability too much to take us all that way. Besides, he'd need to save his strength for when we got there, in case there was any trouble.

"I'll see what I can do," Willis said, and went striding back to where her husband and the other Primes were already moving people in the direction of the vehicles. Nobody thought it was a good idea to hang around here.

Jules rounded on Connor and me. "This is nuts, even for you two. You should be worrying about the Tribe, not a bunch of detainees who we don't even know!"

"We *are* worrying about the Tribe," I said. "We need more people with abilities in this fight than just us, and we especially need them protecting Prime Willis."

He rolled his eyes. "I get that she's your friend and—"

Connor interrupted him, "This isn't about friendship. If, as seems likely, Terence takes the city, then Willis becomes the focus of all opposition to him. If she dies and the only real threat left to Terence is the

Tribe, who do you think he's coming after next?"

Jules blinked. "Oh."

"And," Em put in, "until the accords are truly gone, the Tribe will never be truly safe. The repeal is only the beginning. Now they've got to dismantle everything that went with the accords, like the centers and bureaus of Citizenship and assessments. Even attitudes. That's going to take time, and a government that's committed to change. It's going to take Willis."

I could see that Jules wasn't totally convinced. He wasn't arguing anymore, though, maybe because he could see we *were* all totally convinced. I caught Em's gaze. There was something I had to do for her and Jules both. "Can I talk to you alone for a second?"

We walked away from the others, far enough that they couldn't overhear. "Listen, Em, I wanted to —"

"It's all right," she said. "I know what you're going to say. You need me to go with the Prime."

"Um. Yeah, I do. Somebody's got to take news of everything that's happened back to the Tribe — to *both* Tribes. Jaz needs to understand that a bunch of government people turning up isn't some kind of invasion. But what I was going to say was about Jules."

Em stiffened. I kept going anyway.

"What he did back there, walking into a room with Neville Rose, wearing Connor's face? It's about the stupidest, bravest thing I've ever seen anyone do."

She folded her arms and looked away. She *really* didn't want to talk about this. I wasn't giving up. "Your relationship with Jules is your relationship with Jules, and I don't want to interfere with it, but there could be trouble where we're going. And sometimes we don't have as much time with people as we think." Penelope's voice echoed in my memory: *You know what, Ash? I can smell eucalyptus. . . .* "Just—please don't leave anything unsaid or undone. Not when you might regret it later."

She was silent, gazing into the distance. Then she lifted her chin and marched up to Jules, grabbing hold of his arm and dragging him to the edge of the clearing. I watched as she started talking, accompanying the words with angry, impatient movements of her hands. Jules was silent, letting her talk.

Connor came over to me. He circled his arms around my waist, and I leaned back against him with a sigh.

"Fixing the world, Ashala?" he asked. He was watching Em and Jules, too.

"Fixing *our* world," I replied. "Our Tribe. With any luck."

Em was still talking, although she seemed to be

taking longer breaks between sentences. She'd started to run out of words, and Jules still wasn't speaking at all. She jabbed at his chest, and I didn't need to be able to hear her to know what she'd said. *Aren't you going to say something?*

Jules caught her hand and finally spoke. Not much, just a couple of words. I knew what he'd said as well. *Forgive me.*

For a second longer they stood where they were, Jules clasping Ember's hand and Ember staring at Jules. Then Em tore her hand from his so she could take hold of the front of his shirt and pull his head down to hers for a long, deep kiss.

"World fixed," Connor said, and I could hear the laughter in his voice. And the regret, for what neither of us had been able to fix. We missed Pen. That only made it more important to do everything we could to change things in the way that she'd wanted.

I looked up at Connor and grinned a fierce, wolfy grin. "Let's go free a detention center."

THE RUNAWAY

GEORGIE

Sometimes I knew where to be. Sometimes I didn't. Today I did, and it wasn't in the caves.

I left Daniel sleeping. He was tired from staying up all night to help with the map. I left the map as well, which was showing me the same thing it had shown me ever since I'd taken Mr. Snuffles to the wolves. None of the other people who'd gone to the city were dead, but they all could be. They could be dead in the next moment, or the next, or the next. Ash was in the most danger of all, and because she was in danger the world was, too. Except wherever there was danger there was Jules, and his choices were the difference between living and dying. He was the shelter from the storm. I told that to Daniel, and he said Jules was truly one of us after all.

The trees grew thinner and then they stopped. I was at the lake. It was always quieter here than the rest of the forest, as if it were wrapped in silence. Sometimes I came here to be alone in quiet, only I was never really alone, since Ash's grandpa was in the water. Today I was even more not-alone, because there was a brown desert cat sitting on the shore.

"Hello," I said. "You're Starbeauty."

She turned green eyes away from the water and toward me. You are Georgie. When I come here, you are the one who greets me.

I'd never heard anyone make such perfect sense. "Yes. And this is where I greet you when you come."

Starbeauty inclined her head. You are trying to save her.

"You know Ash is in danger?"

I am the third.

I had known Starbeauty would be here, but I hadn't known she was the third, and that worried me. How was I supposed to help Ash if I missed something so important? "I didn't know that."

You did not need to know it. I knew it.

"But you're here! Shouldn't you be where Ash is?"

My choices are made here. The one whose choices are to be made there is with her already. She paced toward me. Hold out your hand.

I did, and she opened her mouth to drop something into my palm. "What's that?"

A taffa bean.

Ash had a lot of things to say about taffa, and none of them were good things. "I don't think Ash would want me planting taffa vines in the Firstwood."

You do not plant it. You put it beneath your tongue. It will help you to see.

I examined the bean, which was small and shiny and red. "But I don't use it now."

No. You will know when it is time to use the bean. Only it will not show you all things. Because to know the tree you must study the bark. But if you are studying the bark you cannot see the whole of the tree.

I nodded. "No one can know all of near and far."

You have wisdom. It is because you are of cat.

"I am?"

You see the future. Cats see the future. Therefore, you are of cat.

That made perfect sense, too.

There was a sudden rush of air, and Daniel appeared at the edge of the trees. "Georgie. I was worried about—" He stopped as he caught sight of Starbeauty. "Hello."

I am Starbeauty.

"I'm Daniel."

You are honored to meet me.

"Ah—yes, I suppose I am."

She returned her attention to me. He is yours. You are of cat. Therefore he is of cat, and all that is of cat belongs to me. She flicked her tufted ears toward the forest. I wonder what else in this place belongs to me.

"I don't know."

I shall find out.

Starbeauty stalked away, vanishing into the undergrowth. Daniel stared after her. "That cat is exactly like Ash said she was."

"How else would she be?"

He turned toward me and smiled. "No other way. Is Leo with her?"

Leo was who Starbeauty lived with in Spinifex City. Ash said Leo thought Starbeauty was his pet and Starbeauty thought he was hers. "No. When she comes here she comes alone."

Then I frowned, because Daniel was still smiling, and

there was something strange about it. Or there wasn't. It was how he always smiled, and Daniel smiled a lot. Only I had that wrong. Daniel smiled at *me* a lot, and there was nothing strange about it. What was strange was that I'd never understood what it meant before.

"Daniel! You love me."

He went so still he seemed to stop breathing.

"You love me like Connor loves Ash," I said. "And like Jules loves Ember."

"No, Georgie. I love you the way I love you."

I walked forward until I was standing right in front of him. "Are you sure?"

He choked back a laugh. "Am I *sure*? Georgie . . ."

Daniel thought it was funny. I smacked my hand against his shoulder. "It's a serious question! Because you could love anyone, and sometimes people find me hard to understand."

He wasn't smiling anymore. "Have I ever made you feel that way, even for a second?"

"No. But people live for a long time, Daniel. Futures go on and on and on. One day you might want someone everyone understands, and that isn't me."

He reached out to put his hands on either side of my face, brushing his thumb lightly along my cheek. He was shaking, although it wasn't cold. "Georgie,

180

you see things no one else sees, and when I'm with you, *I* see things no one else sees. You make me extraordinary. Why would I ever want to be with anyone else?"

I stared up at him, seeing myself reflected in the green of his eyes. I'd always thought Ash was the only one who could pull me back from a future. I'd been wrong. The picture Daniel had of me was one that would always draw me to wherever he was. Except I was too far away from him even though I was standing close. There was air between us and there shouldn't be. There shouldn't be anything between us.

I threw myself forward so that my entire body was pressed against his and I wrapped my arms around his neck and lifted up my head to kiss him. Then *I* was shaking, but with heat instead of cold, and I finally knew.

This was how it felt to be part of the real world.

THE CODE

ASHALA

We drove, Connor and Jules and me. Well, Connor and Jules did. I didn't know how. So they took shifts at the wheel while I sat in the front passenger seat and dozed.

We'd been driving for about eight hours now, and day had wound into night as we went. I stared out at gungurru trees washed silver by moonlight and wondered what was happening in the city. Was the fighting still going on? Which side was winning? *Probably not ours.* Terence might even be there . . . or, no, I'd bet he wasn't. He'd want to be absolutely sure

Neville had complete control of the city before he went anywhere near the place. It said something about how paranoid Terence was that a man who was basically indestructible was so afraid of abilities. Especially when the aingls had made alterations to their systems that meant not even the ability that had killed Dominic could hurt them now.

It was Connor's turn to drive; Jules was asleep and snoring in the backseat. I shifted to face Connor. "How long before we get there?"

"Three more hours. Four, perhaps."

He knew because he'd been to the center before, back when he'd been an enforcer. And three or more hours meant there was plenty of time for him to tell me the story I hadn't yet heard. "How were you hurt?"

He was silent. Reluctant to talk about it because he didn't want me thinking of it, not when we might be going into another fight. But I needed to hear. "I know you were hurt, and I know how badly. Jules is a mirror. He shows what he sees." So at one point today, there'd been a collar around Connor's neck and a wound to his head.

He sighed. "We were outside the room, right after the taffa had been delivered. Willis's husband had left by then, so it was only us with the guards. Three enforcers came walking around the corner, and one of them looked too young."

So that had been the sense of alarm I felt. Since all the minions were teenagers, Willis had set an age limit on entering the Residence as a security precaution. There shouldn't have been anyone under twenty wandering around that place other than us. "Minion?"

"Yes, as it turned out, although to begin with she was simply a distraction. It meant I was looking *ahead,* and so were Ember and Jules."

Ahead and not behind, where the guards were — and Jules had said that enforcers had turned on other enforcers. "The guards attacked you."

"It didn't seem like that at first. One of them tripped and bumped into me. There was a pain in my arm, nothing too bad! And I didn't pay much attention because the minion — Firestarter — attacked at almost the same time, and the Electrifier and the Blinker showed up. Then I tried to use my ability. And couldn't."

"Not at all?"

"That pain in my arm? Rhondarite dart, sunk into my skin. Before I knew it, there was an electric field across the door, and the enforcers were firing on us or at one another. We had to *retreat.*"

I heard the loathing in that last word. "Minions, streakers, and no ability? If you'd stayed you would've died."

"Doesn't mean I had to like leaving," he growled. "But you're right, and Ember and Jules saw it more clearly than I did. They dragged me out of there and got me to Wentworth. She dug out the dart and Mended me."

Okay, except there was something he was leaving out. "The collar?"

"That I did to myself."

"To *yourself*? Why?"

"Because Jules thought it might be useful for him to have an image of me wearing it in his head. I was going to put it on without closing the lock quite all the way until Wentworth told us about the master code."

Oh. Clever. "Where'd you even get a collar? Was . . . did the enforcers collar one of you?"

"No, three of them tried to collar *Wentworth,* before we got to the infirmary. Nicky attacked them, and Wentworth knocked them out."

Dr. Wentworth's healing ability was so strong she could make people sleep just by touching them — as she'd once said to me, almost everyone needed more rest. And the only one besides us who knew she could do that was Neville, because she'd put him to sleep with her ability once before. He must have sent those enforcers himself. No one else would consider a Mender a threat.

I grinned. "He didn't get any of us."

"What?"

"Neville," I explained. "He didn't get any of the people he most wanted revenge on. You. Me. Belle Willis. Dr. Wentworth." Despite everything, Neville hadn't had nearly as good a day as he would have liked to have had. I leaned back into the seat, the smile lingering on my face at the thought of Neville's plans going wrong. "Tell me the rest."

Connor shrugged. "You basically know it. Jules and I took uniforms from the enforcers who'd come for Wentworth, and Em got some spare Mender robes. Easier for us all to get through the place dressed like that, and, well, Em and Jules had blood on their clothes, too."

I stopped smiling. "They got hurt."

"We had to fight our way to the infirmary, and Jules . . . he kept putting himself between me and danger. I think he feels responsible for Pen. He didn't want anything to happen to me as well. Em took damage trying to protect us both."

Every bit of it would have hurt her before it healed, but I knew that wouldn't have stopped her. Not my Em.

"After that," Connor continued, "Jules and Nicky let themselves get 'captured.' I was waiting outside the window for the chance to get you out. Oh, and we met up with Henry Willis in the infirmary before then. That was when we arranged to get the Primes, and meet up with him and as many people as he could get out of the city at Turtle Rock."

I'd almost lost him, and maybe Jules as well. I felt a sudden sense of panic at how fragile their lives were, how easily taken. . . . No. Not fragile. Strong. My Tribe was strong. We'd made it through.

Connor took one hand off the steering wheel and held it out. I clasped hold of him, reassured by the feel of his hand in mine. Alive. Both of us alive, and Jules as well, still snoring away in the back. *Neville didn't get any of us.*

Then Connor said, "Your turn. Tell me about Neville Rose."

"There's not much to tell. He'd only just arrived when you all showed up."

He smiled, teeth flashing in the darkness. "Try again, Ashala."

Yeah, I hadn't expected to get away with that. "He killed Prime Grant, and he was going to kill the others. But—not me." I ran through all of it, stumbling over the part where Neville had told me I was going to be his audience. When I got to the end, I said, "Making me watch while people suffer and die, over and over? It's the worst thing he could do to me, much worse than killing me. And it really *bothers* me that he knows me well enough to understand that."

"He's evil, and evil knows how to hurt good," Connor answered. "That's not the same as understanding you. If he did, you wouldn't have escaped him both times he's had you captive." His fingers tightened on mine. "You are beyond his comprehension."

I snorted. "I only escaped because I had h—" I stopped, a smile pulling at my lips, and repeated in a different tone of voice, "I only escaped because I had help! *The Tribe* is beyond his comprehension."

A weight I hadn't even realized I was carrying seemed to fall away. *Neville doesn't know me.* Because he didn't know us.

We drove on in silence, enfolded by the dark and connected to each other. We drove for hours as the moon traveled across the sky, looping over our heads as night approached morning. But it was still dark when we neared Detention Center 1.

The place was on a rise, so we saw it for a ways before we reached it. Spotlights lit up the main gates, which were set into a towering composite wall that surrounded the center. Except the wall was early composite, the stuff the recyclers had produced before people had gotten them working properly, which meant it was gray instead of white and rough instead of smooth.

Connor slowed the car as we approached, and we waited in the glare of the spotlights as one of the guards began to walk toward the car. I'd swapped clothes with an enforcer at Turtle Rock and I had a streaker as well. Now I copied Connor's pose, sitting just as a real enforcer would. Shoulders straight and eyes ahead, watchful but not nervous. Maybe I was doing something wrong, because the guard was staring at me. My breathing seemed unnaturally loud and too fast—she must be able to hear it. *Stop. She only knows what you show her.* Jules said that if you truly wanted to pass as something you weren't, you had to wear the identity like a second skin. So I slowed my breathing and shifted toward the guard, meeting her eyes squarely.

I am an enforcer just like you. What're you looking at me for?

It worked. She gave me a brief nod and her gaze drifted to the back, where "Henry" was. People here should recognize him, since he'd accompanied Willis on regular inspection tours. I heard Jules wind down the window and speak in Henry's cheery voice. "Henry Willis to see the Chief Administrator on urgent business. Can you let us in, please?"

The guard peered in at him and stepped back. "Right away, sir!"

She waved to the other guard, and within seconds the big gates opened. We drove through and they shut behind us, sealing us in with a shuddering thud. Connor swung the car around to park it beside some other vehicles. Then he got out to open the door for Jules, and I followed him.

The inside of the center was as gray as the outside, and the lighting was dimmer. Buildings were crowded around the space where we were parked, three stories high and all of them with windows looking down at us. There were no lights in those windows, which wasn't the same as there being no people. It just meant that if anyone was watching, they were in darkness. Perhaps standing to the side of the window, staring down at three figures in the parking lot . . . *Stop imagining things.*

190

If these buildings were offices, there was absolutely no reason for anyone to be in them in the early hours of the morning. Most of the staff would be sleeping in their quarters, and the ones who weren't would be enforcers on patrol.

The door to the building immediately ahead of us opened, and a blond enforcer came hurrying out. "Mr. Willis! So good to have you with us again. I don't think we've met before. I'm Carrie, one of the officers here. The Chief Administrator's sleeping, I'm afraid."

Jules beamed at her. "Quite all right. My fault for arriving unannounced. But I really must speak with her as soon as possible."

"Of course. I've already sent someone to wake her. Please come with me, and you can wait in her office."

Jules walked along behind the enforcer with Henry's bouncing step. Connor and I paced after him, into the building and more grayness. Carrie led us down a long corridor and up a flight of stairs, turning on lights as she went. "Sorry. There's no one in the administration buildings at this hour."

I'd been right that they were offices. That didn't make me feel better. Carrie was nervous. Her eyes kept darting back and forth between Jules and Connor and me. *She could just be wondering what we're doing here.* Worried about a surprise inspection, maybe? Or worried about something else?

She led us up two more flights of stairs and to a large room. I cast a quick glance around as we entered. Tall cupboards across one wall, a shelf holding books on another, and a big desk that held a couple of pictures of a smiling redhead with various other people. *Hello, Chief Administrator Hayne.*

Carrie ushered Jules over to the chairs sitting in front of the desk. "Can I get you anything? Water? Tea?"

"Just the Chief Administrator, thank you," Jules replied, with another of Henry's big smiles.

"I'm sure she won't be long. I'll go check on what's happening."

She scurried out, shutting the door behind her. I waited until the sound of her footsteps disappeared down the corridor outside and said, "Does it seem like something's off to you two?"

Connor was frowning. "She's too young to be a senior officer."

And Willis had said she'd replaced all the senior staff but had only just started in on the juniors. "You think Carrie was here when Neville was?"

He shrugged. "Not necessarily. They rotate junior

officers through different centers. And it *is* four in the morning. All the senior officers might be sleeping. I don't like that none of them came to meet us, though."

I didn't, either, now that he'd pointed it out.

"Best to stay alert," Jules said. He shimmered into himself and began to prowl around, opening drawers to see what was inside. Connor shifted to stand facing the door, ready for trouble if it came. It didn't seem like I'd be much help to either of them, so I wandered to the window in case I could spot anything outside. We were on the opposite side of the building from where the parking lot was, and the window gave a view of the center, which was to say, more gray buildings lit by the dim glow of the night lighting. Also, an exercise yard surrounded by a razor-wire fence. The one in Detention Center 3 had a park in it. This one didn't seem to have so much as a single blade of grass. I suddenly realized that this would have been Neville's office when he ran the place. It was easy to imagine him standing right where I was now, staring at the detainees in the yard. *Choosing his next victim* . . . I stepped away.

Jules had abandoned the desk and gone over to the cupboards, opening one door after another. One of the cupboards had some kind of silver machine in it that I thought looked pretty interesting, but Jules must have seen whatever it was before, because he just shut the door and went on to the next. Except the next door wouldn't open.

He shook the handle. "Locked."

"Careful!" I hissed. "You'll break it."

"Why would this one be locked? None of the others were." He shook it harder.

"Stop do—"

Before I could finish the sentence, the door gave way—and a red-haired woman came tumbling out to land on top of Jules.

He yelped and leaped backward. The woman sprawled across the floor, head lolling and eyes closed. Connor darted over, kneeling to put his hand to her neck. After a moment he shook his head. "No pulse. But no apparent injury, either . . ." He rolled her over. There was a burn mark on the back of her beige robe. "Streaker."

I swallowed. "That's the Chief Administrator. She's in all the photos."

From outside there was the sound of footsteps approaching down the corridor.

Jules grabbed the streaker from my hip and shoved me back, sending me stumbling as he leaped across the Chief Administrator's body to put himself in front of me *and* Connor. The door opened, and two objects came hurtling through the air to crash into the window and clatter to the ground. In the same moment Jules fired twice, and then there was quiet.

I grabbed hold of the desk to catch my balance and glanced around in bewilderment, trying to work out what had happened. "Is everyone all right?"

"We're fine," Connor answered. "You?"

"Yeah. Just . . . surprised." Two enforcers were lying outside the doorway with open, staring eyes and streaker burns to their chests. And on the floor behind me were two more streakers — *the enforcers'*. They'd been armed with them until Connor had taken their weapons away. They'd come here to kill us — no, they'd come here to kill Prime Willis's husband and his guards. With weapons that they shouldn't have had and that must have been smuggled in here.

Neville's people had control of the center.

The door flew shut. "Stand away from the furniture," Connor said. "I'm going to use it as a barricade."

I let go of the desk and backed up to the window. The desk rose upward and the chair and shelves along with it, all floating forward to pile up against the door.

"How do we get o —" Jules began, and stopped as he realized. "Oh. Window."

"That's our escape route," Connor agreed. "But not yet."

He went to the cupboard with the silver device in it, bending down to twist one of the dials.

"What *is* that?" I asked.

"Public address system," Connor replied. "Gets heard all over the center, and I can make it play a recording on a loop, over and over."

I didn't see how that would help — no, I did. "Like the collar code? That's genius!"

"It won't be much help to anyone who doesn't have an ability that can get them out of a cell," he said, pushing at the buttons. "But I don't see any other way to give the detainees a chance." He bent closer to the device and spoke in a calm, clear voice. "Attention all detainees. This facility has been seized by traitors loyal to Neville Rose. Your collar can be unlocked using the following sequence: 367537369."

He sat back, pushed yet another button, and stood. "That's it. Let's get out of here."

I grabbed the streakers off the floor, handing one to Connor and shoving the other into my pocket as the message started to play. "Attention all detainees . . ."

Jules pried open the window, and then the three of us were out and soaring through the night, floating over the buildings to settle onto a nearby rooftop. We lay flat, clinging to the ridge of the roof and looking down over the center.

Lights were flicking on inside buildings. Doors were slamming, and voices raised in anger and panic. I could hear orders being shouted, too, but not well enough to make them out, and the pounding of multiple sets of feet as enforcers ran to—wherever they were running to. Over the top of it all, Connor's voice steadily recited the magic numbers that would set the detainees free: *367537369*.

"Well," I said, "*now* what do we do?"

THE DETAINEES

ASHALA

"Whatever we do, we've got be careful about it," Jules said. "This is going to get real chaotic real fast, and we're in enforcer uniforms, in case you'd forgotten. We're as likely to get killed by someone on our own side as we are by the guards."

He was right about that. "We need to make contact with the detainees. Let them know we're here to help."

Connor inched forward and pointed to a distant rooftop. "If I'm remembering right, that building over there is solitary confinement."

Jules nodded approvingly. "Good idea, flyboy."

"What's a good idea?" I demanded.

"You've got to have caused some serious trouble to get thrown into solitary," Jules explained. "Anyone in there will be a fighter. Our kind of people."

"Also," Connor added, "there's only six cells in the building. We need to make contact with a small group, not have dozens of Illegals using their abilities on us before they realize we're not their enemies."

I grinned. "Let's go make some new friends!"

We hurtled across the rooftops and then down into the center, landing in the narrow gap between solitary confinement and the next building over. Connor's voice wasn't blaring out any longer. They must have broken down the door to the office to cut the announcement, but they'd been too late. I could hear distant shouts and streaker fire. At least some of the detainees were out, and there was a fight going on somewhere, although apparently not here, which seemed strange given that we were near a set of cells. Maybe none of the detainees in solitary had abilities that could free them. Still . . . "Shouldn't there be more guards around?"

Connor shook his head. "Solitary is some distance from the main cell block, which is where they'll be

199

concentrating their resources. We should be okay for a while."

"Don't forget we're being careful," Jules whispered. Pen's death really had affected him; he was usually the most reckless of all of us. He pointed to a high mesh-covered window above. "You two try to see what we're dealing with inside. I'll go keep watch."

He skulked away to hide in the shadows at the edge of the building, peering out into the center. Connor and I drifted upward to the window. It was hard to make out details through the mesh, but I could pick out the main features of the space. A door to my right that must lead outside onto the wide lane that Jules was watching. Directly opposite the door were two desks, positioned on either side of a passageway, only I couldn't see what was down it from this angle.

"No guards at all?" I whispered. "That doesn't seem r—"

I broke off as the door opened and a heavyset enforcer strode in. He shut the door behind him and hurried across the room, past the desks and into the passage.

"That corridor leads to the cells," Connor said. "I think we'd better go in."

We both floated back down, turning toward Jules.

200

He wasn't there.

Then I heard the faint but familiar sizzle of an energy weapon firing from somewhere inside solitary confinement and understood.

The heavyset enforcer *was* Jules. "Oh, that idiot!"

We raced around the corner and into the building. I'd barely closed the door when Jules came stumbling in our direction, wearing his own face. There were three enforcers and an administrator sprawled on the floor behind him, and Jules had one hand clapped to his shoulder. Blood was pouring over his fingers.

Jules staggered. I ran to catch him, lowering him into a chair. Connor began to yank open the drawers of the desk, saying over his shoulder to me, "There should be a first-aid kit in here somewhere. Check the other one!"

I darted across the room to the second desk. *Procedure manual . . . forms . . . more forms . . . first-aid kit!* I flung open the lid and gazed at the contents in dismay. The healfast strips I understood. The small bottles I didn't. I knew how to do first aid with forest herbs, not with this stuff.

Connor had medic training, and he would know. "Connor? Help!"

He was at my side in seconds, grabbing hold of the

kit and racing back to Jules. He leaned over him, trying to pull Jules's hand from his shoulder. Jules wouldn't let him.

"Here." I crossed to Jules's other side. "Give your hand to me."

"'S got blood on it," he objected.

"That's okay, I don't mind. Come on, hold on to me, now." I pried his hand gently away, clasping it in mine.

"I'm dying, aren't I?"

"It's only your shoulder," Connor told him, taking a pair of scissors from the kit and cutting away Jules's shirt. "Stab wound . . . it's deep, but it won't kill you."

"Are you sure? It *really* hurts."

"I'm sure." Connor reached into the kit to take out a cloth, and poured the contents of one of the bottles onto it. "I'm afraid this is going to hurt, too. Try not to yell."

He pushed the cloth against the wound. Jules sucked in a harsh breath, crushing my hand, but was otherwise silent. Connor took away the cloth and held out another one of the bottles to Jules. "You need to drink this."

Jules let go of me to reach for it. He was shaking so badly I knew he'd drop the thing. I grabbed the bottle and held it to Jules's lips as Connor pressed a healfast strip over the wound. By the time Jules had finished drinking, some of the color had come back into his face.

"You shouldn't have come in here alone," I said.

He looked up at me out of half-closed eyes. "Hey, I did pretty good, being as it was four against one. Saved the lives of whoever's in those cells, too. The guards were going to kill 'em."

"*What?*"

Jules tilted his head toward the bodies. "When I got here they were all standing in front of the cells, checking a file to see what the detainee locked inside could do. So they'd know what to expect before they opened the door and — well, let's just say I don't think they were planning on having a friendly chat."

I felt cold all over. *They're killing the detainees.* Picking off the ones whose ability couldn't be used to escape from a locked room before they got released by another detainee who had been able to get out. "We've got to help them!"

"We will," Connor said. "I'll —"

He broke off as there was a distant booming sound, and the building trembled. *Boomer.* But we were feeling the edge of an explosion that had happened somewhere else. Cell block, probably. Either the detainees were fighting back, or someone had lost control of their ability. The people in here had been in collars for a long time, and I really hoped they could manage their abilities well enough to be more of a threat to the guards than they were to one another. Otherwise this would be over fast, and without the guards having to do much of anything at all.

The reverberations eased, and Connor said, "Wait here with Jules. I'll go open the cells."

I leaned back against the desk. But Jules lurched to his feet, staggering after Connor. "*I'm* the one that saved those detainees! Stop trying to steal my glory."

I ran to Jules's side. "You need to sit back down!"

He threw his good arm around my shoulders, dragging me along with him. "We all have to open the cells together. Can't make the right choices if we're not together . . ."

He was a little delirious from either the wound or the medicine or both. And his grip on my shoulder was surprisingly strong—there was no way I'd be able to force him back to the chair, at least not without getting into a fight that would only hurt him worse. Connor hesitated, looking back at us.

"Let the detainees out," I told him. "Then we'll deal

with Jules. We can't stay here anyway; we'll have to get him somewhere safer than this."

"No one needs to deal with me!" Jules objected. "I'm a hero. Stories will be told about me. Statues built. Songs sung . . ."

I helped him along, maneuvering around the bodies on the floor and trying not to stare into their slack faces. I was sorry they were dead in a larger sense—sorry anyone was dead—but I couldn't be sorry about them in particular, given what they'd been about to do. Besides, that could have been Jules, and back at the administrator's office it could have been all of us if Connor and Jules hadn't moved as fast as they did. A shudder ran through me, seeming to linger in my legs and around my heart. *Reaction.* I'd been too close to death too often over the past few days, and it was starting to fray my nerves.

Only two of the six cell doors were closed, and Connor walked up to one of them. He peered into the tiny window set into the door, speaking to whoever was inside. "We're here to help you. I want you to listen to the sound of my voice, because you've heard it before. That was me over the PA system, telling everyone the code. Do you understand?"

He paused. I didn't hear the detainee answer, but they must have nodded because Connor said, "Okay. There's three of us here, and when you come out you'll find we're wearing enforcer uniforms. But we're *not* enforcers."

He stepped away and pulled out his streaker, aimed it at the keypad lock, and fired. The door clicked open and was immediately yanked back from the other side to reveal a brown-skinned woman wearing a white detainee uniform.

Connor rose up into the air until there was clear space between him and the ground. She cast an assessing, dark-eyed gaze over him. "You're Illegals. I understand." Then she surveyed the bodies on the floor. "Did you do that?"

"I did," Jules caroled. "I'm a hero."

"Well, you seem to be injured, hero. Lucky for you I can fix that. I'm a Mender."

Jules gasped. "Don't trust her! Can't be a Mender— they get Exemptions!"

I grabbed the streaker at my hip, pointing it at the stranger. I couldn't see why she'd lie to us, but that didn't mean she wasn't lying. It wasn't totally impossible for a Mender to end up in detention—Stella, the Saur Tribe Mender, had gotten detained after she'd tried to help her Waterbaby best friend escape the enforcers. But Jules was right that it was rare, and after everything we'd been through, I wasn't in a trusting mood.

"Why can't I move?" the woman demanded, glaring at me and Jules. "One of you is, what, some kind of Paralyzer?"

No, it's Connor. She'd seen him levitate and assumed his ability was flying, and I wasn't going to correct the mistake when I wasn't sure I could trust her. For all I knew, she still didn't believe we were here to help her and was telling us her ability was something it wasn't. "How'd a Mender end up in detention?" I asked. "If that is what you are."

"My Exemption was revoked when I refused to treat a Citizen."

That made even less sense. "What kind of Mender refuses to treat a patient?"

She rolled her eyes. "Oh yes, anyone with my ability is supposed to be about the love of all of humanity. In case you hadn't noticed, all of humanity doesn't exactly love us. As far as I'm concerned, Citizens can get sick and die."

Those words had the ring of truth to them, even if it did mean she was the most un-Mender-like Mender I'd ever met. But if she was telling the truth about her ability, she'd have to be unusual to have ended up here.

"Shoot me," she said.

"What?"

"Shoot me!" she repeated impatiently. "Just my foot. Then I'll Mend it, and you'll see."

This was getting ridiculous. "No one's going to shoot you. We'll let you go." Because I didn't see what else we could do. We couldn't keep standing around here, and if she wasn't a Mender and tried to use some other ability on us, I was going to have to trust Connor to stop her.

Jules was shaking his head, but Connor had already released her, because she reached across to drag her nail across her arm, hard enough to draw blood.

"What are you doing?" I demanded.

"Proving what I am," she answered. She put her fingers over the cut for a second before wiping the blood away to reveal undamaged skin. "See?"

She'd been telling the truth all along. "Sorry."

The woman shrugged, tossing her hair back over her shoulder. "I can appreciate a touch of paranoia in an ally. Means you're smart enough to stay alive." Then she jerked her head toward Jules. "Can I fix him now?"

"Go ahead."

The Mender strode forward to put her hand on

Jules's shoulder. After a few minutes she released him and said, "You're good, hero."

Jules let his arm fall away from me, reaching up to pull off the healfast strip. The wound was gone. He jabbed at his now-whole flesh. "Nice work!"

The Mender was already moving away, striding across to the other cell with the closed door. She pounded on it with her fist and called out, "Laurie! It's Shona. Hold on and I'll let you out." She turned to Connor. "How *do* we let him out?"

He pointed his streaker at the door. "Stand aside."

She stepped back, and Connor fired at the lock. The door clicked, and Shona shoved it open all the way. The cell beyond was empty except for an open collar sitting on the floor.

Then there was a stirring of the air and a gangly, freckled man appeared in front of her. "I Ran, Shona! I heard the guards coming, and I Ran very fast and when I Run fast no one can see me and no one can catch me. And no one did!"

"You did good, Laurie," she told him. "Really good." She waved at us. "These are our new friends — ah, whose names I don't know."

Connor pointed at himself. "Connor." Then Jules. "Jules." And finally me. "And this is Ashala Wolf."

"Leader of the Tribe?" Laurie exclaimed. "I thought you were just a story!"

The Tribe had been called a lot of things, but "story" was a new one. "I promise you, we're totally real."

Laurie beamed at me. "Is it true you live with saurs?"

"You can ask about saurs later," Shona told him. "Right now we've got to get everyone out of the cells who hasn't already made it out." She looked at Connor. "If you can spare that streaker, I'd like you to show Laurie how to fire it. He can get to all the cells a lot quicker than anyone else."

Connor handed it to Laurie, showing him the firing button.

Laurie shot a few experimental blasts at the doors. "This is fun!"

"This is *dangerous*," Shona told him. "You need to get to the cells and Run through to shoot all the locks, but you have to do it very fast, because it's going to make the enforcers angry. Too fast to be seen, and too fast to be caught. Okay?"

"Okay!"

Laurie vanished, and a second later the door whipped open and slammed shut.

Connor winced. "I hope no one heard that." He paced to the door, opening it gently to peer out.

Gray light filtered in; the sun had started to rise. *No more hurtling through the skies.* We'd be easy targets for streakers in the daylight, and the fighting I'd overheard earlier had gotten more intense — with the door open there were clear sounds of distant shouts and screams and the sizzle of weapons fire.

"All clear," Connor said. "I think —"

The door suddenly flew all the way open, and Connor was sent staggering. I drew my streaker, aiming it at — I didn't know, air! Then Laurie materialized again. Only now there was a red-haired, sharp-faced woman clinging to his back.

Jules had also pulled his streaker, and his hands were trembling. I hoped the shaking in mine wasn't that visible. He looked over and gave me a half-shrug, as if to say, *You too, huh?* If we weren't careful we'd end up shooting someone out of sheer nerviness. We lowered the weapons, and Laurie set the woman onto her feet.

"Cat was coming to save us," he announced. "Only I told her we were saved already. Now I'm going to save everybody else!"

And he was gone, sending the door slamming for the second time.

The newcomer cast a wary glance at our uniforms. Flames flickered across her fingers.

"They're friends," Shona said. "Illegals. This is Connor, Jules, and Ashala Wolf."

"Ashala Wolf?" The flames vanished. "Aren't you supposed to have some kind of ability that makes the impossible real? Can you help us?"

"My ability is used up right now," I answered. "We'll help any other way we can, though. We've got streakers and —"

"Don't care," Cat interrupted. "I mean, I do, but what I need most right now is a miracle or a Mender."

She switched her attention to Shona and said, "Jacks and Vishan Strongarmed open as many Leafer cells as they could get to. They got almost all of them out, only some are hurt."

I couldn't see why it mattered that Leafers in particular were hurt, but from the expression on Shona's face, it was a disaster. She leaped for the door. "Show me where!"

THE DAY

ASHALA

Shona and Cat hurried out, and the rest of us followed, skulking through the center in the cold dawn light. This place was a gray maze—even the ground was covered in composite, and the buildings were gathered together in haphazard groupings that meant we had to keep twisting and turning back and forth. But we had to be getting nearer to the fighting, because the shouting and weapons fire were growing steadily louder. Then Cat ducked into an alley between two buildings, swinging around to face us as we crowded in after her.

"Everyone's holed up just ahead," she said. "In the dining hall, or what's left of it, at least."

"What's *left* of it?" Shona asked.

"Priya blew part of it up trying to break the composite."

I had no idea why anyone would want to break composite, but it seemed to make sense to Shona, who nodded as if it explained everything.

"Thing is," Cat continued, "to get to the hall you need to—um, perhaps it's easier to show you. Look around the corner to your right."

Connor, Jules, Shona, and I crept to the edge of the alley and peered around. I could see . . . my foot.

I was looking at my foot.

Why was I looking at my foot?

I tried to look ahead again—and stared at my foot. *Oh.*

"A Lookaway?" I asked, turning back to Cat.

"Ten of them," Cat answered. "Standing in a circle around the hall, and every last one staring outward onto the center."

That was smart thinking. Everybody hiding *in* the hall would be gazing at the Lookaways' backs, which meant they wouldn't be affected by the ability. But everyone outside of it would be looking—or *trying* to look—at a Lookaway who was looking at them. Which was impossible.

"I'll go first," Cat said. "That way I can make sure everyone knows you're not enforcers. Give me a little while, then shut your eyes and run in a straight line for about ten meters."

She closed her own eyes and darted out. I reached for Connor's hand, and Jules's. I didn't want to lose track of them, and we were going to have to run blind. There was only one way to approach a Lookaway who was facing in your direction without getting turned around, and that was if you couldn't see them. Shona took hold of Jules's other hand, and we waited for a few minutes. Then the four of us ran out, jogging along in darkness with our feet thudding against the composite ground. The only way I had to tell that I was getting closer to where we were supposed to go was the gradual increase in the battle noises. It was *very* loud now—we were almost on top of the fighting, and it seemed like I'd been running for ages. Surely it had been ten meters already? *What if something went wrong?*

Cat's voice suddenly called out, "Stop! You're here."

I staggered to a halt, blinking my eyes open. In front of me were a lot of detainees, huddled in the shelter of a big pile of rubble. I could see the odd

215

flash of weapons fire over the top of the debris. As I'd thought, we were right at the edge of the fight. Cat grabbed hold of Shona's arm, pulling her over to where wounded people were lying on the ground. That left Jules, Connor, and me staring at the rest of the detainees. There were about fifty of them, and some were staring suspiciously back at us.

The others were digging.

They were gathered around a jagged hole in the composite-covered ground, scooping dirt out of it and into enormous cooking pots that they must have managed to salvage from the dining hall. Twenty—no, twenty-three—pots, and all of them filled up with earth. *Was this what they'd needed to break the composite for?* They certainly seemed to think they had something worth protecting, from the way they were hunching over the pots and glaring at us.

Beside me, Jules muttered, "We don't want your dirt. Really."

"Shhh!" I hissed. "They must have a reason."

"Either they do or they've been in here too long and gone cr—"

He broke off as Shona came striding over, along with an older, gray-bearded man whose shirt was stained with blood, although from the easy way he was moving he wasn't hurt anymore. Shona must have Mended him, and as I watched her approach, I realized *all* the wounded were getting to their feet. *She's good.* In fact she was about as strong a Mender as any I'd ever seen, other than Wentworth.

"This is Bran," Shona said as she reached us. "Bran — Connor, Jules, Ashala. Connor's the one who can fly." She drew in a breath and added, "We need your help. We're losing out there, and we've got to find a way to win, or at least hold out until Laurie can get everyone else free. See those pots?"

"They're kind of hard to miss," I said.

"They're filled with seeds. The wind blows them in from the forests, and we've been collecting them for years and hiding them from the guards. Just in case we ever got a chance to fight back."

I suddenly understood why the detainees were being so protective. *Not dirt.* Weapons. Or the seeds would be, in the hands of a strong Leafer, who could make anything grow as long as it was anchored in earth. Which was why it had mattered that Leafers were hurt. "You're going to attack the enforcers with plants?"

"That's the plan," Bran said. "We Leafers are going to climb up to the top of the rubble so we've got a good view of the fight. Then we move the pots onto the battlefield and make the seeds grow."

"The problem," Shona said, "is that it's not going to be easy to get the pots to where we want them to be. We need them scattered over as much of the fighting as possible, and we don't have anyone who can fly. So, Connor, if you could carry even a few of them across to the other—" She broke off, scowling. "You all find this funny for some reason?"

Jules and Connor and I were grinning, and she didn't know why. Because she didn't know what Connor could really do.

"My ability," Connor said, "is not flying."

He gestured, and there were startled exclamations from the detainees as their pots rose upward to hover above the ground.

Shona's jaw dropped. "Wh—how?"

"He doesn't fly, exactly," I explained. "He controls the air."

The detainees were staring at Connor as if he were the sun come down from the sky to shine upon them.

"You *control* the air?" Bran repeated. "That means—you can—" A fierce grin split his face. "Oh, this is going to be grand! You get the pots out there, lad—we'll do the rest!"

He spun around and raced for the debris, calling out

to the others as he went, "Leafers! Top of the rubble, now!"

Detainees shot to their feet and followed him. Ten . . . twenty . . . thirty . . . *Almost everyone here is a Leafer.* Even if some of them were having difficulty with their abilities, there were more than enough here to compensate for it. *And their Strongarms had prioritized freeing the Leafers from the cells.* These detainees had been thinking about escape for a long time.

Connor, Jules, and I soared up to the top of the rubble, lying flat to peer over the edge as the Leafers climbed up after us. Below was more of the collapsed hall, and directly opposite was a huge building dotted with tiny windows that had to be the cell block. In the space between there and here was chaos.

There were enforcers *everywhere,* shooting and slashing and stabbing, and they moved like the trained fighters they were. I could see individual detainees fighting back—Jumpers leaping in to strike a blow and leaping out again, Strongarms lifting guards up and flinging them across the ground, Waterbabies blasting with spouts of water, and a couple of Firestarters tossing fireballs. But too many of the detainees seemed to be trying to fight with nothing but their fists. Others were gesturing with their hands as if something was supposed to happen, and nothing did. *They're having problems with their abilities.* Against swords they still could probably have taken the enforcers. But not against streakers. The detainees were losing, and they were dying fast.

The Leafers reached the top of the rubble. Connor drew a breath, and pots shot out overhead to hurtle across the battlefield. Streaker fire blazed through the sky as some of the enforcers fired upward, and the pots swerved, zigzagging back and forth as they scattered across the sky over the fight. Connor's shoulder was next to mine, and I could feel the tension in it. *Too many pots, too many streakers* . . . I shifted closer, trying to transfer what strength I had to him. We couldn't let those pots get shot down—if the dirt spilled, the Leafers weren't going to be able to grow the seeds, and this would be for nothing.

The pots careened onward until they'd reached all corners of the battlefield, hovering above the fighting. And Bran shouted, "Now!"

The seeds began to grow.

Stinger nettles surged out and down, wrapping around enforcer heads and sending them shrieking in pain as the toxic hairs on the leaves embedded into their skin. Tussock grasses boiled out, stretching to unnatural lengths to tangle up enforcer hands and pluck streakers from their grasp. Starflowers descended in a pretty shower of pink and white to puff their pollen into enforcer faces and confuse their senses. And from every pot, the slender silver limbs of young gungurrus grew, coiling around and around to encase their pots in wood before flowing to the earth and thickening to form a trunk.

"Let go, lad!" Bran called. "We got this."

Connor shuddered, lowering his head. I pressed closer to him and tightened my grip on my streaker, alert for danger. Only there wasn't any, not to us, because the Lookaway protection was still working. Even with the pots flying out from this direction, none of the enforcers had noticed anything odd about not being able to look this way, or at least not enough to realize it was an ability at work. Which wasn't surprising, since they had more immediate problems.

The pots had become living towers that were dealing green death in every direction. A few of the enforcers were firing uselessly at the gungurru trunks, burning the wood but doing no more than that. The rest of them were struggling with the plants or with the detainees, who were attacking with renewed enthusiasm. Some of those detainees were now armed with the streakers that the tussock grass had stolen, and it hadn't taken them long to figure out how to fire the things. Then there was a sudden roar, and I looked across at the cell block to see detainees pouring out. One after the other went charging into the fight in what seemed like a never-ending stream of people. *Well done, Laurie.* The detainees already in the battle let out a ragged cheer. So did the Leafers on the rubble around us. And I saw it, as clearly as if I'd been standing on the shore in Gull City—the tide had turned. The detainees were going to win this.

I nudged Connor. "It worked. It totally worked!"

He lifted his head. "We should—"

"No!" Jules snapped.

We both looked at him, and he growled, "We shouldn't do *anything*. Whatever idiot, self-sacrificing idea you're about to suggest, no!" He jabbed a finger at Connor. "You were badly hurt back in the city. And you"—he pointed to me—"can't even use your ability! Besides, in case you haven't noticed, this lot are taking care of themselves just fine. So for once, for all of five minutes, can the two of you just stay put and *stop helping people!*"

Connor and I exchanged rueful glances. Then I said, "Well, I suppose. For *five* minutes."

"Possibly even ten," Connor murmured.

Jules didn't think we were funny. He turned his head away, muttering something that sounded like *This is the worst job I've ever had.* Except that didn't make sense, so I must have heard wrong.

We watched the fight for a while longer, but Jules was right that the detainees were looking after themselves just fine. So we floated down to the ground and were immediately recruited by Shona, who needed help to manage the wounded. For the next few hours I held hands and spoke reassuringly, and helped sort people into three groups: hurt . . . a lot hurt . . . *Shona, get over here now!* The remains of the dining hall gradually became a makeshift hospital, with Lookaways guarding the sides but not the front so detainees could find their way in. Eventually, there came a point when I realized there was no one left to help. And everything was quiet; there were no sounds of fighting anymore.

I glanced across at Connor and Jules, who were standing nearby. "Is it over?"

A voice behind me said, "Yes, it's over, Ashala Wolf!"

I spun around to face Laurie. Shona caught sight of him and hurried across to us, reaching out to take hold of his arm. "You're all right, Laure? You're not hurt anywhere?"

"I can Run *much* faster than enforcers."

She checked him over and gave a relieved nod, wiping a weary hand across her forehead. She'd been using her ability for ages now and desperately needed to rest. I couldn't let her yet.

"Shona? If the fighting's over, then there's something everyone here needs to know. Something *really* important." I drew in a breath and launched into the story of the repeal of the Citizenship Accords. Connor and Jules joined in, adding details I'd missed and telling their side of what had happened while I'd been with the Primes.

When we got to the end, Laurie was grinning an enormous grin. "No more accords? Really truly?"

"Well, sort of," I told him. "They're gone, just . . . not around here, if Terence Talbot is in charge of Gull City."

Shona was staring at us with an expression of utter disbelief. I supposed not being an Illegal anymore was a hard thing to absorb. Then she said, "You want us to fight for the *government*?"

Oh. It wasn't the end of the accords that she was finding hard to believe. "We want you to fight against Neville Rose."

Laurie hunched his shoulders. "Neville Rose is a bad man."

I blinked, recognizing the way Laurie said those words. It was the same way I said them. "Neville hurt you."

He stared down at the ground, moving some stray dirt with his foot. Shona put her arm around him. "Laurie was one of the subjects for Rose's experiments. A lot of people here were." Her lip curled into a snarl. "And I was the one Rose got to Mend them once he was done. So that he could start all over again."

I shuddered. "I know. I mean, I didn't know about you, but . . ."

"You know what it's like," Shona said.

"Yeah." I moved a fraction nearer to Connor so that my hand brushed against his. When I'd been held prisoner in Detention Center 3, Connor had been the one who'd had to patch me up and send me back to Neville. It was the hardest thing I'd ever asked of him. An impossible thing, but he'd done it. We did the impossible for each other, and the Tribe.

Shona's gaze roamed across the two of us, and I don't know what she saw in our faces, but she said, "I'll tell everyone to hear you out. Although I don't know if anyone's going to be prepared to do what you're asking." She looked up at Laurie. "Can you go tell everyone what's happened in the city? And that if

225

they want to find out more they should come speak to Ashala?"

He nodded and disappeared. Shona pointed to the rubble. "You need to go sit somewhere where it's easy for people to see you, so they can come and ask you questions if they'd like to. *Don't* go up to anyone yourself, don't pressure anyone for a decision, don't —"

"I know," I interrupted. "In detention you have all your choices taken away. Now everyone here is the boss of themselves, and it's important that they're treated that way."

She let out a sigh of relief. "You do understand. Now go!"

Connor, Jules, and I made our way up the rubble and sat, high enough so people could spot us from a distance and come talk to us — or not. Then I turned my head to the left, toward the battlefield, where detainees were going about the grim task of clearing the area of bodies. There were a lot of people dead, detainee and enforcer both. I wouldn't ever have left the detainees at the mercy of Neville's people, but I wished there'd been another way.

After a while, people came, in groups of twos and threes. Some asked questions. Some just wanted to hear us tell the tale of the repeal of the accords. Many told us they weren't going to join the fight. Others went away without saying anything at all, and I knew they were thinking about it. Before we'd come here I'd figured we'd be bringing detainees back with us straightaway. I knew now that wasn't going to happen. They needed time to make the decision. That was how things were done in this tribe.

We talked through most of the day. When it was clear no one else was coming, I rose, needing to stretch my legs, and walked across the rubble to gaze out over the battlefield. It was empty of bodies now, and there was blood and streaker scorch marks on the composite. And twenty-three strange-looking trees. There wasn't enough soil in the pots for those plants to survive for long, but they wouldn't have to. The Leafers were going to make a garden and encourage the gungurru trunks to sink roots deep into the earth. That was another thing we'd learned in the course of the day—many of the detainees were staying. They thought that between them all they could hold the center against anyone who came to take it back. I thought they probably could, too.

Jules and Connor came to stand on either side of me. "We did it," Jules said. "Guess we're all heroes."

"I think they would've done it without us," I replied. "I mean, more people would have died, but . . . *years.* They spent years collecting those seeds just on the chance that it might help them." I'd imagined Neville before, staring into the exercise yard at detainees who shrank from his gaze. Now I wondered how many of those detainees had been looking away because they'd been looking for seeds. Neville had taken away most of their choices. But they'd held on to their hope.

We were silent, staring out at the battlefield and over the gray center bathed in the long light of the afternoon. Then Connor murmured, "There will come a day when a thousand Illegals descend on your detention centers . . ."

I'd heard those words somewhere before. I looked up at him to find that the corner of his mouth was curving into a smile; he was waiting for me to realize something. And I remembered. Connor was quoting me. Back when I'd believed that Connor was my enemy, because Ember had altered my memories to keep my secrets safe from Neville's interrogation machine, I'd made him a promise. I'd told him that one day Illegals would rise up and destroy every detention center in the world.

I tried to remember how the rest of it went. "Pounders—no, Boomers!—will breach the walls. . . ."

He joined in. "Skychangers will send lightning to strike you all down from above . . ."

". . . and Rumblers will open the earth to swallow you up from below. . . ."

He took a breath, and I took a breath, and we chorused together, "And when that day comes, think of me!"

Connor's laughter rang out over the center and sparkled through his eyes. I rested my head against his shoulder and laughed with him. Jules rolled his eyes at the both of us. But he was smiling as well, as if it made him happy to see us happy.

I put one arm around Connor and the other around Jules and said, "I think it's about time we got back to the Tribe."

THE WHEN

GEORGIE

Ember was back and so was Nicky. They'd arrived yesterday, only they weren't in the Firstwood yet, because Em had needed to help the Prime and all the other people who'd come from Gull City move into Detention Center 3. But she'd mindspoken Jaz, who had mindspoken Daniel and me. That was how I knew Terence Talbot had sent Neville Rose to take over Gull City, and the Citizenship Accords were gone, and Ash and Connor and Jules had gone to save the detainees in Detention Center 1. Or Ash and Connor had, and Jules had gone to save Ash and Connor. Only Ember wouldn't know that because Ember didn't know about the blizzard.

Em wanted to talk to me. She'd told Jaz that, too. She hadn't told him what about, but she was coming home today and then I'd know. Right now I was making my map.

Helper chirped a question. I was holding a piece of vine, and I must have been holding it for a while, because he wanted to know when I was going to do something with it.

I let it fall. "I don't know where it goes," I told him. I'd been mapping all morning and couldn't seem to get anything right. Whenever I tied futures together I had to untie them again. "None of the futures connect. Or they all do."

Everything is and everything is not.

I turned to where Starbeauty was lounging in a patch of sunlight. "I don't understand."

Who is the Prime of Gull City?

"Belle Willis." I frowned. "Except she doesn't have the city anymore." Now I did understand. "Everything is and everything is not! Belle Willis is the Prime of Gull City, but she isn't, because Terence Talbot is calling himself the Prime and he has the city. And the Citizenship Accords are gone, but they're not, because no one's let all the detainees out yet."

231

Exactly so. All is in motion in opposite directions.

That was why I couldn't map. No one future was more likely than another. "When will things stop being in motion?"

The world is good. The world is bad. What is the difference?

"Choice." I understood even more now. "We're waiting on people's choices. Like Jules, and . . . No." This was bigger than that. "Everyone's choices. All the people, everywhere in the world."

Yes. When enough choices are made, a direction will emerge. Then you and yours must make your choices.

"What about you?"

My choice is to help you. She rose to her feet, shaking herself off. *Someone approaches.*

I went to the entrance of the cave and waited for whoever was coming to get here. After a while there was a scuffling sound and Nicky bounded in. He leaped around me, trying to lick my face.

What are you?

Nicky dropped onto all fours, staring at Starbeauty with his ears pricked up and his nose quivering. "Woof!"

She turned her head away from him. *You are not of cat.*

Nicky whined. Starbeauty wouldn't look at him. He whined again. She still wouldn't look.

Nicky went running out, and I said, "He just wants to be friends."

That which is not-cat must know its place. She tilted her head to one side. He is returning.

There was the scuffling sound again and Nicky came back in, carrying a stick. He took it up to Starbeauty, dropped it in front of her, and sat. "Woof!"

She turned a green gaze on me. Why has he brought me this wooden object?

"It's his favorite stick," I explained. "He likes to carry it around the forest."

Ah! She flicked her ears at Nicky. You have presented me with your most treasured possession.

Nicky wagged his tail.

It is a worthy gift.

His tail wagged even harder, thumping steadily against the floor.

You may escort me around the Firstwood and show me the places that are not known to humans.

"Woof!"

Nicky bounced out, and Starbeauty followed. When she reached the entrance she looked back over her

233

shoulder at me. *I am trusting you to take care of my stick.*

"The spiders will make sure it's safe."

See that they do. And this is when.

"When what?"

She stalked off without answering. Perhaps I already knew the answer. If I did, I didn't know that I knew. I'd have to wait to understand or for Starbeauty to explain more.

I began to map again, but it was the same as before. Every time I made a connection, I had to unmake it. I tried anyway, and I was still trying when there were footsteps in the passage and Ember came into the cave.

"Em, you're back!" I hugged her and she hugged me. Then she said, "Terence has taken over the city."

"For certain?"

She nodded. "Willis got a messenger, right before I left. Things are very serious, Georgie. Which is why I need you to tell me what's going on. Everything that's going on."

I took in a deep breath for all the words I would need and said, "The Tribe is in the forest and Daniel is with the Tribe. They're sad because we told them what you told us about Pen. They knew anyway when Mr. Snuffles howled, but they didn't know for sure and now they do. I am making my map, and Nicky and Starbeauty are visiting the places not known to humans."

"*Starbeauty?* Leo's cat is here?"

"Yes. But Leo isn't."

"What's she — Actually, never mind, we can discuss this later. Georgie, when I said I wanted you to tell me what's going on, I meant what's *really* going on. I want to know what you told Jules."

I didn't say anything. Sometimes if I didn't speak for long enough, people stopped expecting an answer. But Ember still looked like she was expecting an answer, and Ember didn't age the way organic beings did. She might be able to expect an answer for a very long time.

She frowned at me. "I *know* there's something happening. I've had the entire journey back from the city to think about this, and too many things aren't adding up. Jules lied to me, which he never does. It's not like him to disobey Ash, either, because he's been trying to be a part of the Tribe, even though people don't always see it. And he was talking to you and Daniel before we went to the city."

I wished Daniel were here. If he were, he'd know how to distract Ember. I wasn't sure what words to use and I had to be careful what I said. Ember was good at taking words apart and finding out what they meant even when you didn't want her to know.

She sighed. "Georgie, I understand you're not always sure when you tell people things, or if you tell people things—whatever it is, if there's a time that you tell me, this is when!"

This is when. Starbeauty had said that. Now Ember had said it, too. But Ember had said it twice, because she'd said it once before this. No, she hadn't. I'd *heard* it before, in a future. I'd been seeing this moment. I hadn't known why it mattered. Now I did. "You're the fourth!"

"I'm the what?"

"Jules was the first, and Penelope the second, and Starbeauty the third, and you are the fourth! So I can tell you." I frowned. "Except I said I wouldn't unless Jules was here."

"Don't stop talking now!"

But I did, because I'd made a promise to Jules. Promises were important. Except Starbeauty had said this was when, and Starbeauty understood futures better than Jules. Futures were more important than promises. I was going to have to tell her. "Ash is *going* to die."

Em swayed. I caught her arm before she fell. "It's all right! We think we can stop it."

She grabbed on to me, her fingers digging into my skin. "How?"

So I explained about the choices and why they mattered, and about the blizzard that would come if we lost Ash or Connor, because either of them dying was the same. When I finished, she said, "And Jules *knew* all this?"

"Yes."

She let me go and looked past me, staring out at the forest as if she wasn't seeing the trees. "He never told me. He never said a word, just let me be mad at him, let me think he'd betrayed us. . . ." Her gaze returned to me. "Do you know if he's alive? Do you know if any of them are?"

"They're alive. I think. I mean, if Ash or Connor were dead, the blizzard would be here, and I saw in my map when Pen died."

"So you believe they're alive. I'm going to believe that as well. I'm going to believe that, and I'm going to—I'm going to—"

She didn't finish the sentence, which was strange

because Ember liked sentences to have a proper ending. Maybe she hadn't understood what she was supposed to do?

"Choose," I said. "You have to choose."

"*I know that!*"

I took a step away from her.

"Sorry," Ember said. "I'm sorry, I didn't mean to yell. This is a lot to cope with at once, but I shouldn't have shouted. Are you certain they're alive?"

"No."

She choked back a laugh. "Sorry again. That was a stupid question."

"They're *probably* alive."

"I should have gone with them."

I shook my head. "Your choices didn't matter then. They matter now, and now you're here. So this is where you need to be."

"I hope you're right about that."

I hoped I was, too.

She turned away and began to pace, striding back and forth across the cave. Em always paced when she was working something out. I returned to my map, picking up the vine I'd let go of before and tying it to another one. No, that was wrong. I untied it and tried another. No, that was wrong as well. I tried another, and another, until I started being able to make connections without having to untie them. Then I had to stop, because it was getting hard to tie the knots with my hands so numb from the cold. . . .

I dropped the vine. *My hands are cold.* Only it wasn't cold here in the real world. I scanned the connections. Ash and Connor and Jules were still alive as far as I could tell, but the blizzard was closer. So close I was feeling it through the vines that made the map. I'd been waiting for people everywhere to make choices. They had, and they were the wrong ones. The world was moving in the direction of its end. *Now me and mine have to make our choices.* And in this world where other people were choosing wrong, our choices were fewer and harder.

"Georgie?"

I turned. Ember was standing behind me with a small silver box in her hands. I'd never seen it before. Had it been somewhere in the cave? I glanced around, but I couldn't see any other boxes. The light coming in through the cave opening was softer, though, which meant it was much later in the day. I'd been mapping for a long time. Ember must have been thinking for a long time. Maybe she'd brought the box from somewhere else. Or built it herself. "Did you make that, Em?"

"My dad did, a long time ago. It's a type of—communicator. I'm going to use it to send a message to my family."

"But aren't your family bad, except for Leo and Nicky and your dad?" Only then I remembered that Ash thought Hoffman was bad, too, only not a bad person. A bad father.

"My family is . . . complicated," Ember said. "But this isn't really about them. It's about getting more time. We need time for Ash's ability to come back, and for her and Connor to fully recover from the injuries they got in the city, and for Willis to gather allies and support. But I think Terence's next move is going to be coming here, and we'll be all out of time."

"You think he'll come to get Ash?"

"Or Willis, and then Ash. Or both of them at once. We need to stop him from coming for as long as we can, and this . . ." She held up the box. "This will do that."

I stared at the box in amazement. "It *makes* time?"

"Ah—in a way. It summons my family to a special sort of meeting called a Conclave. Once a Conclave's been set, none of us can act against the interests of any of the others, not before the meeting and not for one week afterward. And since I'm part of the Tribe, coming after us counts as acting against me. Coming after Willis does as well, because the Tribe is known to be sheltering her."

That meant Ash would be safe from Terence until the meeting. Perhaps Ash could be safe for a long time. "Maybe you could make the meeting a hundred years from now!"

"I wish I could. But I can only make it four weeks from now. That's the maximum amount of time there can be before a Conclave."

It was still a good idea. Only there was something I didn't understand. "Why does it make you sad?"

"What makes you think I'm sad?"

"Your mouth looks like an upside-down smile."

Em straightened her mouth out. She wasn't fooling me. "You're still sad, Em."

She sighed. "I know. Conclaves . . . They're special, Georgie. None of us have ever broken the rules of one, not even Terence, because—well, we're family. We all need to know that whether it's now or hundreds of years from now, there'll always be a way for us all to come together. But after *this* Conclave, there probably won't be another one."

"Why not?"

"Because my dad won't be there." She bent to the box on the ground. "Dad's the one who calls Conclaves. This is his device, and everyone will be expecting to see him. They don't know I've got the device, and he's . . . sleeping."

Ember's dad was in the tunnels somewhere beneath the Firstwood because something had gone wrong with his head, and Em had shut him down when she hadn't been able to fix him. "Couldn't you tell the others he had to be somewhere else?"

Em shook her head. "There's no excuse good enough to miss a Conclave. Well, the truth, perhaps—but I can't tell them that. Dad made me promise I never would. He didn't want to live without his mind, and he was terrified the others would wake him even though they couldn't repair what was wrong." She sighed. "When he's not there . . . we won't have come together as a family, and the promise of the Conclave will be broken."

Her mouth had gone upside down again. "I'm sorry, Em."

She shrugged. "It has to be done."

"I'm sorry anyway."

"I know you are. And thank you." She sat on the floor

beside the box, reaching out for it. Then she stopped. "I don't suppose it's possible for you to tell me if this will change things without me doing it?"

I shook my head. "You have to make the choice before the choice matters."

"Just thought I'd ask." She opened a panel in the top of the box. There were buttons inside, and Ember pressed them. She pressed them until the box lit up with swirling lights. Then she closed the panel and stood up.

"Is that it?" I asked. "How does your family see the lights?"

"They don't need to see the lights. I've just sent a signal that only they will receive. In four weeks, my family is going to meet at the Prime's Residence in Gull City. Until then, Ash is safe." Her gaze went to my map, and she asked hopefully, "Can you tell now? Whether it's made a difference?"

"I can try."

I went back to my map and began connecting futures. Only there were too many possibilities. Things were . . . complicated. Helper suddenly scurried across the wall, getting in my way and making me lose hold of the vine I had in my hand.

My hands. I looked at one and then the other,

and pressed them both together to make sure. "My hands are warm!"

"Does that mean something?"

"It means the blizzard's further away." I grinned at Em. "You did it!"

She sagged. "Good. Except, Georgie, I don't believe it's a blizzard you're Seeing."

"It isn't?"

Em shook her head. "It's an apt description, though, because in a blizzard people can't see anything but snow or hear anything but wind, and they become so cold they can't feel anything, either. That's what's going to happen to the world without Ash, only it's not a storm. It's disconnection."

That made such complete sense I didn't know why I hadn't understood it before. "That's why only Ash can stop it! Because Sleepwalking is her ability and not her power. Her power is to connect."

"Yes." She put her hands on my shoulders. "Listen, Georgie, I don't know if you've thought about how all this ends. There's probably going to come a time when you'll have to tell Ash about what we've been doing. Once she's safe, I mean, when all this is over and there's no more blizzard. And she'll be mad. She'll say she wasn't worth it."

Her face shifted. She was still Ember, but this was an Ember I hadn't seen before. This Ember was old, so much older than me. "I carry human history in my head, and that means I know what the world looks like when people don't care for one another and the earth. So I want you to know that there is no price—and I mean *none*—that's too high to pay to stop that world from happening again."

Ash looked into the now. I looked ahead. But Ember? She looked back.

I gazed into her eyes, letting her see that I'd listened, and said the words I always hoped people would say to me. "I understand you."

THE CENTER

ASHALA

I was soaring across the grasslands with Connor at my side, on our way to meet with the Prime.

It was two and a half weeks since we'd returned from Detention Center 1 to find that the Tribe was well and Georgie and Daniel were together. I was glad of it; they were a good match and they'd taken good care of everyone while we'd been gone, especially Mr. Snuffles. The little pug waddled around the forest with the Pack, fat and glossy and healthy, and seemed to think he was a wolf himself now.

Today's meeting with Willis would be the third one we'd had since we'd come back, and so far she hadn't had much good news to share. In the city, Neville was stamping out any remaining resistance with the same ruthless efficiency with which he'd once run a detention center, and it seemed like any of Willis's supporters who hadn't died in the initial battle had been arrested since. Terence had moved into the Prime's Residence and was spreading nasty stories that Willis had allied herself with a group of renegades who'd blown up the station, murdered Prime Grant, and led an uprising at Detention Center 1. But at least Neville and Terence hadn't come here. Em's Conclave idea had worked, even though I hadn't been sure about it at first and still wasn't happy about her going to Gull City for it. In fact, I was hoping to talk her out of going at all. Or see if Jules would, although the two of them hadn't quite worked things out between them yet. I knew because they were having lots of low-voiced, intense conversations that always stopped when I approached.

Connor and I began to descend, drifting downward until we landed among the grasses. We never flew directly into or out of the center; there was too much chance of getting accidentally shot by one of the sentries on the walls, who were on the lookout for a minion attack. So we walked, strolling over the long stretch of white gravel that separated the center from the edge of the grass. The place looked much the same as it always had from the outside, except for the green flag that flew from the top of the composite wall. Green was good, because it meant no one had breached the barricade that had been set up across the road that ran from the highway to the center. If any kind of army ever did come this way, the enforcers on the barricade would use their radios to get a message back here, and a red flag would be flown.

The guards standing on either side of the gates pushed them open for us, and we stepped into a hum of voices and activity. The inside was where the center had changed—it had never been so busy, not even when it actually was a detention center. Every enforcer and government official loyal to Willis who'd made it out of Gull City was in this place, along with the entire former staff of Detention Center 2. Some of the families who'd been in detention there had come here as well, although most had chosen to take their chances on their own after they'd been freed. And there were ex-detainees of Detention Center 1 around, too—not as many as I'd hoped might join the fight, but more than I'd expected.

Connor and I wound our way through the bustling people to Willis's office. It was in one of the buildings that overlooked the park, which was a nice view to have now that they'd taken down the high wire fence that had once imprisoned the grass and trees.

We'd almost reached it when we heard the scream. Someone was under attack!

I took off in the direction of the sound with Connor at my side. We pelted past composite buildings, around a corner—and came skidding to a halt. *Not an attack?*

Shona, Cat, Laurie, and some other ex-detainees were standing near the edge of the park. An enforcer was sitting on the ground in front of them, being tended to by Wentworth, and while I couldn't see how bad his injuries were from here, I could smell the horribly familiar smell of burned flesh. Next to Wentworth were a bunch of other enforcers, all of them on their feet and glaring at Cat.

A gray-haired man jabbed a finger toward her. "You can't just lob fireballs around like that! This was supposed to be a training exercise."

"Yes, and I was *training* everyone to get out of the way when I'm throwing fire," Cat replied. "It's not my fault Alex didn't learn fast enough."

"He could have been seriously hurt!"

Shona rolled her eyes. "Oh, the poor baby, got a little bit burned—"

"Shona!" That was Wentworth. The tall Mender rose and swept a stern gaze across the detainees. "You need to be more careful. I realize you've been hurt by people wearing enforcer uniforms, but *these* enforcers are your allies, and we're all fighting the same enemy." Then she shifted her attention to the enforcers. "And as for you—accidents happen in training. Alex will be fine. And if you can't learn to work with people with abilities, how do you imagine you're going to protect the Prime or anybody else?"

No one said anything to that. Not loud enough to be properly heard, anyway. Wentworth sighed. "All right. Everyone take a break, and then we can start the exercise over."

Detainees and enforcers stalked off in opposite directions, and Wentworth went back to the injured man. Laurie caught sight of us and waved. Then he vanished and reappeared right in front of me. "Hello, Ashala Wolf! Hello, Connor!"

"Hey, Laurie." I nodded toward the park. "Have there been a lot of fights like that?"

He shrugged. "We're scared of the enforcers and

the enforcers are scared of us. Also, we're not the kind of Illegals they were expecting."

I frowned. "Exactly what kind of Illegals were they expecting?"

"Grateful ones."

That didn't make sense to me. Connor said, "You mean they think former Illegals should be grateful to Citizens for getting rid of the accords."

"Yes. But Shona says freedom is something everyone should have and no one should have to feel grateful for getting it, and besides we're just as good as any of them and none of us should forget it."

I muddled my way through to the end of that sentence and smiled. "Shona's right."

"I know. Are you all right, Ashala Wolf? There's no trouble in the Firstwood?"

"No. We're just here to meet with the Prime."

"I'll go tell her you're coming!"

He vanished again, and we continued on. I cast a glance back over my shoulder as we went and was pleased to find that some of the ex-detainees and enforcers were now talking to one another, apparently friends, or as much friends as they ever had been. Laurie materialized among them and waved again, pointing at something to my left.

I turned my head to find that the Prime was emerging from the building ahead. She ushered us inside, down a corridor to the large bright room she was using as her office. We sat where we always sat, in the two armchairs in front of Willis's cluttered desk. Or at least we did once we'd moved the files that were on the chairs. Every surface in the room was covered in paper, and if it got piled any higher on the desk we'd have trouble seeing Willis over the top of it.

I gazed at her across the papers, thinking that she looked even more tired than she had when I'd last seen her—or, no, not tired. Glum.

"Is something wrong?" I asked.

She sighed. "Primes McAllister and Lopez aren't going to be able to send as many enforcers to help us take back Gull City as they thought they could. Prime Zhao has promised support, too, but she's also going to have trouble sending substantial numbers of people."

Connor frowned. "How come?"

"They're all having issues in their own cities. Spinifex City is in the midst of some kind of taffa crisis, and as for Fern City and Cloud City . . . I'm afraid not everyone is taking the changes well. There have been protests. Fights. Instances of ex-detainees being beaten up, and of them losing control of their abilities and hurting people." She shook her head. "No one has died yet, but there's been a lot of ugliness."

Laurie's voice echoed in my memory. *We're scared of the enforcers and the enforcers are scared of us.* I supposed it had been stupid to expect otherwise. Except I had, and my disappointment was bitter. "Is it happening everywhere? All the other cities, too?"

Her expression hardened. "No, because nothing's changed in the other cities. Primes Kettridge and Singh won't support the repeal. They're demanding a new vote with *all* the Primes present. And Mangrove City is refusing to do anything until after an election's been held to replace Prime Grant."

"Terence killed Grant!" I spluttered. "And tried to kill the rest of you. Don't they care about that?"

"They don't believe it," she replied. "Not even with Primes McAllister and Lopez telling everyone what Terence and Neville did. There's no proof, you see, and I hate to say it, but . . ." Her lip curled. "I think it's easier for them to believe that Illegals did those things than that a Citizen did."

Connor made a frustrated noise. "Surely they must know what Neville Rose is capable of! He was about to undergo an Adjustment for breaking three sets of accords before Terence broke him out of custody."

"I'm afraid too many people still think of Neville Rose as someone who did bad things for good reasons," Willis replied. "He always did claim everything he did was to protect Gull City from an Illegal threat. And if people believe Illegals are responsible for the things that have happened since, it only goes to prove to them that he was right to be concerned."

I slumped in my chair, feeling like I'd been slugged in the gut. After everything we'd been through, and everything we'd done — after everything *Penelope* had done — it hadn't been enough. We'd taken away the laws that made it okay to hate and fear us, but not the fear or the hate itself. And it sounded like if some of the Primes had their way, that hate and fear would bring those laws right back.

Willis cast a concerned glance at me. "It isn't all bad, Ashala. We've got a sizable force here now. Even with minions, it would be difficult for Terence to overrun this place. And once we get reinforcements from the Primes who are willing to help us, we should have enough people to take back the city."

"When will the other enforcers arrive?" Connor asked.

"Another couple of weeks, I think. We're going to—"

Whatever else Willis was saying was lost beneath

the sound of a shout inside my head. **Hey, Ash!**

I'm with the Prime, Jaz. Is this important?

Yes. Connor's with you, right? I'll tell him to distract her.

There was a moment of silence, and then Connor leaned toward Willis and asked a question we already knew the answer to. "How is the training progressing with the ex-detainees and the enforcers?"

Willis launched into an explanation, and I called out to Jaz, *What is it?*

First of all, you can't react to what I'm going to say in front of the Prime. You know you usually show whatever you're thinking on your face, right?

I'm fine. Tell me what it is.

Have you got a blank face?

Just tell me!

Terence is here.

My legs acted all on their own and shot me to my feet.

Connor and Willis both stared at me, and I started babbling. "Um—sorry. I just remembered, I have somewhere to be. . . ." *Jaz, WHERE IS HE?*

On the grasslands. He says he's here to talk. Pepper caught him, and Wanders-Too-Far and Gnaws-the-Bones are guarding him.

255

Anxiety tightened my chest so fast I almost gasped for air. *Jaz's baby sister was alone with Terence.* . . . No, she wasn't. Pepper couldn't have better protection than two gigantic saurs. I drew in a breath and said, "I'm sorry, Prime Willis. The thing is, I promised I'd do something with some of my Tribe today, and I got so caught up I *completely* forgot. If we don't leave now we'll be too late getting back, and I don't want to let them down. We can come back the day after tomorrow, if that's okay."

"Of course you must go," Willis said. "I'll see you soon." She smiled a weary smile at us. "With any luck I'll have better news for you by then."

Connor wants to know why you just leaped into the air like something bit you on the bum. Well, okay, he didn't say the bum bit, I added that myself. But he said the leaping bit. Way to keep your cool, Ash.

Tell him what's happening. And stop mindspeaking me for a moment!

Willis opened the door for us, and as I passed by her, she said, "Ashala? If there's anything I can help with, please do let me know."

I met her shrewd gaze. She didn't believe the explanation I'd given for leaving, but she wasn't going to press me. "Thanks. I will."

Willis closed the door after us, and Connor and I hurried out into the center, moving as fast as we could without attracting too much attention. We couldn't bring anyone else into this, not without risking Terence being attacked and Conclave rules being broken. *And he says he's here to talk.* Which might or might not be true.

I took hold of Connor's arm and whispered, "I'm going to get more details out of Jaz." Then I called out in my head, *We're on our way. Where is Terence exactly?*

At the Traveler, where it meets Little Blue.

The Traveler was the saur name for a river that meandered across the grasslands, and Little Blue was the stream it connected up with. Even flying, we were a few hours away. *How'd he get so far into the grasslands without Em warning us he was coming?*

She did warn us. That's *how* Pepper caught them — Em told her where she needed to go. But Em said there wasn't much time between her sensing them coming and them getting here. She thinks the Blinker can move people farther and faster than we thought.

The Blinker's here, too? He's incredibly dangerous! Tell Pepper to be careful; he can vanish in an instant—

She knows! Stop panicking.

What does Terence want to talk about?

Won't say. But it has to be to you or Em or both of you. Daniel's Running Em to Terence, and Em says you should let her handle this. But she's about an hour farther away from Terence than you are.

Too long. *Tell her we can't wait.*

The gates loomed up ahead of us. *We're leaving now. Let me know if anything changes!*

Will do, Ash.

His voice went silent, and I communicated everything he'd said in quick sentences to Connor as we moved through the gates.

Then we were in the sky, and flying toward an aingl.

THE AINGL

ASHALA

The world contained nothing but the rush of air for what seemed like forever. Then we finally began to descend, plunging to the ground to land about twenty meters away from a big river, a small stream, two saurs, and three people.

Terence Talbot was standing by the banks of the Traveler, a thin figure in Gull City blue being loomed over by the massive bulk of Wanders-Too-Far. The Blinker was farther away, with Gnaws-the-Bones half-curved around him. And Pepper was marching up and down in front of them all with her chest puffed out and her black pigtails bobbing. She came running over to bounce to a halt in front of us, eyes shining with pride. "Wanders and me caught an aingl *and* a minion."

"Have they given you any trouble?" I asked.

"No," Pepper replied with a disappointed sigh. "Actually, they've been kind of boring."

Boring was good. Boring was great. But I didn't say so out loud because I knew Pepper would never agree with me. Then Wanders's voice rolled into my mind.

Eats-the-Fire says that Holds-the-Secrets says we cannot eat the aingl. Or the smaller one.

Eats-the-Fire was Jaz's saur name, and Holds-the-Secrets was Ember's. *No, you can't. We're in a sort of truce with Terence.*

But you are Leads-the-Pack. Holds-the-Secrets has to do what you say.

Another voice chimed in, deeper and older. *Gnaws.* **It would only take two bites to finish them both.**

You can't eat them! Besides, I'm not sure you could *kill Terence. He's made of some pretty tough material.*

Pepper sniffed. "Saurs can eat *anything*. Tough material just takes longer."

Gnaws put in hopefully, **I am a very patient eater.**

No one's eating anyone! At least, not unless he attacks us

260

first. Out loud I added, "Pepper, Connor and I are going to talk to Terence. You keep watch, okay?"

I didn't want her too close to Terence, although I supposed no distance was really safe with the Blinker around. Pepper resumed her marching, and Connor and I continued on. With every step I took, I got angrier. I was furious that Terence was here, in *my* place, near *my* Tribe. I wanted to reach into his chest, rip out whatever passed for a heart, and—*Oh.* This anger wasn't mine. Or not all mine.

I grabbed hold of Connor's arm, stopping him from going any farther. "If we attack him we're the ones breaking the Conclave rules."

"I know that, Ashala." His voice was calm. Rational. Which was good, except I knew the sheer fury that lurked beneath the surface. He was angry for what had happened to Penelope, and for what Terence had done to me, and for the person Terence had taken from Connor before that. Back when he'd been an Assessor, Terence had been in charge of an Assessment that had gone wrong and resulted in the death of Connor's mother.

"You want to rip his heart out," I said.

"Wanting to rip someone's heart out isn't the same as doing it."

261

I almost laughed at that. *"Connor . . ."*

"You don't need to worry that I will lose control," he told me, and I heard the resolve in his voice; he had his rage in check. "But, Ashala, I won't allow him to harm any of us. If he attacks . . ."

Now *my* anger came through, spilling out into a wolf's smile. "If he attacks, we attack right back. And I guess we find out how tough aingls really are."

We loped on, side by side. As we got close, I muttered to Connor, "Let me do the talking. He knows me a bit, but he doesn't know you at all, and I'd prefer to keep it that way." *You're too near to this. Don't let him bait you into giving him anything of what you are.* I didn't know if it was because of what I had said or what I hadn't, but Connor nodded agreement.

We stopped a wary distance from Terence. He looked much older than when I'd seen him last, with gray running through the brown of his hair and lines around his mouth. This was the face of Prime Talbot, rather than the younger ordinary Citizen he'd been pretending to be when I'd met him in Spinifex City.

His gaze met mine, then dropped to my neck. A hint of a smile touched his lips and warmed his eyes, as though he were contemplating a pleasant memory. I shivered, remembering the feel of his fingers around my throat. Then I lifted my chin, baring my neck to him. Daring him to try again. *He gets no part of me, either.* Especially not my fear. "Hello, Terence."

"Ashala Wolf." His voice was as soft and precise as I remembered. His nose wrinkled as if he'd smelled something bad, an automatic reaction of revulsion, and I remembered that, too. It was how he reacted to anyone with an ability.

Terence's gaze drifted to Connor. "You are the one who used to be an enforcer. Neville Rose has spoken to me of you."

Connor said absolutely nothing. Just watched him with a face devoid of emotion that gave Terence no clues as to what he was thinking or feeling. Terence didn't seem to know what to make of it, and after a few seconds he turned his attention back to me. "Where is my sister?"

"She's on her way," I answered. "But she'll be a while."

An emotion I couldn't identify flickered across his face. "I cannot wait. I have come to issue an invitation to the Conclave. I am assuming that Ember has told you about our family meeting?"

Even for Terence, this wasn't making much sense. "Ember's already going to the Conclave."

"The invitation is not for Ember. It is for you."

"*Me?*"

He gave a slow nod. All his mannerisms tended to be a little slow and not quite natural. "Some of my siblings wish to meet you. I have explained to them that you remake reality, you see. And that you will make it so that we do not exist."

It was such a ridiculous idea I would've laughed, if it had been at all funny. "I'd never do that. I *can't* do that."

"You can, and you will."

There was nothing to be gained in talking sense to Terence, but I couldn't stop myself from pointing out the obvious. "If I could kill you, why didn't I do it when *you* tried to kill *me?*"

"That was before. Your ability has evolved. You cured the Primes, and your ability will only increase in strength as you grow older." His licked his thin lips. "One day you will decide we should not be, and we will not."

No, no, no . . . He was afraid. He truly believed what he was saying, and that meant the other aingls would hear it as truth. With the exception of Ember, they couldn't knowingly lie to one another, but they could say any kind of nonsense if they believed it themselves.

264

Terence had told a group of powerful synthetic life-forms that I was going to kill them, and death was the aingls' oldest and deepest fear.

I could feel something closing around me, like one of the cages they'd put animals into in the old world, and with it came a clawing panic. Or maybe that was Connor, because he saw the trap, too. Going to the Conclave meant walking into a city run by my enemies and a room full of aingls who might well try to kill me. *Not* going to the Conclave meant there was a good chance some of the aingls would come looking for me, and they'd come looking here. A choice between me in danger and the Tribe in danger was no choice at all.

I glared at Terence. "I'll be there."

"I am pleased to hear it." He hesitated, then added, "You will tell my sister that I could not stay."

He hadn't phrased that as a question. But he was watching me with his pale eyes, waiting for a response.

"Um. I'll tell her."

"You will tell her something else also. You will tell her that she understood once."

Again not a question, and yet there was the faintest hint of a plea in his tone. For some reason it really mattered to him that I passed the message on. "I'll tell her that, too."

"Good. Now I am going to depart." His voice rose at the end of the sentence, making it the third time he'd come close to asking a question without actually doing so. *He's worried I'm going to try to stop him.* Terence was so delusional it was almost pitiful. Except those delusions had ended Pen's life, and they might end mine before this was through.

Connor gestured to the minion. "Come over, but walk. Don't use your ability."

The Blinker stalked across to us, scowling at Connor and at me. Then he turned his attention to Terence and his expression shifted into adoration tinged with awe. Alexander Hoffman had put "gods" at the top of his list of the evils of the old world, and seeing the Blinker idolize someone as flawed as Terence made it easy to understand why.

"Are you all right, sir?" the Blinker asked.

"I am well," Terence answered. He held out his arm, and his nose wrinkled just like it had before. He didn't like the Blinker touching him. He didn't want anyone with an ability touching him. I stared at the Blinker's hazel eyes, willing him to see. *Don't you understand he hates you?*

But all the Blinker did was reach out to place his hand

reverently on Terence's elbow. Both of them vanished.

I swiveled toward Pepper. *Call Em! Tell her to make sure Terence is moving away from the Firstwood and not toward it!*

The silence was filled with the sounds of saur claws tearing through grass as Wanders and Gnaws began to patrol the area. They skittered in a loose circle around us, heads darting back and forth and blue tongues flickering out to lick the air, which was how they smelled. They didn't seem to find anything, and in a few seconds Pepper's voice came into my head. **She says they're definitely moving in the direction of the city and it's going to take her another half an hour to get here and are you all right?**

Tell her I'm fine. We can talk when she gets here. Tell her—Actually, did you overhear everything Terence said? I figured she had. The Saur Tribe had excellent hearing on account of their bond with saurs, and if Pepper hadn't been able to hear, I suspected Wanders would have relayed the whole thing to her.

Yep. I heard.

Tell her all of it.

Pepper went quiet again. I looked at Connor. "Em says Terence is moving away."

"Hardly surprising," he growled. "He's done what

he came here to do now that you've been forced to go to the Conclave. He's using the aingls to get to you."

I didn't say anything. I was thinking about the look on Terence's face when he'd realized he wouldn't see Em today. I knew what it was now. *Disappointment.* And when he'd said that she'd understood once, he'd meant she'd understood the things he had to do to protect them all from abilities.

"He's not only using the aingls to get to me," I said. "It's the other way around as well."

He frowned. "What?"

"He's using *me* to get to *them*. Terence has his city back, and I think he wants other things back as well. I think he wants things to be like they were when the other aingls all looked up to him. He's the big brother, and he's making me the danger that brought them all together before." The danger for which they'd created the Citizenship Accords. If Terence could convince the aingls they were under immediate threat again, there was no end to the lengths they'd go to in order to protect themselves, and not just from me but anyone with an ability.

Except Terence would make very sure they started with me.

Connor knew it, too. He put his hands on my

shoulders and said in a low, intense voice, "Terence doesn't hurt you. Not you, not me, not the Tribe. Not any of us."

He sounded fierce. Inside he was howling, and I understood why. Him losing me to Terence was like me losing him to Neville. He couldn't bear the thought of it. *I* couldn't bear the thought of it. I reached up, tangling my hands in his hair and staring into the blue wildness of his eyes. "Terence doesn't end us." *Neville doesn't end us.* I said it with absolute certainty, because I knew they couldn't even if they did. Connor and I went on, in this life or the next.

He bent his head until it was resting against mine, and for a moment we stood there in silence, each one listening to the other breathe.

Ash?

I raised my head. *Yeah?*

Em says she'll come out here for a while to make sure Terence doesn't turn back, but you and Connor should head for the Firstwood. Where it's safe. Like right now.

Okay, tell her we're going.

"Em wants us to go back to the Firstwood," I told Connor.

"Mmph."

He didn't want to let go of me. I didn't want to let go of him right now, either. *Or ever, if it comes to that.*

"Walk," I said. "We could walk for a while. You probably shouldn't use your ability for a bit anyway, with all the flying you've done today."

He nodded and shifted to put an arm around my shoulders. I looked for Pepper and found that she was riding on Wanders's back.

We're going now, Pepper. You be careful, okay?

You worry too much, Ash.

And Wanders's voice came right on top of hers. **We are saur.**

Tougher than anything. I hoped they were.

I leaned against Connor, and together we walked back toward the forest without letting go of each other. *Now, or ever.*

THE SLEEPER

"I don't know what to do!" Em said.

She had said that many times as she'd paced back and forth across the cave. She'd said it yesterday as well, when she'd come back from the grasslands after she'd made sure Terence was really gone. But we hadn't had everyone gathered together yesterday, and today we did. All the people whose choices mattered were here, and Daniel as well. Starbeauty was lounging in the corner, and Jules was sitting beside her. Daniel was standing by the map with his shoulders resting against the wall. Helper was here, too, but he wasn't helping at the moment because he was asleep.

Jules held out his hand to Ember. "Quit pacing, Red. You're making me tired just watching you."

She let him pull her down beside him, and he said, "How're you doing with that weapon?"

Em had been building a weapon that looked like a streaker but wasn't. She said it was a copy of something her sister Delta had once made, and she said that if she could replicate Delta's design correctly, the weapon would make an aingl unconscious for a few hours. Everyone thought being able to make Terence unconscious was a good idea, even if he wasn't unconscious for very long.

"It's progressing," Em said. "But it's hardly a solution to this! I was trying to—I mean, the weapon is just to give us some protection against Terence, not all of them."

"Is it all of 'em, though?" Jules asked. "Who's the biggest threat? Other than Terence, obviously."

My pet is not a problem. He is an excellent pet.

That made Ember smile, but her smile went away again fast. "No, Leo's not a problem. He's basically on our side as long as whatever we're doing doesn't affect taffa. And Delta might not be a problem, either, because she hates Terence. She hasn't forgiven him for giving the circuits that were all that was left of Dominic to Neville Rose."

"Do the others know Terence did that?" Jules asked. "Couldn't you use it to start a fight?"

Ember shrugged. "I don't know if they know or not. Even if they don't, finding out might not make them mad enough at Terence to turn against him, not when he's telling them Ash is going to kill them. And if they think Ash is a genuine threat, they'll be able to justify her death."

That mattered, because Ember's dad had made it so the aingls couldn't kill unless they were sure the death was justified. Em said that if an aingl killed without being sure a death was necessary, they shut down, which was like being dead for them. Em also said that Terence saw threats everywhere, so it wasn't hard for him to kill.

Ember sank her head into her hands. "I've *done* this," she whispered. "I called the Conclave. I made the wrong choice."

Jules put his arm around her. I said crossly, "You did not make the wrong choice. The blizzard was much closer before you called the Conclave. You made the right choice. Now we just need another one."

Then Daniel said, "What about moving the Conclave? To here?"

Em raised her head again. "We can't bring my family to the Firstwood!"

"Not the forest. The Steeps."

The Steeps was behind the center. I'd never been there. Daniel had, and he said nothing grew there and the rocks went on forever.

"Gull City is dangerous," Daniel pointed out. "And Terence has proved he can get here fast from wherever he is, so keeping him in the city for the Conclave doesn't appear to be a particular advantage. Em, wouldn't it be better to have Ash—and you—closer to us? Because we all know we're not going to be able to stop Ash from going."

Em nodded slowly. "You're right. It would be better to move it, and I can do that. But it's not going to be enough, and I don't see any other choices that will help Ash."

You require the fifth.

Ember stared at Starbeauty. "The fifth person whose choices matter?" Then she stared at me. "Georgie, who is it?"

"I don't know. I haven't Seen."

Your not knowing and not Seeing is not important,

274

nor is my knowing and Seeing. What matters is that the fifth is known to himself.

"So who is he, then?" Jules asked. Starbeauty was silent, and Jules reached across to scratch behind her ears. "Come on, beautiful, give us a name."

She ignored him, licking at her paws. Above me, the spiders suddenly chittered, passing on a message from other spiders elsewhere in the caves.

"Ash and Connor are coming," I said. That meant it must be later, because that was when we'd arranged for Ash and Connor to meet us to talk about the Conclave. Then we'd come earlier so we could talk about choices without them. "Everyone stop talking."

Everybody did, and everybody had still stopped talking when Ash and Connor walked into the cave. They both paused in the entrance, looking around at us with puzzled expressions.

"You're all very quiet," Ash said.

Had I done it wrong? Maybe I should have told them all to keep talking instead. But Daniel knew what to say.

"Actually, we were just discussing moving the Conclave." He explained why.

"Good idea," Connor said.

Ash looked doubtful. "I don't know if I like all the

aingls being here. What if they decide to come after the Tribe?"

"All it really means," Ember said, "is that they'll get here a bit quicker than they would have if they'd come from the city. I don't think they'll come for us anyway, not personally. If they decide the Tribe is a threat, they're more likely to send in enforcers, or help Terence do so. And that they can do from anywhere."

Ash opened her mouth to speak. Before she could, Nicky came bounding in, barking madly. He ran in a circle around Ash and Connor and tore back out. Then he barked from the passageway. "Woof, woof, WOOF!"

"He wants us to follow him," Ash said. She stuck her head out the entrance and said, "Nicky? Did you get your new stick wedged into a crevice again?"

Nicky whined.

"I've told you to stop trying to bury it in the caves!"

"Woof!"

She looked back at us. "Give me a minute. I'll just go find his stick."

Ash went out and Connor followed her.

Starbeauty rose and flicked her ears at Jules. *I have a name for you.*

"Oh, yeah? Who is it?"

Nicky.

Jules gasped and scrambled to his feet, pulling Ember up with him, and the both of them tore after Ash and Connor. Daniel and I went to go, too, but Starbeauty said, Wait.

We looked at her and she said, Daniel is required here.

"I am?" Daniel asked. "Required for what?"

You are required for vine. She stalked over to my pile of vines in the corner of the cave and sat beside it. There will be much mapping to be done, and more vine is needed. More is needed now.

I stared at the pile and felt bad. I had been letting it get too low.

"Go," Daniel said, bending down to brush a kiss against my cheek. "I'll get your vine."

That was only a small kiss and it wasn't enough. So I pulled his head down to mine for a much better kiss, a kiss that made me dizzy and happy and real. When it was done I whispered against his skin, "I love you, Daniel."

"I love you, Georgie."

I let him go and skipped after the others. The spiders told me they had gone into the warm black of the deeper passages, so I took a solar lamp from a cave and ran until I caught up.

When I found them, Ash and Connor had lights, too, and they were holding them up to show the way as everyone trailed after Nicky.

Then Nicky stopped. Ash shone her lamp over gray stone. We were at a dead end.

Jules sighed. "That dog's taken a wrong turn somewhere."

But Ember said, "No. He hasn't."

She moved to the stone and put her hands on it, pressing. Something clicked and the wall slid up into the ceiling. Light flooded out, and I threw up a hand to shield my face. Then I peeked through my fingers into a passage that wasn't made of rock. It was shiny and silver, and there were lights running along the sides of the floor.

Nicky barked again. "Good boy," Ash said. "Good boy for finding . . . whatever this is."

"It's the tunnels," Ember said. "The ones that run beneath the Firstwood. This is where they connect to the caves."

Em went wandering into the passage, and everyone else wandered after her. I reached out to touch the walls. They were cool and smooth and flat. My spiders wouldn't like it here. It was too bright, and too cold, and there were no crevices to hide in.

Ember knelt down next to Nicky, taking his head in her hands and staring into his eyes. "Are you trying to tell me what I think you are?"

"Woof!"

"I didn't know you spoke dog, Em!" I said.

"I don't." She stood up. "But sometimes I understand what Nicky is saying. I think he's brought us here because of my dad. These tunnels are where he's . . . sleeping."

Ash cast a suspicious glance up at the ceiling. "Is it going to collapse or something? Do we need to move your dad?"

Ember shook her head. "No. This part is completely stable. This isn't about moving him. It's about waking him up."

"I didn't think you could," I said. "Because his head is broken."

"If I can fix him," Em said, "then it's okay to wake him, and if I'm understanding Nicky right, he knows how to fix him. And once he's fixed . . . my dad could make a difference to the Conclave."

"How?" I asked, in the same moment that Ash and Connor and Jules asked the same thing.

Em looked around at everyone. "Eight aingls." She counted them off on her fingers. "Me. Nicky. Leo. Not threats. Delta, possibly not a threat because she's mad at Terence, only . . . I don't know. That leaves Terence himself, Katya, Maleki, and Nova. We can't do anything about Terence. As to everyone else . . ." She sighed. "We all love Dad, even though he's—well, sometimes he's not the best dad. So if he makes it clear that he won't be happy about Ash dying, some of my brothers and sisters might leave her alone. It won't solve the Terence problem, of course. But it might hold off the others."

Fixing Ember's dad sounded like a good idea. But Jules shook his head. "No offense, sweetheart, but are you so sure your dad is going to tell 'em he wants wolfgirl alive? Isn't he a little . . . unreliable?"

"He's a *lot* unreliable," Ember said. "But he'll want to protect Ash. Because she's going to make him better."

I stared at Ash. "I didn't know you could fix Ember's dad, Ash!"

"I didn't know, either, Georgie," Ash said. "Em? Since when have you thought I can do this?"

"Since now, because Nicky thinks so. That's why he brought us here. I'm fairly certain he believes that you can help Dad the same way you helped him."

I didn't understand what that meant. Maybe the others did and someone would tell me. Then Jules said, "Think you're going to have to explain that a bit more, Red."

Ember drew in a deep breath, which was good, because it meant a big explanation was coming. "Dominic was dead. All that was left of him were those few circuits that Neville put in an interrogation machine. Then Neville hooked that machine up to you, Ash, and you brought Dominic back. Only as Nicky, instead of Dominic. You made him new."

Ash nodded. "I get all that, Em, but I don't see why that means I could help your dad."

"When Nicky was the machine and you were connected to him, you weren't conscious. You were in a state that was close enough to Sleepwalking for your ability to work. That's *how* you brought him back. And Nicky still has some kind of link to you. I think he can use it to connect you to Dad's mind in the same way you were once connected to him."

Jules frowned. "And then, what, Ash can make your dad's mind new?"

Ember threw out her hands. "I don't know! Dad's suffering from some kind of progressive instability that was caused by transferring his consciousness from his original organic body into a synthetic one. I've never been able to figure out how to repair it. All I know is, Nicky thinks Ash can. Or at least that she has a chance."

Nicky bounded over to Ash and sat at her feet, thumping his tail on the floor. She patted his head and said, "Well, if he believes I can do it, I'll give it a try." She looked at Em. "Do you need any special equipment or anything?"

Ember shook her head. "There's a lot of stuff stored in the room where Dad is. Things I was using to work on him. I'll have all I need there—but we might be away from the Tribe for a while. I really don't know how long it's going to take."

"Don't worry about that," I told her. "Me and Daniel will take care of the Tribe." We were good at taking care of the Tribe, and these tunnels were no place for spiders anyway. I needed to be up in the warm rock, and with my map. Now that this choice had been made, I could feel futures shifting and changing and becoming. My hand twitched, wanting vines to map them. "You all go bring Ember's dad back."

"Everyone come with me, then!" Em said. She marched off down the tunnels, and everybody followed her. As they turned the corner, Nicky glanced back at me. His head was held high and his doggy mouth was set into a firm line. Like Em, I understood him even though I didn't speak dog.

My name is Nicky and I am going to save Ashala Wolf.

THE BUNKER

ASHALA

So this was the great Alexander Hoffman.

He was lying on a table, and he looked pretty much as he had in the memories Ember had once shared with me — red hair, a short beard, and a lined, intelligent face. There was a small black disc on his forehead displaying a series of numbers that Em said indicated the level of instability in his brain. If I couldn't change that, she wouldn't wake him up. I reached out to touch him, brushing my hand over the Spinifex City–yellow fabric of his sleeve and then against his wrist. His skin was unexpectedly cold, and I jumped back, bumping into Connor, who was standing behind me.

He caught my elbow to steady me and spoke in my ear, his breath warm against my skin. "He's not going to bite you, Ashala."

"I know! I just . . . it's *Hoffman*."

He said nothing, but I knew he was smiling. He thought the way I was reacting to Hoffman was funny, which I guessed it was. I couldn't help it. I'd grown up admiring Hoffman-the-hero, and I couldn't quite manage to merge that Hoffman with the one who'd built himself a family only to abandon them. Despite everything I now knew about Ember's dad, I was still a bit awestruck by him.

I stepped back to the table. *He's just an ordinary man . . . who predicted the end of the old world . . . discovered the Balance . . . invented the technology that saved humanity . . .* This wasn't helping. I stopped looking at Hoffman and looked at the rest of the room instead. Ember was sitting on the floor in the corner, surrounded by bits of technological clutter that she'd taken from the shelves that lined the wall behind her. For the past half hour she'd been busy assembling wires and circuits into . . . well, something that she said we were going to need. Jules and Nicky were both wandering around the room, except Nicky was sniffing along the floor, and Jules was taking things off shelves to examine them before putting them back, generally in a different place from where he'd gotten them.

Ember glanced up at me. "I'm almost done, Ash. Can you move another table next to Dad? You and Nicky will need something to lie on."

Connor and I went to the far end of the room, where more tables were shoved haphazardly against the wall. We grabbed hold of the biggest one, pushing it next to Hoffman. Then we helped Nicky onto the top of it before I climbed up beside him.

Within a few minutes, Ember came hurrying over, and Jules strolled after her. Em was holding something in her hands—a thin circle of wires, connected by trailing cords to two other bands.

I swallowed. "That looks kind of like the thing that was put on my head when I was in the detention center with Neville."

"It is. Or an adapted version of it." Em held up the circles. "One on you, one on Dad, and one on Nicky. If this works the way it's supposed to, Nicky will be able to use it to link you to Dad through him."

She reached up to set the loop onto my head.

I suppressed a sudden surge of panic as the cool metal touched my skin. *This isn't the same as before. You're not Neville Rose's prisoner.* Em put the second loop on Nicky, who rolled onto his side. I stretched out beside him, and he tipped back his head to gaze soulfully at me. Not the same at all, and yet it was, because Nicky had been with me when I was a prisoner, his spirit trapped in the interrogation machine. We were both free now. Em attached the final loop to her dad and said, "Okay, Ash. Now you . . ." She stopped and sighed. "Actually, I'm not really sure. Nicky's in charge of this. Maybe close your eyes, see if anything happens?"

I shut my eyes tight. Nothing happened. After a few minutes of boring darkness, I opened my eyes again. "Sorry, Em, it's not—"

I sat up with a gasp.

There was a gray sky above my head, and around me were the remains of fallen buildings. I scrambled to my feet, my gaze darting across twisted wreckage that seemed to go on forever. Some of the wreckage was shattered glass or warped metal, but a lot of it was made of a material that I'd never seen before, something hard and gray and not composite, not even early composite. And the few buildings that were still standing were so high they seemed to be trying to reach the sky itself. I'd never seen buildings that tall before. I hadn't even known it was possible to make buildings that tall. *Is this Hoffman's mind?* It had to be, only nothing here made sense and nothing was whole. I wasn't sure I could fix this. I wasn't sure anyone could.

The earth suddenly shook, sending me stumbling. A massive crack opened up in the distance, cutting a jagged path across the ground until it struck one of the remaining tall buildings. The crack vanished. But the building shuddered and began to collapse.

Debris rained down in heavy chunks of gray, smacking into the earth around me and shattering into pieces. Splinters of rock came flying out, and I threw up my arms to cover my face and head as they spattered into my body, stinging my flesh. I sprinted, away from the building and the danger falling from the sky, careening across the fallen city with no idea of where I was going.

"Woof!"

Nicky? I staggered to a halt, lowering my arms to find him standing a few meters away. He took off, barking at me to follow.

"Nicky, wait up!" I chased after him, tripping and stumbling as the ground shook beneath my feet. Then

288

he bounded up a massive heap of debris, disappearing over the top. I followed, skidding down the other side into empty space.

Nicky leaped about my legs, nuzzling at my hand. I patted him and looked around. We'd come to the end of the city. Everything from this point on was flat emptiness, with the exception of the single squat structure rising up from the ground ahead. Some kind of bunker? Like the city, it was made of a gray material that I couldn't identify, and it had no windows, only a large heavy-looking door. A flash of light shot out of the bunker and streaked high overhead. I spun to watch as the light arced down to strike the earth, setting the ground rumbling and opening a crack that went scissoring into the city beyond.

"Woof!"

"I get it," I told him. "I think." Thanks to the way my ability worked, I'd had lots of practice interpreting what I saw in weird landscapes of the unconscious.

"The cracks are the instability? Which makes the city his mind, and the bunker the source of whatever's wrong." I turned to look at Nicky. "That's why you brought me here."

He licked my hand as if to say, *Good human.*

"Guess I better go inside, then."

Nicky flopped down onto the ground, put his head on his paws, and whined. He wasn't coming with me. Whatever was inside was for me to see.

I strode to the bunker and turned the door handle. The door swung inward to reveal a gray floor with a square hole in it containing a ladder that descended into the ground. I peered downward, but it stretched so far I couldn't see the end. I began to climb, my feet thudding against each rung. The ladder was made of a kind of silver material I'd never seen before, and it was cold. Everything was cold, which wasn't right, because I was going into the earth, and it should have been warm like the caves were. But I could hear the soft hum of some kind of machinery at work; this place was being artificially cooled.

I climbed until my arms and legs were aching from the effort, and still the ladder stretched on. Finally, I made it to the bottom, stepping off into a long tunnel. Lights shone down from the ceiling, glaring over the stark gray walls and floor. I could hear movement somewhere in the distance. *Someone's in here with me.*

I swallowed and crept forward, following the tunnel until it connected with another, bigger passageway. Some kind of main corridor? It seemed like it, because it was wider than all the tunnels that branched off it. I skulked along the corridor, trying to spy some clue that would tell me what this place was and why I was here. Then I heard the distinctive thudding of footsteps headed my way.

I darted into one of the side passages, pressing myself flat against the wall and peering around the corner to watch as a man stepped into the main corridor. A large overweight man with golden skin, a flat nose, and white-blond hair, who moved with the grace of a cat. He was wearing khaki pants and a white shirt instead of Spinifex City–yellow robes, but it was impossible not to recognize Leo.

I sagged in relief and stepped out in front of him. "Hey, Leo! It's me, Ash—"

He walked straight at me and *through* me, as if I were mist. I staggered back, bumping into the wall. *I'm not really here.* I poked at my arm. It seemed solid enough to me. Obviously not to him. I stared after Leo to see him turn down a side passage, and hurried to follow. It was better to be with Leo than alone in this creepy place, even if he couldn't see me. Besides, it wasn't like I had any other indication of where I should be going.

I trailed behind Leo, padding down the corridor at his back until he came to a door. He pulled it open to step inside, and I darted in before the door swung shut. I was in a big square room, every wall of which was covered with screens that showed mysterious numbers and charts. Sitting in front of the screens were . . . *aingls?* There was Delta—her black hair was cropped a lot shorter than when I'd seen her last, but it was her. On the other side of the room was a round blond woman I didn't recognize. Katya or Nova, maybe? Then there was a man with a hawk-like nose, brown skin, and black hair tied in a ponytail at the base of his neck. *Maleki?* And strolling between them was Alexander Hoffman.

Leo walked up to his father, and the two of them began a low-voiced conversation. I waved experimentally at Hoffman. He didn't react. It didn't seem like he or anyone else could see me, any more than Leo could. I wandered around the room, trying to figure out exactly what was going on. The screens I didn't get at all, and the aingls were wearing strange sorts of clothes. None of them were dressed in the color of a city, and everything they had on seemed a bit grubby and worn out, as if they'd been wearing those clothes for a long time.

I jumped at the sound of Hoffman's deep, gravelly voice. "Delta? How is Europe doing?"

She turned to him. "The quakes are getting worse.

292

We project losses at thirty percent of the population."

"That's a better outlook than Africa," Hoffman said, looking toward the brown-skinned man with the hawk nose. "Losses there are running at—what, Maleki, fifty-five percent?"

"Sixty," Maleki replied. "If things continue this way, there won't be enough survivors to sustain a human population, even assuming there's anything left of the earth to live upon."

I didn't know what an Africa was, or a Europe, for that matter, but I understood quakes and fears about humanity surviving. That, plus the clothes that weren't from cities, plus the building materials that I couldn't recognize, equaled one unbelievable thing. *This is the Reckoning.* I'd gone back in time to when the earth tore itself apart after humanity had abused it for so long—or, no, I couldn't have traveled in time, because I was in Hoffman's head. I was in Hoffman's *memories.*

Hoffman heaved a sigh. "If everyone had just listened to me . . . I suppose there's no point in revisiting that now. We must identify areas of relative safety and send people there. What—"

Before he could finish that sentence, the door to the room banged open and someone shouted, "Everybody freeze! Put your hands up! Now!"

I swiveled, gaping. Six people dressed in brown uniforms had crowded inside the room, blocking the doorway and pointing black stick things at Hoffman and the others. Weapons? They had to be weapons, because Hoffman was slowly raising his hands, and so was everyone else. Whatever those stick things were, they must be able to hurt an aingl. And the uniforms . . . enforcers of some kind? But if they were enforcers, they worked for the government. Why would the government, any government, be after Hoffman?

I watched as the enforcers parted to allow a short blond woman to come marching through. She inclined her head at Hoffman. "Professor. I'm sorry we have to meet again under these circumstances."

He nodded back at her. "General. I'm sorry we have to meet again at all."

One of the enforcers snapped—"Show some respect!"—only to fall silent when the General subjected him to an icy glare. She returned her attention to Hoffman, offering him a smile that might have been pleasant if it hadn't been so false. "There's no need for this to be difficult, Professor. Simply give us the code, and we'll be on our way."

"If I give you the code, you will use the device, and

as I have told the people you work for a thousand times over, the technology is flawed. The device will stabilize a small area of land in its immediate vicinity. However it will *de*stabilize the earth everywhere else."

"We're willing to take that chance."

"I am not." Hoffman lowered his hands to his sides. The enforcers shifted uneasily, and the General snapped, "Nobody shoot!"

"Yes, that's right," Hoffman said. "Nobody shoot. Because I am far too valuable to kill. We are *all* far too valuable to kill. There is no one else who understands what is happening to this planet as well as we do." He folded his arms, lip curling as he surveyed the General. "So I wish you'd stop pretending to threaten us. You're making yourself look quite ridiculous."

The General sighed. "You're right that you are too valuable to kill." She turned and motioned to someone in the corridor behind her. "But your family is not."

More enforcers came forward, shoving two people in front of them, and I let out a cry of dismay that no one heard. *Ember.* And right beside her was a brown-haired boy with oddly familiar dark eyes, who looked to be a few years younger than she was. The enforcers pushed them onto their knees and stood with the weapons pressed against their heads.

I surged forward, trying to wrest the weapons from their grasp. It was useless, of course. My hands passed right through theirs. They didn't even know I was there. I *wasn't* here. This had all happened a long time ago.

I stepped back, glaring at the General as she moved to stand between Ember and the boy. She rested one hand on each of their shoulders and said, "Ember? Dominic? Why don't you tell your father how much you want to live?"

Em lifted her chin and stayed silent. Dominic glanced at her and then did the same, copying his big sister.

"Your choice, Professor," the General said. "Give me what I want or watch them die."

Every gaze in the room was focused on Hoffman, and Hoffman's gaze was focused on Ember and Dominic. Leo leaned in to whisper to him, "It's all right, Professor. Just give her the code, and we'll deal with whatever happens after that. Maybe you're wrong about the flaws in the device."

"Ah, Leo." Hoffman sighed. "We both know I am never wrong. If the device is used, it will result in the death of millions. Perhaps billions. Perhaps even humanity itself." He kept his eyes locked on Ember and Dominic, and shook his head. "I am sorry, my children."

The General gestured, and there was a sharp cracking sound. Dominic slumped to the floor.

Ember wailed, and I dived to Dominic's side, trying to stop the blood pouring out of his skull even though his eyes were open and staring. Ember was sobbing and struggling with the guard who held her, and I couldn't help her. I couldn't do anything but watch.

The General drew her own weapon. "Last chance, Professor!"

Hoffman said nothing. The General fired. And the lights went out.

The enforcers started shouting as a buzzing noise filled the air, seeming to vibrate unpleasantly against my skin. There were a bunch of strange clicking noises that I didn't understand until I heard someone yell, "The guns won't fire! They've done something to them!" That was followed by sizzling sounds I understood all too well. *Energy weapons.* Then everything went silent, and the lights flicked back on.

I was sitting among the dead. Bodies were sprawled all around me, gazing sightlessly upward. The enforcers. The General. And—no, no, no! *Ember.*

Someone was screaming. *I* was screaming. I clapped

my hand over my mouth to stop myself and crawled over to Em. This was all wrong. It had to be wrong. Em wasn't dead, and Dominic hadn't died like this. He'd been killed by someone with an ability, not by enforcers. This couldn't be the real world.

A stricken voice spoke. "Professor, I'm so sorry! We thought we'd be in time."

Terence? My head jerked up. Terence was standing in the middle of the bodies, wearing a pair of odd red glasses and holding an energy weapon in his hand. Beside him was a tall black woman, and she had glasses, too, but no weapon—well, not unless that metal sphere thing she was holding was a weapon.

"You almost were in time," Hoffman said. His gaze wandered vaguely around the room, focusing on the sphere in the woman's hand. "The jammer worked well. And the night-vision glasses also? Good. Very good. I suppose this was an opportunity for a field test—" He stopped speaking as his legs went out from under him. Leo and Delta rushed forward to catch him.

"You're in shock, Professor," Delta said, holding on to Hoffman with one hand and using the other to wipe at the tears streaming down her cheeks. "You need to sit d—"

"No!" Hoffman flung them off. "We must leave.

The location of this base is compromised, and more of them will be coming."

"We should be safe for a while," Terence said. "We could wait long enough to bury them."

But Hoffman shook his head. "We pack up the essentials, we set the self-destruct, and we go." The aingls exchanged uncertain glances. Hoffman glared at them. "How many times do I have to tell you? Our work is the only thing that matters. Something of humanity must survive. Now *move*."

They obeyed him, rushing around the room to shove papers and files and bits of technology into cases. Hoffman went to one of the screens and pressed at the keys beneath it. Whatever he did made flashing numbers appear on all the screens, and I realized it was a clock, counting backward from thirty minutes.

Hoffman turned his attention to the aingls, hurrying them along and herding them out. Leo was the last, and he came to kneel at my side, bending down to press a kiss to Ember's cheek, and then to Dominic's. Hoffman put an impatient hand on his shoulder. "Come on, Leo! We have to get out of here before this place becomes a smoking ruin."

Smoking ruin? The *self-destruct*. I understood now

what the clock was counting down to and I didn't care. I shifted so that I was sitting between Ember and Dominic. Then I reached out my hands to hover over theirs. It was the closest I could get to holding their hands without touching them.

"You're not alone," I whispered. "I'm right here with you, and you're not alone."

I stayed until the world exploded.

THE FAMILY

ASHALA

When the world came back I was outside the bunker, sitting on the ground, and Nicky was sitting in front of me. I sprang forward, flinging my arms around him and burying my face in his fur. "You're okay! Nicky, you're okay!"

He licked the side of my head and then tried to wriggle free. I let him go and he took off, darting over the piles of wreckage toward the city.

I sprinted after him. I hadn't even made it to the top of the pile when everything seemed to blink and

I found myself right back at the bunker. I tried again only to have the same thing happen, except that this time when I was flung back I heard a faint "woof" in my head. *I'm supposed to stay here?* The bunker looked completely intact—had the whole thing somehow reset? I didn't want to go back in, especially not if I was going to have to live through the same thing twice over. But maybe I hadn't done something that I was meant to do.

A voice spoke from behind me. "Hello."

I spun around. Alexander Hoffman was standing a few paces away. He looked me up and down and shook his head. "I must say, you're an odd incarnation of my consciousness. I don't believe I've ever seen you before, although I must have. At some point your face lodged in my memory, and I have reproduced it. For what purpose, I wonder?"

"You can see me?"

"Obviously. You're oddly slow on the uptake for a manifestation of my mind." He cast an uneasy glance around. "Strange that any part of me would be here. I don't like to come here."

"I'm not a part of you! I'm a friend of Ember's, and I came here to help." Although I was a long way away from being able to do that. The bunker had to be the key, but I hadn't understood it. Maybe that was why *this* Hoffman, a Hoffman I could talk to, was here.

I waved my hand at the bunker. "What happened in there?"

"You're me. You know that already. Why are you asking such pointless questions?"

"I already I told you, I'm not you! My name is Ashala Wolf, and your daughter sent me here to help you, which I can't do unless I understand what happened. And I don't. How could those weapons even hurt any of you? You're aingls; you're supposed to be virtually indestructible. Besides, Dominic never even died like that!"

His brows drew together in a frown. "Could it be that you're not part of my mind after all?" He walked in a slow circle around me, examining me as if I were a puzzle to be solved. "If you are not me, then say something to me I would never say to myself."

That was easy. "You got something wrong."

He stopped. "I did not!"

"You should never have left Em and the others all by themselves to guide humanity in the new world. If you'd been there, the Citizenship Accords might never have happened."

He sniffed. "That is a patently ridiculous remark."

Then a gleam of humor crept into his eyes. "But it is also something I would never say to myself. Hello, Ashala Wolf."

He held out his hand to me. "Alexander Hoffman."

I shook it. "Hi. Now can we talk about what happened? Please? Because I really don't want to have to go back in there."

He sighed. "I can understand that, I suppose." He released my hand and walked up to the bunker, his steps growing slower and more reluctant as he drew nearer to it. "This is where they died. My children."

"Em and Dominic?"

He nodded. "I'd lost their mother in one of the floods years before, when Dom was little more than a baby. Ember and Dominic survived, until this moment." He looked over his shoulder at me. "They weren't aingls. There were no aingls then. I hadn't invented that technology yet. They were organic, fragile human beings who could be killed by perfectly ordinary human weapons."

That didn't make sense. "How could there have been no aingls when all the others were there? Leo, and Delta, and even Terence . . ." I stopped, suddenly getting it. "They were organic back then, too. When you built the aingls, you based them on people you knew." No, not just people he'd known. "People you'd lost?"

"Oh yes, they all died. Those were dangerous times. There were so many, many things that could kill you. . . . Environmental catastrophes. Religious cults. Governments, such as they were. And men and women made vicious by the simple ruthlessness of survival. Believe me when I tell you that you never want to live through the end of the world."

They all died. But not Hoffman, because he'd still been alive to build a synthetic body for himself, and later, synthetic replicas of the others. "You were the last. And you were lonely."

He gave an irritated shake of his head. "Loneliness had nothing to do with it. The work was all that mattered, and I was not as efficient without them. They were my research team, and I required their assistance. And *of course* I left them all alone to manage things in the new world! That was what they were created for."

"Even Ember and Dominic?"

"Especially Ember and Dominic. The two of them were based on *my* children, after all. They inherited their intelligence from me. Genuises, the both of them. Well, Dominic always was more like his mother. Ember, though . . ." His lips curved into a proud smile. "She is her father's daughter."

Her father's daughter. I could see that, clearer than I ever had before. Hoffman had been able to do whatever it took to survive, and so could Ember. It was how she'd created the Citizenship Accords in the first place. But, as Em herself had once said, survival wasn't life. It was just existence, and she wanted to be a better person than the one who'd done what it took to survive. She *was* a better person. That was why she tormented herself over the Citizenship Accords. Hoffman was a better person, too. Even if he didn't know it. *Her father's daughter. His daughter's father.* "You never forgave yourself. For letting Em and Dominic die."

"Nonsense! Billions would have died if I'd given up that code. I did the only thing that could have been done."

"If you're so sure about that, why didn't you ever tell her?" Because I knew he hadn't. Em carried the weight of a lot of things, but not of this.

"She has records enough of the harshness of these times. She didn't need this as well." He was silent for a moment, then added, "I told Dominic once. He said it was the right choice."

I heard the defensiveness in his tone and waited him out. Eventually he spoke, in a voice so low I had to move closer to catch his words. "The only thing is . . . two years later the government of the time cracked the code anyway, and used the device. So I might as well have saved them, in the end." His mouth twisted into a bitter, self-mocking curve. "As it turns out, no one can be extraordinary enough to account for every variable. Not even me."

I finally understood. "You're the one who's doing this."

"Doing what?"

"This!" I waved my hand around at the bunker, the wreckage, and the ruins of the city beyond. "The instability. You're doing it to yourself. Because losing your mind is the worst possible punishment for yourself that you can think of."

"Ridiculous!" he spluttered. "Arrant nonsense!"

I knew I was right. "Maybe if you'd had a normal life span, it wouldn't have mattered so much. But this has been eating away at you for hundreds of years."

"You are a very stupid girl."

I ignored him. I understood what was wrong with Hoffman now. I just wasn't sure how to fix it. He wanted to be forgiven. That was why he'd told Dominic but not

Em, because he hadn't been certain she would forgive. He was safe with Dominic. I knew that because the essence of Dominic was in Nicky, and like all dogs, Nicky had an infinite capacity for forgiveness. Except for the first time it occurred to me to wonder — could Nicky forgive because he was a dog, or had Dominic become Nicky because he could forgive? *And do I dream because I'm a Sleepwalker, or am I a Sleepwalker because I dream?* I shook my head at myself. I couldn't be solving Grandpa's riddles now.

I folded my arms, studying Hoffman and thinking. Dominic forgiving him hadn't been enough. Hoffman needed to forgive himself. A grin broke over my face. I knew how to do that. Because I'd once had to forgive myself for failing to save my little sister, Cassie, killed during a Citizenship Assessment. It had been Georgie who'd helped me see that hating myself for that was no way to value who Cassie had been, just as Hoffman hating himself was no way to value who Ember and Dominic had been. And I knew that Em would forgive him, or at least *my* Ember would, the one who'd created the Citizenship Accords. She understood what it was to regret a choice.

I closed my eyes and focused, letting myself feel the forgiveness I'd given to myself. And the forgiveness I'd given Jules for Penelope, and Em for the Citizenship Accords, and the bigger forgiveness I gave to all of the Tribe for anything that they'd done before they were Tribe. The first thing everyone got when they came to us was the chance to start over and become new. That was the chance Hoffman needed now. I held out my hands, imagining that forgiveness flowing from my heart and down my arms and into my grasp. Imagining it into reality.

When I opened my eyes again I was holding a small shining ball.

"What is that?" Hoffman asked.

"A present." I offered the ball to him. "Here."

He reached out to take it. The second his fingers touched it, the ball unraveled, becoming shining mist-like strands that flowed over his body and sank into his flesh. His eyes widened —

— and he vanished.

Everything vanished. *Did it work?* I had no idea, and it didn't seem like there was anything more I could do about it if it hadn't. I was alone in blackness and I was grateful for the peace. My chest felt bruised, as if my heart had taken a hit, and it had. I'd seen Ember die. I'd seen Dominic die. *They're not dead.* Only they were. The Ember who'd died hadn't been my Em, and the

Dominic who'd died hadn't been my Nicky. I mourned them anyway.

I drifted for what seemed like forever, soothed by the quiet dark and with no desire to wake — until there was a sudden searing pain in my arm.

My eyes flew open and I sat up, gasping. I was on the table in the room where Hoffman had been sleeping, only he wasn't sleeping now. He was standing a few meters away, and Jules was between us.

Hoffman was holding up one hand, and sparks were dancing between his fingers. "It was merely a small electric shock. I assure you, she hasn't been permanently damaged. She's awake now, see?"

Jules cast a quick glance back at me and came striding over. "Are you okay? I only took my eyes off the guy for a second, I swear!"

"I'm fine. I think." I looked down at my arm. It didn't seem to be injured, and the burning sensation was fading.

"I told you," Hoffman said. "No permanent damage. And really, how long were you intending to allow her to sleep?"

"How long *have* I been asleep?" I asked.

"Four days."

My mouth fell open. That was a long time. The

Conclave was less than a week away, and . . . *Where is everybody?* The room was empty except for Hoffman, Jules, and me. "Where did everyone go?"

"Leo turned up," Jules replied. "He ran into Pepper, and Em and Connor went to bring him here."

In other words, Pepper and Wanders had taken Leo prisoner, and Em and Connor were going to free him.

"And," Jules continued, "if you're wondering where the dog is, Georgie took him out for a walk."

So Nicky was all right, and Hoffman didn't know a thing about him or Jules wouldn't be talking in code. *Everything's all right. Everyone's all right.*

"If the two of you are *quite* finished catching up," Hoffman said, "I have some important questions to ask." He walked over, holding out his hand. "Allow me to introduce myself. My name is Alexander Hoffman. You probably know me better as the savior of humankind."

I shook his hand. Again. But he didn't seem to remember the first time. And this Hoffman wasn't the same as the one I'd met inside his mind. That had been Hoffman when he was wounded and vulnerable. This was Hoffman when he was healed.

So far I liked the hurt Hoffman better.

"I'm Ashala Wolf." I noticed he wasn't wearing the

311

disc on his head that Em had been using to monitor his instability, and glanced at Jules, raising my eyebrows in a question.

Jules snorted. "Oh yeah, he's all better. Aren't you, Professor?"

"I am indeed recovered. Now, Ashala, you really must tell me about Neville Rose."

Neville? I stared at Hoffman in bewilderment. "Um, he used to be the Chief Administrator of a det—"

"I know all that! I need to know *who* he is, not his employment history. It's vital information if we are to prevent Terence from doing more damage to this world than he already has."

I couldn't understand why Hoffman was so focused on Neville with the Conclave looming over us. "Do you know about the Conclave? We're worried about the other aingls."

Hoffman waved an impatient hand. "You need have no fear of my children; none of them will touch you once they realize you are under my personal protection."

I exchanged a glance with Jules, who shrugged. "Em says it'll probably be enough to stop Katya and Delta from coming after you. Not Terence, though, and possibly not Nova or Maleki."

"She might be correct in that," Hoffman conceded. "But we can deal with Terence and Nova and Maleki. It is most important that we look beyond the Conclave. We stand at a critical point in human history. This is the closest we've been to the end of the Citizenship Accords in over two hundred years, and I need to understand Neville Rose."

It must have been obvious that I still wasn't getting it, because he heaved a sigh and said, "I believe Rose to have been largely responsible for many of Terence's actions. The creation of these—minions, I believe you call them?—and the takeover of Gull City? It would never have occurred to Terence to do either without someone putting the idea into his head. The first requires too much subtlety, and the second is too bold."

Now he was making sense to me. "You think Neville is the key to stopping Terence."

Jules rolled his eyes. "You could've just said that before, you know."

"If I paused to explain my thought processes to lesser minds, it would consume my existence. Ashala—*tell* me about Neville. My daughter says you understand him better than anyone."

"He's—well, he's . . ." I thought for a moment. "I

had a taffa dream about him once." Hoffman would know about taffa dreams; he'd lived in Spinifex City. "I saw him standing on a hill of bodies, not just humans but animals and plants as well. The death of the world." I shivered at the memory. "But I don't think he'll actually kill everything. I think he'll do it by making it okay to kill."

"Interesting. Explain!"

"Neville enjoys hurting people. But most of the time, he doesn't *look* like someone who enjoys hurting people—he comes across like a friendly grandfather. And when he talks about abilities being unnatural, he sounds sorry about it. Regretful, you know?" I remembered what Willis had said about him and added, "He's done the most terrible things and there're *still* people who think he did them for the right reasons. Neville . . . makes it seem reasonable to hate. Reasonable to do anything to anyone, in the name of preserving the Balance. When the whole time all he's really interested in is getting his hands on more victims."

"Ah." Hoffman nodded in satisfaction. "Psychopaths always do tend to flourish in oppressive regimes—yes, I believe I understand him." He beamed at me. "An insightful analysis, Ashala. Thank you. Now we must leave."

314

He turned and went striding out the door. Jules took a quick step after him, then glanced back at me, obviously torn.

"Go," I told him. "I'm fine, I promise."

Jules sprinted after Hoffman, and I climbed off the table, leaning on the edge of it until I was sure my legs would support my weight. Then I went out into the tunnels, where Jules and Hoffman were arguing.

"Fine, then," Jules was saying. "Go off on your own. You'll get lost in the cave system and someone'll probably find you wandering around in, oh, a year or so."

"I need to think," Hoffman snapped. "I require pacing space. That room is much too confined. These tunnels are much too confined!"

I could sympathize with that. I didn't like being underground, either, not with the memory of the bunker still lingering.

"We can go into the forest," I said. "There's heaps of, um, pacing space there."

"An excellent notion," Hoffman exclaimed. "Let us depart."

The three of us starting walking, winding our way down the passages and then through the caves and finally out into the Firstwood. Hoffman took an instant interest in the plants, which apparently included some species he didn't recognize, and went hurrying off into the trees, running from one leaf or stalk or flower to the next. Jules rolled his eyes and followed him.

I stayed where I was, just outside the cave entrance. My legs were still weak; I was in no condition to go chasing after Hoffman, and I could trust Jules to make sure Ember's dad didn't get into any trouble. I tipped back my head, inhaling the eucalyptus in the air and enjoying the feel of the sun on my face. *I'm going to sleep outside tonight.* I was going to sleep outside for a while, with nothing around me but the trees and nothing above but the moon and the stars.

"Ashala Wolf!"

I jumped, twisting to see Leo careening through the forest on some kind of — *flying machine?* His feet were resting on a small white platform out of which came a T-shaped pole that rose up to chest height, and his hands were clasped around either end of the T. The entire device zoomed through the air, zigzagging between the trees and sending Leo's Spinifex City–yellow robe flapping around him. Connor and Em were flying above Leo, higher in the canopy, and they came drifting down to land at my side.

Leo stopped his vehicle and jumped off, leaving

it hovering as he hurried over. *Something's wrong.* Leo looked bad. His skin was sallow, his cheeks were sunken, and there were dark shadows under his eyes. If he weren't an aingl, I would have thought he was sick.

"Have you dreamed, Ashala?" he demanded.

"Um. Dreamed what?"

"You would know if you had dreamed!"

I cast a puzzled glance at Ember, who shook her head. "He's been like this the whole way here. I haven't been able to get any sense out of him at all." Then, "Ash? You're staring at me."

I was drinking in the sight of her alive and here and not dead in some cold underground room. But I wasn't going to tell her that. Now wasn't the time, and anyway I didn't know if I was ever going to be able to talk to Em about what I'd seen in her father's mind. "Sorry, Em, just . . . lost in thought, I guess." I felt a steady sense of reassurance emanating from Connor; he knew I was upset about something. I used the comfort of his presence to banish the memory of the bunker and returned my attention to Leo, who was turning in a slow circle and surveying the forest as if he was expecting to find something.

"In my dream," he said, "I came here. I came here,

and you were here, and I found the dreams. It's been the only dream anyone has dreamed for weeks; it must be right!"

I sighed. "Leo, I don't understand."

"The taffa dreams are gone!"

Everything suddenly became clear. Leo was obsessed with taffa dreams. He believed they gave glimpses into worlds beyond this one and would eventually show him Peter, the long-dead love of his life. If the dreams were gone, that possibility had been taken away, which was why Leo looked so ill. *Not sick. Heartsick.* The reason there'd been problems with the dreams was obvious, but I wasn't sure Leo knew it. The last time I'd seen him he'd thought Starbeauty was an ordinary desert cat who he called Misty.

I opened my mouth to speak with no real idea of what I was going to say — and closed it again when Starbeauty herself emerged from the trees. She stalked up to Leo and sat at his feet. **Hello, my pet.**

His mouth fell open. "I . . . you . . . *Misty*?"

No. I am Starbeauty.

And a deep voice exclaimed, "Extraordinary!"

Hoffman had returned, and Jules with him. Jules sauntered over to perch on a nearby rock, and Hoffman strode across to Starbeauty, staring down at her with a fascinated expression.

"Hello there, Father," Leo said.

Hoffman waved an impatient hand. "Yes, yes, Leo, I noticed you there. Now, this feline . . . telepathy? Some kind of advanced intelligence, perhaps?"

I didn't usually talk about spirits to people who didn't already know about them. But Starbeauty seemed to have decided to reveal herself, so I said, "She's an ancient spirit."

"Ancient spirit?" Hoffman frowned. "You surely don't believe in gods, Ashala! There are no gods."

They believe in me.

He scowled down at her. "And you think yourself to be a god?"

I think myself to be an earth spirit.

"But . . . you expect people to worship you? Obey your commands?"

People *do* worship me and obey my commands.

"Because you tell them you are a god?"

Because I tell them I am a cat.

This conversation had the potential to go on for a really long time.

"Ancient earth spirits aren't like the gods you wrote

about," I told Hoffman. "It's more like . . . well, there's the Balance, and it's in everything and it *is* everything. And the Balance shows itself in lots of ways, and some of those ways have names and personalities. They're ancient spirits." Then to Leo I said, "It isn't taffa that causes the dreams. It's Starbeauty."

His face lit up with hope, and he dropped to the ground beside her in a single graceful motion. "Why did you take the dreams away? Did I do something wrong? How do I get them back? I'll do anything!"

I took the dreams so that you would follow a dream here to find them again. But that is not what you are truly here to find. She looked over her shoulder into the trees. You may come out now.

Nicky came bounding out of the undergrowth and pelted over to Leo. I cast a panicked glance at Em, who gave me a helpless shrug back. She didn't know how Hoffman and Leo were going to react, either, but it was too late to do anything about it now.

Nicky stopped in front of Leo, his head almost level with Leo's own, since Leo was still sitting, and grinned a doggy grin. Leo gazed at Nicky in bemusement. "I'm not sure I —" Then he gasped. *"Dominic?"*

"Woof!"

"Don't be ridiculous," Hoffman said sharply. "It

320

cannot possibly . . ." His voice trailed off as he stared at Nicky. "It *can't* be." Hoffman sank to the ground, reaching out to rest a shaking hand on Nicky's head. "My son? Is it you?"

"Woof!"

"He's not the same," Em said. "He's Nicky now, not Dominic, and this is his second life. Neither of you can take him apart to turn him back into what he was, because that's not what he is."

Leo looked up at her and said in a raw, stunned voice, "Little sister, how could you think I would ever hurt him?"

Her gaze fell before his. "I'm sorry, Leo. I wasn't sure. We both know the others—"

"I am not the others!"

Ember flinched, and Hoffman said, "I think we can all agree Dominic appears to be perfectly content in this form. Let us focus on the more important issue—how is this possible?"

"It's possible because of Ash," Ember replied. She walked over to sit beside her father and brother. Then she drew in a breath and told them about how Dominic had become an interrogation machine before becoming Nicky.

When she'd finished, Leo stared down at Nicky and

whispered, "I thought when we died we just ended, and wherever Peter had gone, it was a path I could never follow. The taffa seemed to be the only way I'd ever see him. I thought there was never any possibility of a second life for an aingl, because we don't have . . ."

He didn't finish the sentence, but he didn't need to. Ember had once thought the same thing, that being synthetic instead of organic somehow made her less human, with no spirit to go to the Balance.

Starbeauty directed a stern green gaze at Leo. **You are a foolish pet. Your end is not your end.**

Tears began to leak out of Leo's eyes. Em put one arm around him and the other around Hoffman and drew them in close. Starbeauty watched them for a moment, then padded back into the forest with the satisfied air of a cat whose work was done.

This wasn't a moment for us. It wasn't a moment for anyone but Ember's family. And after everything I had seen in the bunker and all I knew about the aingls, it seemed so right that these four—Ember, Nicky, Hoffman, and Leo—should be together, in this moment, in this life. So I took Connor's hand and motioned to Jules to follow us.

The three of us walked away, leaving the aingls to their grief and their joy and one another.

THE FUTURE

GEORGIE

Two days from now was the Conclave and tonight was dinner. Everyone was gathered around the cooking fire in the Overhang, and the air was filled with the smell of vegetable soup and eucalyptus and smoke. All the Tribe was here, along with Starbeauty, and Ember's dad, and Ember's brother Leo, who was sitting very still so as not to wake Rosa, who'd fallen asleep in his lap.

Everyone who was going to the Conclave would be leaving early tomorrow morning. They wouldn't reach the meeting place in time otherwise, not when they had to cross the grasslands and then travel into the Steeps. Em and Jules and Starbeauty were going, along with Ash and Connor and Ember's dad. That meant tonight was our last chance to bring together all the people whose choices mattered before the Conclave happened. So that was what we were doing. Em and Jules and Nicky were already waiting in the caves, but Starbeauty was still here, and so were Daniel and I. Starbeauty was going to leave when we did, but Daniel and I couldn't go yet, not until we'd talked to Ash and Connor. They were speaking to everyone, and if they missed out on speaking to us they might come looking. We didn't want them to find our meeting.

Daniel leaned in closer to me and said, "You go talk to them now, and while you're doing that I'll go get Starbeauty. Then *I'll* talk to them, and I can leave." He nodded at Ash and Connor and added, "Quick, before they get into a conversation with somebody else."

I stood up and hurried over to where Ash and Connor were standing at the edge of the rock. As soon as she saw me coming, Ash opened her mouth to talk, but before she could say any words I said some instead.

"It's all right. You don't have to ask me what I did today or how I'm feeling, the way you've been doing with everybody else. I know."

"Know what?" Ash asked.

"That you're not asking about people's days or feelings at all. You're saying good-bye. So that if you don't come back from the Conclave, everyone will remember that you asked something about them the last time they saw you, and know that you love us."

Ash and Connor looked at each other and then at me. Ash came closer and whispered, "Do you think anyone else knows that?"

"Yes. Everyone."

"Really?"

"Really."

Ash's face fell, but Connor smiled. "I guess we're not as clever as we think we are," he said. "And I definitely won't ask you about your day, Georgie. But I will tell you that I am glad to have been your friend, and I do love you."

He leaned in to kiss my cheek and moved away. Ash took hold of my arm. "Walk with me for a while."

We climbed down off the rock and into the trees, and as we went I said, "You don't need to say good-bye. You're going to be okay, and so is Connor."

"Oh, yeah? You *See* that?"

No. Maybe. "Yes."

She laughed. "Liar! Thanks for trying to make me

feel better, though." Then she stopped and turned to face me, letting go of my arm.

"Georgie, if something does happen to me, Ember's going to take it hard. I'm not saying you won't be sad, too, but . . ."

"I won't be sad like Ember is. Because I don't get sad the way she does. Nobody does."

"Yeah. So you might need to run things without her for a while. Until she feels better. I want—I *need* to know that you'll all go on without me."

We won't. Nothing goes on without you. Except it was no good telling her that. I thought she might even believe it now if Starbeauty told her, too, but no one could stop Ash from being Ash or Connor from being Connor. They thought they were the people who saved and not the ones who were saved, and they both looked into the now. They wouldn't let anyone die for them today even if it stopped a blizzard from coming tomorrow.

"I made you a party once," I said. "Do you remember? I brought all the Tribe together and we had a party."

"I remember. It was right after the fight at the center. When we saved Belle Willis from Terence."

"That wasn't why I made the party. I made it because of what happened before that. Terence almost killed you. You shouldn't have gone after him alone, Ash. Do you remember what I told you at the party?"

"I . . ." She frowned. "I said I needed the Tribe. And you said the Tribe needed me more."

"I wanted you to see how much you mattered to us. Because sometimes you're not good at mattering to yourself."

She breathed in deeply and then out again. "I know. But I'm better at it than I used to be."

I nodded because that was true. "You're not the same as after Cassie died. For a while after that if you'd lost someone else, it could have made you . . . not-you. Now if you lose people, it hurts you, but it doesn't . . ."

"Break me," Ash said. She didn't sound happy. She looked down at the ground and added in a low voice, "It just—doesn't seem right that it *doesn't* break me. That I should able to go on when they don't. When Pen didn't."

"You're not good at being the person who lives." I reached out to hold her head so she had to look at me. "But the Tribe needs you to be that person. So you have to fight for yourself the way you'd fight for any of us. You have to fight *hard.* Promise me!"

Ash was quiet, staring at me. Then she said, "I don't know what's going to happen at the Conclave. And I don't know what's going to happen after, with the accords and—everything!" She reached up and clasped my wrists. "But I promise you if there's ever a time when I don't come back, it won't be because I haven't tried as hard as I possibly could to come home."

I took my hands away and she hugged me. "I love you, Georgie."

"Love you, too, Ash."

She let me go, and the two of us walked back together to the Overhang. Daniel was still there, only now he had Starbeauty with him and he was talking to Connor. He'd have to talk to Ash as well before he could leave, and that would take a while, because she'd started speaking to Micah. He gave me a look across the campfire, and I knew the look meant *Go; I'll catch up.* So I climbed down from the rocks and went to the caves, wandering through the passages to the cavern where I'd told everyone to meet me. It wasn't the same place where we'd been meeting before. It was a bigger cave, with no opening onto the forest, and it was where I'd built my new map. When I got there, everyone was looking at it.

The map was on the ceiling and it was made of webbing instead of vines. My spiders had bound lots of thin strands of webbing together to make bigger strands that were the thickness of my little finger, and all of the strands had tiny pieces of quartz stuck to them that Daniel had collected from the forest. I'd told the spiders where the strands needed to go, and they'd made a map that covered the entire ceiling, hanging down above everyone's heads. Then I'd put solar lamps across the floor and pointed them up so they shone across the strands and made the quartz glitter.

As I came into the cave, Em said, "Georgie, this is beautiful!"

From inside the map, Helper chirped proudly. Jules backed away from the sound, and Helper let out a gleeful chitter.

"This isn't like your other maps," Ember said. "What does it mean?"

"We have to wait for Daniel," I said. "When he comes here is when I tell you."

Ember and Jules wandered around the cave, and

Nicky flopped in a corner, licking at his paws. Then there were footsteps outside, and Daniel came, and so did Starbeauty. But behind them was somebody else.

"Dad!" Em gasped. "What are you doing here? Did you want me for something?'

Em's dad ignored her, walking into the middle of the cave and staring at my map. "What an extraordinary creation! How was such a thing achieved?"

Daniel said, "Starbeauty says he's the sixth."

"There's a sixth now?" Jules said. "And it's *him*?" He turned toward me. "You sure about that?"

"No! I didn't even know there was a sixth!"

Some things cannot be known until they are known. Now is when this is known. Starbeauty paced across to me and sat at my feet. Bringing you the sixth was my last choice.

"Are you going back to Spinifex City?"

This is not a matter of who goes and who does not. It is a matter of choices ending. I can no longer change what is to be. She flicked her ears at Jules. You cannot, either.

"I'm off the hook, huh? Can't say I'm sorry about that." Only he was sorry; I could hear it in his voice. He looked at Ember and added, "But don't think you're leaving me behind, Red. I'm coming with you to the Conclave whether my choices matter or not."

Hoffman was frowning, and he was frowning at all of us. "Would someone please explain to me what you are all talking about?"

I explained. It took a long time because first I had to talk about my ability, since Hoffman didn't know what it was. Then we all took turns telling him about everything that happened since I'd Seen Ash was going to die, and how the world would end if she did, and what he had to do to stop it.

When we'd finished, Hoffman heaved a sigh and said, "Must I save humanity again? It really is becoming rather tiresome."

"Dad!" Ember hissed.

"I'm *joking*, Ember. Obviously the girl cannot be allowed to die. Who is going to repair me if I ever suffer another episode of instability?"

"Do you understand what you need to do?" Ember demanded. "Make the choice you wouldn't have made if you didn't know about the danger?"

"Yes, thank you, Ember, I am quite capable of understanding a perfectly logical explanation." He looked upward and added, "I take it, then, that this is one of your 'maps,' Georgie? Of the things that are to be?"

"Yes," I said. "And no."

I walked until I was standing in the center of the cave, and Daniel walked with me. I reached up to brush my fingers against one of the strands. "The spiders made this webbing specially. It's lots of strands wound together. So it's connected on the inside." I let my hand fall. "Then the strands link to other strands. So it's connected on the outside, too. And all of it together—it's the future if Ash lives."

Daniel added quietly, "Georgie wanted you to see what you were all fighting for."

Everyone looked up, and so did I. It wasn't quite the future I saw in my head. Nothing could be as shining and hopeful as that. But with the white webbing glowing silver in the light and the quartz glittering, it was enough.

"I *want* this future," Ember said.

"We all want this future," Hoffman said. "What you are speaking of, Georgie, is a true Balance. Harmony within and without. Besides"—he nodded at his daughter—"it is a family affair now. The people whose choices matter are you, me, and Dominic."

"Nicky!" Ember insisted.

Hoffman shrugged and turned his attention to me. "My understanding of the plan for tomorrow is that Dominic will be some distance into the grasslands in order to place him in sufficient range of Ashala to activate her ability, should it be required. But are you quite certain he should not be in the vicinity of the Conclave itself?"

His next choice is not made at the Conclave. Starbeauty rolled to her feet and came over to stand with us. He must trust you to preserve her life. You must trust him to preserve her chance. Both are required to make the future.

"Are you implying that there is a difference between Dominic's choices and ours?" Hoffman demanded. "And what, precisely, is Ashala's 'chance'?"

Starbeauty yawned. Explanations are not of cat.

Hoffman kept staring at her as if she were going to say something else even though she'd just told him she wasn't. Ember understood there were no more words coming from Starbeauty. She looked over at me and said, "Is there anything more you can tell us that might help, Georgie?"

I shook my head. They knew the danger was greater

than ever before because it was all we'd been talking about over the past few days as the Conclave drew nearer. They didn't know what the blizzard was doing to me, but it wouldn't help them to know that I was always so cold now that my bones ached with it or that it sometimes hurt to breathe because it felt like I was inhaling ice. "I haven't Seen anything else." Except I hadn't Seen the sixth. "Starbeauty?"

What has needed to be said has been said. She stalked to the entrance and gazed back at everyone else. **We are now elsewhere.**

"Hold on a moment!" Hoffman protested. "I still have questions!"

Em gave him a push toward Starbeauty. "When an ancient spirit—or Georgie—tells you it's time to be elsewhere, you go elsewhere."

Ember and Jules took Hoffman away, past Starbeauty and into the passages, and Nicky trotted after them. Starbeauty stayed where she was, looking back at Daniel and me. Her tail was in the air, but her ears were flat. Something was making her sad, and I knew what it was because she would have understood the map in the way the others didn't. She could tear it with her claw. I could break it with my hand. The possibility of the future where Ash lived was fragile and easy to destroy.

In whatever is to come you must know yourselves to be of cat. We do not fall. Even when we do.

Then she was gone, disappearing into the passages after the others.

I turned and threw my arms around Daniel and held on very tight. The space inside his arms had become the only space where I wasn't cold. The blizzard was taking my warmth, and if we couldn't stop it, it would take everyone else's, too. I was afraid for Ash and for Connor and for all of us.

Daniel whispered against my ear, "Georgie? Let's Run."

He lifted me up, and I wrapped my arms around his neck. Everything blurred, and when everything stopped blurring we were somewhere else, and then somewhere else, then somewhere else again. We lay by one of the small pools where the markings on the backs of the star frogs were glowing, and Daniel looked up at the stars in the sky while I looked down at the ones in the water. We sat in one of the hollows where the night jasmine bloomed, and Daniel made me a crown of flowers. We stood at the edge of the cliffs and watched the hawks soaring across the face of the moon. Sometimes we talked and sometimes we didn't, and in one of the times when we did, Daniel said to me, "I will love you always and forever and in all the futures you can See and the ones you can't."

We lived in each other's arms and shared each other's worlds, and for one whole night, I looked into the now.

THE CONCLAVE

ASHALA

Aingls were ahead. But we couldn't see them yet.

Em said we had about another ten minutes to go before we reached the staging area of the old rhondarite mine. That was the location she'd sent out to her family using the Conclave-calling device, and that was where they would be, waiting. *Lurking . . . Stop it.* I was as safe as I could get, surrounded by my own aingls — Ember at my side. Leo hovering along on his flyer in front of us, using one arm to steer and the other to hold Starbeauty against his chest. And Hoffman striding along next to Leo. We'd left Connor and Jules a ways back, sheltering in one of the many crevasses in the jagged white rocks that made up the Steeps. They hadn't liked staying behind, but as Hoffman had put it, a Conclave was an "invitation-only event." There was nothing to be gained by breaking the rules, and besides, if there was any trouble we could contact them pretty much immediately. We could warn the Tribe, too, because we'd set up a sort of mindspeaking relay system. Pepper and Wanders were in the forests near the center, close enough that we could reach them from here. And once we'd reached them, they could mindspeak Jaz on the grasslands, and Jaz could reach Georgie or Daniel.

I rubbed at my chest. It was tight and getting tighter with every step we took, even though I knew I wasn't likely to die today, not when I had Hoffman and Leo to defend me as well as Ember. The three of them wouldn't let the others kill me no matter what happened at the Conclave, and Em was carrying the weapon that would paralyze an aingl in her pocket. It was the days that came after today that worried me. Because if the aingls decided I was a threat — that the Tribe was a threat — we'd never have a safe day again. They could come for us at any time, and I knew they'd never give up, not if they thought they were fighting for their lives.

The wind suddenly picked up, and with it came the scent of eucalyptus. A Firstwood wind. I inhaled the familiar, comforting smell and seemed to inhale something else with it. A sense of calm filled me, pouring into my lungs and expanding outward across my chest. My concerns abruptly seemed to be small things, not worth worrying myself over. They would pass, as all things did. Night would follow day, and the seasons would shift, and all that was would live and die and live again. *And the Tribe will endure forever. . . .*

I blinked. What had that been? But I knew. Grandpa, reaching out to comfort me from afar. And he had.

"Ash? You all right?"

"Fine," I told Em. Then I studied her face and asked, "You?" Because there was danger ahead for her as well, the danger of the bleakness that threatened to overwhelm whenever she had to deal with her family.

"I'm fine, too."

"Are you sure?"

She smiled. Ember's whole face changed when she smiled, but never quite like this. She looked totally at peace with herself and the world. "I'm not sad."

"Good." She seemed to be doing much better at

coping with her family. It must have helped her to be with Hoffman and Leo and Nicky. Maybe the repeal of the accords had helped as well, even if it hadn't turned out as we'd hoped.

Ember glanced at her dad and shifted closer to me. "Listen, Ash, I wanted to say to you—I know Dad can be a little . . . Well, he is who he is. But he can be a real asset. He can do everything I can do with nanomites and everything, and he knows as much about human history. More, actually, and—"

"Em," I interrupted, "if you want your dad to stay in the Firstwood for a while, he can."

"Oh. Well, yes, I would like him to stay. I mean, I think it would be good for everyone if he stayed."

Silly Em. You don't need a reason other than him being your dad. "Then he stays."

She smiled that same smile of contentment again, and I smiled back. Then I caught a glimpse of something in the distance and looked up to see black wings flapping through the skies. *Crows.* Two—no, three of them, soaring overhead.

I nudged Ember. "Your crows are here."

"I know," she answered. "They've come to be with me."

There was a sudden heaviness to her voice, and I

frowned. Maybe she was sad after all? Before I could ask her about it, the road began to slope sharply upward and Em said, "This is it, Ash. The staging area for the mine should be over the top of this rise."

We can talk about her family later. We'd probably have plenty more to discuss after today anyway. I drew in another calming breath. I could still taste the eucalyptus in the air, and I tried to pull as much of it as I could into my lungs as we walked up, and up. It seemed to take forever before we neared the crest of the rise. Leo and Hoffman got there first. Em and I arrived a few minutes later, and all of us looked down at what was below.

The road we were on ran into a big flat area and then out of it again, twisting away through the jagged white cliffs that loomed over the flat space on all sides. In the center of it were the aingls. Most I recognized immediately—Terence in Gull City blue, Delta in Cloud City white, and Maleki in Jet City black. Then there were the two I didn't know but had seen in the bunker, the black woman and the blond one, both in Wattle City gray. Flyers were hovering in a neat row behind where the aingls were standing, and the aingls themselves were staring at us.

Hoffman went striding downward. He reached the

bottom of the hill and kept on going, flinging his arms wide open. "My children!"

With the exception of Terence, everyone came running. They crowded around him, all trying to hug him at once and talking over one another as they vied for his attention. Em had been right; the aingls loved their dad. *Putting me under his protection might actually work.* I didn't want to get too hopeful, though. Once they got over being happy to see him, they'd probably start to remember the times he'd let them down, and if they didn't, Terence would remind them. Besides which, I knew they feared dying more than they loved him, because the one thing they'd never been prepared to do for their father was get rid of the Citizenship Accords.

Leo stepped off his flyer. He put Starbeauty onto the ground, and she padded away to perch on the rocks. I will observe.

Ember and I started down the hill, and Leo hurried to join us, pacing along at my side. Em leaned in to whisper to me as we went, "The one dressed in black is Maleki. The blond one wearing gray is Katya, and the other one is Nova."

I'd already recognized Maleki, but she didn't know I'd seen him before, in the bunker. My gaze slid over the other aingls to where Terence was watching his brothers and sisters bounce around Hoffman like puppies. Terence's face was rigid and his mouth pressed into a thin line. Fury, and pain. *He wants his family back.* If he'd been anyone else I would've felt sorry for him. But not for a man who took other people's families away.

The moment we reached the base of the hill, Terence jabbed a finger in my direction and shouted, "There she is! That is the girl who will kill us all!"

The aingls stopped talking and swiveled to stare right at me. Ember and Leo moved closer, sheltering me between them. I looked back at the aingls, trying to appear—*trustworthy? Harmless?* But I knew I could never be harmless enough, because whatever Terence had been telling them about me had worked. They were afraid. Delta went very still and Maleki shifted uneasily on his feet. Katya took an anxious step back and Nova stepped forward, standing in front of Katya to shield her. *I'm not your enemy!* There was no point in saying so. They were like the people in the city who thought all Illegals were killers, the ones who Jules had said were made vicious and stupid by fear.

I swallowed. I might be safe for today, but one way or another these people were coming for me, and I didn't think anyone was going to be able to stop them.

Then Hoffman said, "Ashala Wolf saved my life."

There was a stunned silence that was broken by Terence. "I don't believe it! When and how were you in danger of dying, Father?"

"I wasn't 'in danger' of dying," Hoffman answered. "I was dead. I had to shut myself down, you see. Because . . ." He bent his head and ran a hand over his face, shading his eyes. When he looked up again, his expression was haunted. "Because I was insane."

I stifled a startled exclamation as the aingls stared at him in horror. I hadn't expected Hoffman to tell the truth, and from the expression on Em's face, neither had she. I'd never considered for a second that Hoffman would be willing to expose a weakness. He wasn't a man who did that.

"There was some kind of instability," Hoffman continued wearily, "caused by transferring my consciousness to an artificial body."

"You should have come to me!" Delta said. "Or to Ember. We could have repaired you."

He *had* gone to Em, but Delta didn't know that, any more than Hoffman himself knew what the true cause of his instability had been. Hoffman patted her shoulder. "There was no way to repair me, my dear.

Believe me, I tried. I was getting a little worse every day, forgetting things — forgetting numbers, Delta!"

Katya's lower lip trembled. "But I don't want you to be insane, Father."

"I'm not insane," Hoffman told her. "At least, not anymore." He gestured toward me. "Because she saved my mind. Ember found me, you see, and Ashala used her ability to heal the instability. So before you all decide to kill this girl, you should know — without her your father would be dead."

The aingls were looking at me again, this time with a strange variety of expressions. Terence was white with rage. Nova was wary, and Maleki thoughtful. Delta was studying me with an intense, creepily detached stare, as if she'd like to take me apart and find out what was inside. But Katya — Katya was gazing at me with something approaching adoration. She turned to grab hold of Nova's sleeve, pulling at it. "We can't let Terence hurt her, Nova. Not after she saved Dad. You have to protect her."

Nova glanced uncertainly from Katya to me. She opened her mouth and closed it again. Frowned. Then seemed to come to a decision. "You're right, Katya. She cannot be harmed. Terence, I will not permit it."

Terence snarled, "This man is not our father."

345

"Terence!" Hoffman spread his arms wide. "I know we've had our differences, but really . . ."

"That's not what I mean. You're an Illegal."

There were gasps of alarm at that, and Terence continued, "There's an Illegal who can appear to be anyone. Delta can confirm that."

"That Illegal is dead," Ember snapped, and I hoped Terence believed her, because none of us wanted him knowing Jules was still alive.

"Then it's another Illegal with the same ability! Think about it, all of you. Is he *acting* like Father?"

"Of course I'm your father, and I'll prove it," Hoffman said. He looked around and then walked over to pick up a rock from the ground—a piece of rhondarite, left behind by the miners. "If I had an ability, I couldn't use it while touching rhondarite." He held it up, letting them see his hand clenched around it, then allowed it to fall. "Although I do understand why you might think that I'm not acting like myself. I was . . . lost, for a long time. And when I was found again, I realized I'd been wrong, about so many things." He gazed at each of his children in turn. "I've been wrong in the way I've treated all of you."

There was a collective intake of breath. Maleki and Katya were mouthing the word "wrong" as if they'd never heard it before. Not even the revelation of Hoffman's insanity seemed to have shocked the aingls as much as him admitting a mistake. *I bet he never has.*

Hoffman gave a sorrowful shake of his head and continued, "I should never have left you all by yourselves to guide humanity in the new world."

My mouth fell open. That was exactly what I'd said to him, inside his mind when he'd asked me to prove I wasn't him by saying something he'd never say to himself. *Oh, you bastard. You remembered all along.*

"But you *did* leave," Terence pointed out coldly. "Don't be fooled by this, any of you—he always leaves! What makes any of you believe he'll be any different this time?"

None of the aingls were paying attention to Terence any longer. They were all staring at Hoffman, transfixed by this new version of their father. Hoffman stood with his shoulders bowed, staring back at them out of pain-filled eyes. He looked humble. Vulnerable. Sad.

"I haven't done right by any of you," he said quietly. "I'd like the chance to make up for it, if you'll give it to me."

"Of course we'll give you a chance!" Katya said. "We love you, Father!" She flew to his side, and every aingl but Terence, Ember, and Leo followed.

347

Leo folded his arms, watching as the aingls embraced Hoffman one by one, and murmured, "Even for Father, this is quite the performance."

Ember whispered back, "It could be real. Some of it could be real!"

"Believe what you wish, little sister. But anyone who puts their faith in our father is doomed to disappointment."

"I don't believe that. I can't."

I wished I could tell Em that Leo was wrong and she was right. I wasn't sure. Hoffman was . . . complicated.

There was a strange hissing, whistling noise coming from somewhere. Someone was breathing heavily and fast, sucking in air past their teeth. *Terence.* He lurched toward his brothers and sisters and burst out, "I'm the one who kept everyone safe! It was me! All these years, it's been me. Not him. Never *him*!" He rounded on me, his thin chest heaving. "And you . . . you should be dead. You should be dead, with the others!"

Others?

"What others, Terence?" Hoffman demanded sharply.

"The other ones who could hurt us! The ones I've saved you from. There've been a few, over the years — a Liquefier boy about a decade back, who could make anything melt — I protected you all!"

He'd killed them. *Dead, with the others.* I was chilled in a way that had nothing to do with the wind off the rocks. The other aingls were gaping at Terence; they hadn't known this. Ember hadn't known this. I cast an anxious glance at her to find that she was staring at Terence, and she looked suddenly . . . old.

She spoke in a harsh, accusing tone to her brother. "You said Liquefier *boy*, Terence. A child? Were they all children?"

He shrugged irritably. "Not quite children, but they were young, of course. That is when you have to act." He took a pleading step in her direction. "You taught me that, sister. You said when we created detention that we had to target the young. They wouldn't resist, wouldn't be able to use their abilities as well as —" He broke off. "Why are you crying?"

Tears were winding down Ember's face in silent streams. I'd never seen anyone cry without making a sound before. I reached out to put my arm around her. She threw me off, moving away from me and toward Terence. She stopped right in front of him, staring up at him out of a face that seemed to have aged ever further within the past few seconds. Ember had become as old and weathered and layered as the stone that surrounded us, and when she spoke, her voice was as unyielding. "Terence, you are my brother and I loved you once. But something went wrong with you, and you are bad, and you are never going to *stop*. Unless someone stops you."

Ember pulled the paralyzer weapon from her pocket and fired.

Terence went down, slumping limply to the ground.

In the same instant, Ember did, too, her eyes rolling back in her head as her body twitched and jerked.

The weapon burst into flame. I tore over and kicked it out of her hand. Then I dropped to her side, hovering uselessly. Leo arrived on her other side, and the two of us exchanged frantic glances. I didn't want to touch her for fear of causing her more pain, and I didn't understand what was happening. The aingls couldn't kill, but Em had only paralyzed Terence; she shouldn't have been reacting like this! Maybe something had gone wrong with the weapon and it had hurt her as well?

She went limp. "Em?" I shook her. "Em?"

Then Hoffman was there, bending over Em, pulling back her eyelids to stare into her eyes. He let her go and went over to Terence, doing the same thing to him. When he straightened, his face was gray.

"She's killed him," he said. "And probably herself."

That wasn't right. It couldn't be right, because

Ember couldn't die. Hoffman had misunderstood. "No, she's — that weapon, it only knocks someone out temporarily. Terence isn't . . ."

My voice trailed off. Hoffman was shaking his head, gazing grimly at the melted goo that was all that remained of the weapon. "I don't know what she told you it did," he said. "But I can assure you, Terence is gone."

She'd killed someone. But Ember could do that as long as she thought the death was justifiable. "Then — she just needs time! To resolve the death."

There was a big hand on my arm. Clasping it gently. *Leo.* "Ashala? She isn't moving. That means she isn't fighting anymore. If she'd resolved it, she would've come out of it by now."

I glared at him. "You're wrong! She just needs more time."

And Katya said, in a small voice, "Daddy?"

The aingls were huddled together. They were staring at their father out of wide, shocked eyes and very definitely *not* looking at Terence or Ember. In fact they'd backed up, right to the edge of where the rocks rose upward and as far away as they could get from where Terence and Ember lay. *Death.* The aingls' oldest fear.

"You must go home, my children," Hoffman said. "Go to Spinifex City, to my house—" He glanced at Leo. "I presume it is still there?" Leo nodded, and Hoffman continued, "I will deal with the . . . with the bodies. Then I will come to you in Spinifex City, and we will be a family again."

Leo's hand tightened on my arm. "I'll go with them and make sure they *do* go to the city. You look after Ember. Don't leave her with Father."

"I won't. The Tribe won't."

Leo bent to press a kiss to Ember's cheek, just as he had with the other Ember, the dead Ember—no. This Ember wasn't dead. She *wasn't*. Then he rose, striding toward Maleki, Katya, Nova, and Delta. They were trying to climb onto the flyers, but they seemed to be having difficulty, like they'd forgotten how to do the simplest things. Leo began to help them one at a time, speaking in a low, reassuring voice. "Come on now, put your foot there, that's it. We have to go now. We'll be together, all of us together, and Father will come."

I wasn't sure he believed that. I wasn't sure I did. But the aingls seemed to, or were in too much shock to argue. I turned my attention back to Em, holding on tightly to her hand so she'd know I was there. For a second I thought she was moving, and my heart leaped in hope. Then I realized it was me; I was trembling so badly I was shaking her.

Something soft brushed against my arm. *Starbeauty.* She didn't say a thing, simply pressed against me and purred, a deep rumble that vibrated out of her body and into mine. The rumble of the purr seemed to absorb my shaking and carry it away, out of me and into the ground below. Then she stalked off, padding over to Leo, who scooped her up into his arms.

The aingls began to fly. One after another they hovered upward over the rocks, heading away from the Firstwood and out of the Steeps. Leo stepped onto the last flyer and joined them. The moment they were out of sight, Hoffman grabbed hold of Terence's shoulders and began to drag him across the ground.

"We'll conceal him in the rocks," he said. "I can retrieve him later. Too difficult to carry the both of them now, I think, and it isn't as if he's going anywhere."

I didn't answer him. There was nothing to say. Or there was, but not to him. *I have to call Pepper.* I had to tell Connor and Jules to come. But maybe Ember would wake up. Maybe she'd wake up in the next second. Then I could tell them that she was okay. I could tell Jules that she was okay.

Then there was an anguished sound from behind me, and I knew. Jules was already here. I twisted to see him tearing down the rocks with Connor behind him. *Of course they're here.* They would have started heading in this direction the moment Connor sensed my distress.

Jules crashed to the ground, cradling Ember's head in his hands. "Wh— How?"

"The weapon," I said. "It killed. She killed Terence."

"She killed? Then— she just needs time! To resolve the death." He pushed her hair gently back from her still face. "It's all right, Red. You did it to save Ashala. You did it to save a life, and I'm right here. You just need time."

"That's what I said," I told him, pleased to finally be talking to someone who understood. "She just needs time and, and not to be alone. She can't be alone."

I glanced up at Connor, hoping he understood, too. But he was looking at Hoffman, who was shaking his head. Hoffman was a very stupid man. Ember was going to be *fine*.

Connor walked across to us, crouching down to clasp hold of my shoulder and reaching over Ember to grip Jules's arm. When he spoke, his voice was as gentle as the fall of a leaf to the forest floor. "Let's get her back to the Firstwood."

THE BATTLE

ASHALA

It had been almost half an hour since Ember di—No, I wouldn't say it. I wouldn't even think it. *Fell asleep.* Ember was just asleep, that was all, and she'd wake up eventually. I knew she'd wake up. She had to wake up.

We were soaring along the road, back toward the center. Hoffman was on a flyer—Leo's, because Leo had taken Terence's and left his own at the top of the rise. Connor was carrying Jules and me through the air, and Jules was holding Ember in his arms. Jules hadn't stopped speaking to her since we'd left the meeting place, and his voice was growing hoarse, but he kept on talking. Mostly he was saying the same thing, over and over: *Wake up, Red. You have to wake up.* Behind us were the crows, dipping through the sky and calling, *caw, caw, caw* . . . Ember hadn't stirred, not for Jules and not for the crows, either. *Oh, Em. He wasn't worth it. He wasn't worth you.*

I should have known what she was going to do. All the clues had been there. I just hadn't understood them. The way she'd been talking about Hoffman, for a start. She'd been telling me to let him stay so I'd have someone who could do the same things she could after she was gone. Her smile, and how she'd told me she wasn't sad, letting me know she was happy with her choice. And the crows, of course. *They've come to be with me. They've come to be with me when I* . . . I stopped my thoughts. I wasn't ever going to complete the sentence that Em herself had never said, at least not out loud. I suddenly, desperately wanted Georgie here to help me make sense of this. To look into her futures and See that Ember was going to wake up. To tell me this *wasn't* the real world.

Hoffman stopped his flyer, waving to the rest of us. "Everybody on the ground, please. *Now.*"

We drifted to the earth. Jules immediately carried

357

Em over to the rocks and sat down, still talking to her and ignoring the rest of us. Connor and I turned toward Hoffman.

"What's wrong?" I asked.

"Perhaps nothing," he answered. "Quiet for a second, please." He tipped his head to one side, tapping at his temple, and frowned. "There's something . . . I need more power."

He stepped off the flyer and knelt to yank a panel from the front, revealing a mess of wires inside. Then he pulled one of the wires free and shoved it into the flesh of his arm. I gasped as blood spurted out.

"What are you *doing*?" I started toward him, but he waved me back.

"Stay where you are. This is nothing."

He closed his eyes, sitting there with blood dripping off his arm and spattering down against the white rock. *He must be using the flyer as an energy source.* I'd had no idea he could do that, and it must have been hurting him—or perhaps it wasn't. Hoffman had made his children so that they'd experience pain exactly as an organic being would, but I wasn't sure he'd done the same with the body he'd built for himself. After a second, he opened his eyes and said, "There's a signal. I think it's coming from Terence."

"He's alive?" I exclaimed.

Jules looked up from Ember, his face alight with hope. "If Ember didn't kill him, she'll—"

Hoffman shook his head. "No. He is most definitely not alive. This signal is some kind of dead man's switch." He noticed my confusion and added impatiently, "A device that automatically activates if someone dies. His body is sending a signal out to whoever has the appropriate apparatus to receive it. Someone knows he's gone."

Connor and I exchanged glances. "Neville," he said grimly. "Or the minions. If they know he's dead . . ."

I nodded agreement and called out in my mind, *Pepper! Any trouble where you are?*

Nope. Everything's quiet.

We think the minions might be on their way. Warn everyone.

I strode over to Jules, knelt down beside him, and said, "I need you to stay here, Jules. With Em."

He gazed at me out of sunken, hollow eyes. "I can help you."

"You can't do that and take care of Ember, not in a fight. And if we've got any chance of getting her back, she can't be left alone." Because being alone was the thing that sent Em spiraling into bleakness, and knowing she wasn't was what tied her to the

359

world. I brushed Em's curls back from her face. "You understand that, Jules. Because you understand her."

From behind me, Hoffman said, "Your place is here now, lad. Don't worry about your friends. I'll be with them."

I wasn't sure I would have found that particularly reassuring, but it seemed to make Jules feel better. He shifted, holding Em awkwardly with one arm as he reached to pull a streaker from his pocket. He and Connor were both carrying the ones we'd brought home with us from Detention Center 1.

"Here. You might need this."

I took it and embraced him and Em both. Then I rose, turning to find that Hoffman was jamming the panel back onto his flyer. He climbed onto it, gazing at me expectantly, and I looked at Connor. "Let's go."

"Brace yourself," he warned. "Because this is going to be *fast*."

We shot upward and hurtled through the skies, so fast the skin was pushed back from my cheekbones, and I had to shut my eyes against the sting of the wind. Then Pepper's voice sounded in my head. **Red flag, Ash!**

The barricade had been breached. Whoever was coming was still about two hours away. *Pepper, we're flying. Tell Connor.* I knew there was no point in me trying to communicate with him; the wind would steal my words.

Silence, then: **Told him, Ash. He says they must have been on the road before. Which totally doesn't make sense, but he said you'd understand.**

I did. There hadn't been enough time since Terence had died for any kind of army to get here from the city, not if they'd left after he'd been killed. They had to have been on the road before then. Which meant Terence had been going to attack regardless of the outcome of the Conclave — or, no, I supposed it was possible he'd had some way to turn them back if the Conclave had gone his way. But the only thing that would have satisfied him would have been my death. *He was always coming for us.* I could see, in my mind's eyes, the convoy of trucks rolling toward the center and the grasslands, each one filled with enforcers . . . and probably minions. . . . *I have to get there before—*

Pepper's voice screamed into my mind. **Ash, Ash, Ash, Ash! The grasslands are under attack!**

My entire body went ice-cold. *How did they get there so fast?*

It's not enforcers; it's minions. The Blinker . . . and he's got a Firestarter with him—I have to go!

The silence in my head was suddenly deafening. There was a Firestarter on the grasslands, and I wasn't there and neither was Connor. Anything could be happening. Anyone could be dying. I tried to suck in air, but it was too thick and tasted strange. Smoke. I was inhaling smoke. Something was on fire. The center, or the grasslands, or both, and *I wasn't there!*

It seemed like forever before we plunged downward to the earth. I stumbled as my feet hit the ground, and righted myself. I was standing at the front of the center, near the main gates. Connor and Hoffman were with me, and ahead was the long flat stretch of gravel between the center and the grasslands.

Beyond that was fire and chaos.

The grasslands were a nightmare of smoke and heat. Saurs were screeching and rolling, trying to put the inferno out, and I could smell flesh burning. Only it couldn't be the lizards, because their armored scales protected them from fire. It was people who burned. There were still forms lying to our right, but they must still have been alive, because they were being swarmed around by Wentworth and Shona and other red-robed Menders. As I watched, Bran came tearing from the grasslands, running straight to Wentworth with a small burned body clutched to his chest. Small enough to be

Pepper—no, it wasn't her. She was standing on the gravel at the edge of the grass with her head tipped back to the sky above. *She's trying to make it rain.* Pepper was a powerful Skychanger, but it could take a while for her ability to have an effect, and anyway, rain alone wasn't going to fix this.

I screamed out in my head, *Nicky, help, help, help! I need to Sleepwalk!* There was no response. Then Connor made a choked, hurt sound, as if someone had struck him in the chest. And I knew why because I smelled it, too. There was a new scent mixed into the smoke. *Eucalyptus.*

The Firstwood was burning.

I surged forward only to be yanked back by a powerful hand on my shoulder. *Hoffman.* He'd abandoned his flyer and was standing right behind me, and he was still holding on. "Let me go!"

He tightened his grip. "What good do you think you could possibly do?"

"If I put myself in danger, Nicky might—"

"No." That was Connor, only he wasn't speaking to me. He was staring into the flames ahead. His mouth was set in a hard line, and his eyes had darkened with rage, shifting from blue to almost black. He raised his hands and took a single step forward. After a moment

his breathing grew harsh and he began to tremble. Connor was trying to do something, and whatever it was, it was taking an enormous effort.

I shook Hoffman off. He let me go this time, and I moved across to Connor, who was muttering to himself, "It's all just air. . . . Everything is encompassed by air, and I control the air. . . . *I control the air* . . . and air flows and moves and is hot. . . . Where are the places where the air is hot? . . . Where are places where something hungers? . . . I control the air. . . . I control the air and You. Can't. Have. *Any!*"

The fires went out.

I gasped, blinked, and looked again. They were still out. There was plenty of smoke and charred earth but no flames whatsoever, and while the Firstwood was too far away for me to make out any small fires burning there, I was willing to bet there were none. I looked up at Connor. "What did you do?"

"Took away the oxygen." He smiled faintly. "Fire can't live without air, you see."

His eyes rolled back in his head, and he collapsed. I caught him, staggering under his weight, and hissed at Hoffman, "Get a Mender!"

Hoffman sprinted across the gravel, and I lowered Connor to the ground. He drew in a stuttering breath and was quiet so long I began to worry he wouldn't draw another. Then he breathed again, only there was a rattling sound to it that terrified me. I put my hand on his chest, trying to pour my strength into him. "Breathe, Connor. You have to breathe." I tried not to hear Jules's desperate voice echoing in my memory: *Wake up, Red. You have to wake up.* Ember wasn't dead, and Connor wasn't going to die. I wasn't losing anyone. Not today.

Hoffman came tearing back, bringing Wentworth with him. "What happened?" she demanded. "How was he hurt?"

"He used his ability to put out the fires. I think it was too much."

"He put out the fires?" She shook her head. "You two really are extraordinary." She bent to take Connor's hand in hers. For what seemed like forever, nothing happened. Unless — was his breathing growing easier? Yes, it was, it definitely was, and the rattling noise was gone.

Pepper's voice rang out in my head. **Ash! Connor okay?** She was staring at us from where she stood at the edge of the grass.

Wentworth's healing him, I told her. *Where are the minions?*

Gone. Don't seem to be coming back. We're all watching for them.

Is everyone okay?

None of my Tribe is dead. Don't know about yours. I'll ask Jaz!

She went silent and I focused on Connor. His breathing was even better. In fact, it was close to normal. He blinked open his eyes, and Wentworth smiled at him. "You'll be fine, although you're not going to be able to use your ability for quite some time. And you need to rest. Not"—she sighed—"that I suppose you actually will. But please try."

She straightened and went hurrying back to her other patients. Connor looked at me. "Tribe?"

"Don't know. Pepper's finding out. The Saur Tribe's okay."

"Help me up."

"Don't," Hoffman said. "The Mender said to rest."

Connor shook his head. "This isn't over."

He was right. The enforcers were still coming, and the minions would be back—and with the Blinker on their side, they'd be back soon.

I wrapped my arm around Connor's waist, supporting him as he rose to his feet. Pepper's voice came again. **Ash, Jaz says—**

Only I never found out what Jaz said. There was a thumping sound that reverberated around us, and then a sharp cracking. And someone grabbed hold of my shirt and *threw* me.

I went soaring through the air. From behind me I heard a tremendous crashing noise and then I was crashing, too, tumbling to the earth. For a second I lay still, staring dazedly up at the sky. What had just happened?

"Ashala? Are you all right?"

Connor. I sat up cautiously, to find he was doing the same a few meters away from me. I was bruised all over, but nothing seemed to be broken. "I think so. You?"

He nodded. Then he focused on something behind me and paled.

I twisted to look back at the center and found that the main gates and part of the wall around them were gone. It was now a heap of composite rubble, and there were enforcers and Menders working frantically at the wreckage. *Because people are trapped.* And Connor and I had been standing right there. How had we gotten out? *Hoffman.* Someone had picked up us up and thrown us farther than any normal human being ever could have. But now I couldn't see him anywhere.

"I think Hoffman must be caught in the rubble—we've got to get him out!"

He shook his head.

"Connor—"

"Hoffman will survive, Ashala! And him helping us is for nothing if we don't find the minions. That thumping sound? It had to be a Pounder."

Of course it had, banging a fist against the base of the wall. Except too much of the wall had fallen for it to have been the work of only one. "Pounders," I corrected him.

He nodded in agreement and searched around on the ground for something. In a second I realized what. The streaker. His must have fallen when we were thrown. Mine probably had as well. I looked around and spotted it, shoving it back into my pocket. Connor found his and we pelted to the center. As we got close I saw that Pepper was hurt. She was sitting with one hand held to a bleeding head, and Wanders was in front of her, hissing and keeping the Menders at bay. "Find the Pounders," I told Connor. "I'll deal with this."

I ran to Wanders, calling out in my head, *It's all right, Wanders; they just want to heal her.* He didn't seem to be listening to me. I got closer, weaving between the Menders, most of whom were hurrying either to the patients or to the wreckage. Three were hurrying away. . . . Wait, three who were hurrying *away*? I stopped, turning toward the three Menders. The three *young* Menders. As I watched, one of them glanced to the side, and I only saw him in profile, but it was enough. I'd never forget that face. It belonged to the Boomer I'd seen at the station.

"Minions!" I shouted, pointing at them with one hand and reaching for my streaker with the other. Before I'd gotten hold of it, there was an enraged screech and Wanders-Too-Far came skittering across the gravel with impossible saur speed. He tore through the minions, crushing one Pounder under his feet, sending another one flying with a sweep of his tail, and locking his jaws around the Boomer. The second before his jaws snapped shut, the Boomer raised his hands, clapping them together.

Boom. It was a small explosion. Tiny, really. Only it spattered the gravel in the deep, rich red of Wanders's blood.

I ran to him. The Boomer was on the ground, broken and dead. And Wanders . . .

He was still alive; I could see his mighty chest moving. But all of his tail was gone, and most of his back leg, and blood was pouring out like a river.

THE RUSE

ASHALA

I raced to Wanders, screaming, "Mender! We need a Mender!"

Wentworth came running, and Connor, too. I fell to the gravel beside the fallen saur, cradling his big lizard head. Wentworth darted over to the remains of his tail and leg, and Connor stood over us with the streaker in his hand, watching for more trouble.

I am gone.

"No. *No.* Just hold on, Wanders. Wentworth's going to fix you, you'll see."

She cannot! He twisted, flinging me off and snapping at the Mender. Blood gushed even faster from his terrible wounds, and he let out an agonized scream. Wentworth scurried backward.

"She's a Mender!" I shouted. "It's okay, she's trying to help."

Someone else yelled, "No, Ash. She has to stop."

Pepper was staggering in our direction with one hand held to the wound on her head, struggling with Shona, who was running alongside and trying to heal her. She spoke again, in my mind this time. **He wouldn't be able to hunt, or run, or move. Saurs can't live if they can't be saur, Ash.**

And right on top of her voice came Wanders. **I am gone. Let me go.**

I stared down at him. His blue tongue was lolling out and his breath was whistling through his teeth. Tears started to leak from my eyes, and my chest was hurting so bad I knew this time my heart really was broken and it was broken forever. Pepper was right. If it had been a wolf, a wolf who couldn't run, couldn't hunt, I knew what the Pack would have done.

Wanders was saur. Tougher than anything.

But not tougher than this.

Wentworth edged forward again. I couldn't speak

for crying, but I shook my head at her. "You can't. . . . You can't. . . ." I reached up one hand to scrub the tears from my face and forced words out of my aching throat. "He wouldn't be able to hunt or — function. He's a *saur;* it's not like you could give him crutches or something. . . ."

Realization dawned on her face, and her shoulders slumped.

Pepper reached us and fell down beside Wanders and me. The wound on her head wasn't bleeding anymore; Shona must have managed to heal it. I put one arm around her, hugging her small body close. Wanders gazed up at her. His golden eyes were clouded with pain, except I could still see the love in them for Pepper. **We have wandered far together, you and I.**

She stroked his scales. "We've wandered the farthest, the very farthest. There'll never be another saur like you, not ever. . . ."

Wentworth suddenly spoke, in a low, urgent tone. "Ashala?"

I looked miserably over at her.

"Some lizards can regrow their tails. Can saurs?"

I shrugged impatiently. "They can regrow the end if something happens to it, but his entire tail is gone, and his leg!"

"It doesn't matter," she answered. "The point is, it's *in* him, the ability to regrow flesh. I might be able to make him whole."

It sounded impossible. It should have been impossible. But Wentworth was the strongest Mender I'd ever seen. I turned back to Pepper and Wanders. "If anyone can do this, she can. Please let her try."

And Wentworth added quickly, "If I can't do it, I promise you I'll let him go. If nothing else, I can take away some of the pain."

Pepper said nothing. Wanders did. **She can try.**

I nodded at Wentworth, who leaped forward. She settled next to Wanders, placing her brown hands gently against his black scales. I put my own hand on Wanders's neck, just to let him know that I was there and that he was with people who loved him. He'd closed his eyes, but I heard his voice faintly in my head. **You were the first human I ever met.**

"You were the first saur I ever met."

Gnaws-the-Bones would have eaten you. Or Tramples-My-Enemies. Or Hunts-the-Small.

"I know. I met exactly the right saur at exactly the right time. You saved me, Wanders." I bent to press a salty kiss to his scales. He didn't speak again.

Pepper made a choking sound, and I thought, *That's*

373

it. He's gone. But then she gasped, "Ash! Look!"

I glanced up, following the direction of her gaze to where Wentworth was sitting absolutely straight, staring at nothing. Beneath her hands, bones were growing out of what remained of Wanders's leg. My mouth dropped open as the bones stretched out to form a skeleton, and in the same moment, cartilage shot out of what was left of his tail. Wentworth started to shake and struggle for breath; she was pushing her ability to its limit and beyond. Wanders was being healed from the inside out, and it was happening faster and faster—veins appeared, and muscle, and blood and scales over the top of it all. The scales were pale blue instead of black, and his tail looked shorter than it should have been. Wentworth had done it. Wanders-Too-Far was whole.

Wentworth shuddered, slumping as Wanders raised his head to look down at himself. **I am not gone?**

The big saur began to rise. Pepper and I scrambled out of his way, and Connor dashed over to help Wentworth get clear. Wanders rolled to his feet and shook himself. He pranced, cautiously at first and then with greater confidence, swishing his new tail from side to side. Then he threw back his head and let out a saur screech. **I am here!** Pepper pelted over to him,

374

throwing her arms around the blue scales of his new leg and holding on as if she'd never let go.

Laughter bubbled up inside me, and it hurt because my throat was raw from the tears, but it was a good hurt. I looked over at Wentworth, wanting to share the moment with her. "You did it, Doc!"

She was lying limp and still in Connor's arms. And Connor was feeling for a pulse. In a second he raised his head and yelled, "Mender!"

No, no, no . . . I took a step toward them but slowed as Shona and another Mender went running past me. I didn't want to get in their way. The two of them crowded around Wentworth, asking Connor a few low-voiced questions. *Wentworth's okay. She has to be okay.* . . . After a moment the other Mender shook his head, and then Shona did.

"She can't be dead!" I protested. "She was fine just seconds ago!"

Shona sighed. "Healing the saur must have taken everything she had. She's gone."

I couldn't absorb it. My mind kept stupidly insisting that she *couldn't* be gone. But she was. Rae Wentworth, who'd saved my life more times than I could count — who'd saved Daniel's life after Neville had stabbed him — was dead. *My friend is dead.* Everything was spinning. The jump from happiness to sadness had been too abrupt, and I was disoriented, unable to get my bearings. I looked at Connor, who looked back at me — and his eyes widened in dismay, fixing on something behind me. He leaped up, reaching for his streaker, just as someone gripped my arm from behind.

Connor disappeared. *Everything* disappeared. The whole world vanished from existence, plunging me into darkness. For the space of three heartbeats, I could see nothing and feel nothing. Then the world came back.

Only I wasn't where I'd been before. I was standing on top of — a truck? I just had time to register that when someone shoved me from behind and I went hurtling toward the ground below. The streaker tumbled from my pocket, and I grabbed for it. But my grasping fingers missed, and I landed awkwardly, right on top of my arm. White-hot pain shot through me, and in the same moment, someone clasped something cold around my neck. *Rhondarite.*

I rolled to take my weight off my injured arm — and found myself staring up at Neville Rose.

He smiled his monster's smile and said, "Ashala. It's *so* nice to see you again."

I struggled to my feet, cradling my arm against my chest. My gaze darted left and right as I tried to grasp what had happened. The Blinker. He'd taken me from where I'd been and brought me . . . here. Wherever this was. No, I knew where it was. Trees, vegetation. A nearby road, with composite blocks that had been smashed through. *The barricade.* I was two hours from the center, at the edge of a big clearing that Neville was using as a camp of some kind. There was a tent, and another truck, and a bunch of enforcers. But it wasn't Neville's main army. It couldn't be, because there weren't nearly enough people here. The rest of them must still have been on their way to the center.

The Blinker appeared at Neville's side, and Neville put a friendly hand on his shoulder. "Well done, Aaron."

The Blinker stared at the ground. "I couldn't get the others, sir. I'm afraid they're dead." He winced as Neville's grip on his shoulder tightened.

I eyed the enforcers in the clearing and pitched my voice to carry. "Oh, they're *definitely* dead. Eaten by a saur." There were a few frightened reactions to that, and I started inventing gory details with enthusiasm. "Two of them got squashed and the other one had his guts torn right out of —"

"Enough!" Neville snapped. I subsided into silence, pleased to have gotten to him. Surprised to have gotten to him, actually — I would've thought it would take a lot more to provoke him. On the other hand, I supposed things weren't going so well for him today, given that Connor had put out the fires, and Wanders had killed the Pounders and the Boomer. Maybe we were winning? *Yeah, if we could just find a way to deal with whatever other minions are here, plus all the enforcers in the trucks, we'll be fine.* Not to mention that I was now a prisoner wearing rhondarite, which interfered with mindspeaking the same way it did with abilities. We weren't winning. But we hadn't lost yet.

Neville pointed to the tent at the side of the clearing. "That way, if you please, Ashala. Oh, and if you're thinking of trying to escape that collar with the master code — don't. I've made the Gull City collars quite secure again."

Figures. I moved reluctantly to the tent, hunching my shoulders. I hated having Neville at my back with a streaker in his hand. I hated having him at my back period. Every instinct I had was screaming at me to turn and face the bad thing breathing behind me. I forced myself to keep looking ahead as I reached the tent and stepped inside.

No one here. Just a desk with papers scattered across it, a chair behind the desk, and another chair in front of it. *Command post?* Neville waved me toward the chair in front of the desk. I walked over and sat down, still cradling my arm, which was either broken or badly sprained. Either way, the pain was starting to make me nauseous.

Neville sat on the edge of the desk. *Too close. Too close to me.* I gritted my teeth, trying to control the urge to lean back and put a few more centimeters of air between us.

Then Neville said, "Tell me where he is."

I stared back at him, puzzled. "Who?"

"Terence! I know it was you, Ashala—and I know you understand what he is. No one else could have harmed him. Where is he?"

My mind raced. Neville knew what Terence was but not *where* he was. Terence hadn't trusted him that far, and I certainly wasn't going to enlighten him.

"He's gone," I lied. "Completely destroyed. There's nothing left."

"I don't believe you." He gave me a slow, considering stare. "I'll bargain with you. We'll have prisoners by the end of today. I'll let you save one of them. One innocent life, rescued because of you. As long as you tell me where he is now."

He *really* wanted Terence, and I couldn't understand why. *For the minions?* But they might not even know he was dead. "I told you, he's gone."

"He can't be completely gone!" Neville snapped. "He is immortal!"

And I suddenly got it. I heard it in his voice, in the longing when he spoke the word "immortal." Jules had said Terence didn't deal well with anyone who wasn't under his complete control. I'd be willing to bet this was how he'd controlled Neville, with the promise of living forever. Except it had been a lie.

Only Ember, Delta, and Hoffman understood how to build bodies and transfer a consciousness into them. But Neville clearly didn't know that. He probably didn't even know there were other aingls, or he wouldn't have been so focused on finding Terence. And I never wanted him to find out.

"He's *gone,*" I repeated, and remembering what Terence had feared, I added, "I used my ability to make a reality where he doesn't exist."

Neville's eyes narrowed. He wasn't sure if I was telling the truth. I lifted my head and met his gaze, doing my best to give nothing away. Finally, Neville said, "Perhaps you did. Or perhaps you didn't." Gleeful anticipation flashed across his face. "I wonder how many people I'm going to have to hurt in front of you before I find out?"

I bared my teeth at him. "You can hurt as many people as you like. I can only tell you the truth." And was pleased to see a flicker of uncertainty in his expression.

He opened his mouth to say something else but was interrupted by movement at the tent opening. The Blinker poked his head through. "We're ready to go, sir."

Neville nodded. "Come inside."

The Blinker came into the tent, and five other people followed him. One I recognized — the Electrifier. The others I didn't, but they were all young. *Minions.* Two — the Electrifier and one other — were in enforcer black.

The other three were dressed in the khaki color of the Tribe.

"You and your group of friends left some clothes behind in Gull City," Neville said. "We thought we'd use them."

Well, that wasn't very smart. Did he truly believe the Tribe wouldn't recognize an impostor? Only . . . Neville *was* smart. Which meant I was missing something.

Neville strolled over to the minions. "Why don't I

381

explain our plan to you, Ashala?" He gestured to the Electrifier and the other one who wasn't wearing Tribe clothes, a short dark-haired girl. "Aaron is going to take these two to your grasslands and your Firstwood. I fear your Tribe is not going to have a good day."

Two minions. The Electrifier was incredibly powerful, and the other one could be the Firestarter. Connor wouldn't be able to put out those fires again. . . . My heart was throwing itself against my ribs like they were a cage it was trying to escape. I tried to send my feelings out to Connor. *Danger! Danger coming!* But he was a long way away, and I had no idea if he'd pick up on my emotions or if he'd be able to interpret what I was warning him about if he did.

Neville moved on, gesturing to the three in Tribe clothes. "These three, however, are going to the center. How long do you think it will take people to realize they are impostors?"

Long enough. Even a few seconds of hesitation on the part of the enforcers or ex-detainees at the center would be enough for the minions to inflict enormous damage. And they'd hesitate. They wouldn't attack until they were sure the minions weren't members of the Tribe.

"Terence is dead, you know," I told the minions.

"I killed him myself. You're doing this for nothing."

The only response I got was looks of contemptuous disbelief. They thought I was lying, and I had no way to convince them otherwise. Neville adopted the same expression, playing with us all, and I glared my hatred at him. Then he smiled his false, pleasant smile and said, "I wonder if you've discovered that abilities can be more powerful when combined?"

I tried to keep my face blank, but I obviously didn't succeed, because his smile widened. "People with the same ability can use it in conjunction with others to great effect. Like three Boomers together, for example."

One minion Boomer had brought down half the station. Three Boomers, with abilities that were more powerful when combined . . . I swallowed. "It won't work. You'll be caught."

"I don't think we will, especially when your Tribe is going to be distracted dealing with other things." The Electrifier smiled a cold smile. My stomach roiled at the thought of what waves of electricity would do to the Tribe, the trees, the animals . . . *And the other one has to be the Firestarter.* Everything was going to burn. Again.

Neville waved at the Boomers and continued, "I

think you'll find that they'll do exactly what they're supposed to. Detention Center Three will be destroyed, with Prime Willis and all her government inside."

The center was huge — they couldn't *possibly* cause an explosion that big! But I wasn't sure of that. Especially when it suddenly made sense why he'd knocked down the wall around the gates, creating a giant pile of debris that would stop him from getting into the center. If what he was telling me was true, he didn't need a way in. But he'd stopped everyone else from getting out.

And any witnesses who survived the attack would have seen three people in Tribe clothes carry it out.

Neville watched me process the implications and said, "It's a good plan, don't you think?"

Yes. I wasn't going to say it. Instead I leaned back, pretending an unconcern I didn't feel. "It's okay, I guess. Only you're not even sure it's going to work, or you wouldn't be sending an army as well."

"I'm afraid you still don't understand." He shook his head in mock sympathy. "I'm *not* sending an army. Those trucks making their way to the center are empty, apart from the drivers. My enforcers are still in Gull City."

384

That couldn't be true. It couldn't possibly be true.

Except it could.

If Neville thought he could blow up the center, then the trucks could be . . . a ruse. A distraction. And while everyone was preparing for them to arrive, the real danger was sneaking in with the Blinker. Wearing Tribe clothes.

We'll beat them. We will. But I didn't know how many of the Saur Tribe or my Tribe had been hurt in the fire. Ember was . . . sleeping. Hoffman was buried under a wall. Wentworth was dead. Connor couldn't use his ability. And I was captured. I tried to tell myself it didn't matter, that we'd beat them anyway.

But I couldn't seem to stop two voices from echoing in my memory. First Wentworth's: *You two really are extraordinary.*

Then Hoffman: *No one can be extraordinary enough to account for every variable.*

THE BEAN

GEORGIE

The Firstwood was burning.

The animals were fleeing and so was the Tribe. Above us were crows and hawks and mudlarks and yellowcrests, around our feet were lizards and pebble mice and hoppers, and all of them were crying out their fear. Helper was clinging to my hair, and we were running for the big rock ledge above the Overhang, because rocks didn't burn and there was water there, too.

We tore through the forest with the Tribe dogs sprinting alongside, herding the little ones when they wandered out of line. Then Daniel pointed behind me and shouted, "Georgie! Look!"

I looked. The fires were out. The trees and the ground were charred and smoking, but nothing burned anymore. I kept looking in case the fires came back. But they didn't.

The Tribe yelled and laughed and hugged one another. Jaz's voice sounded inside my head. **Georgie? Are the fires gone there, too?**

Yes! What happened?

Don't know. The fires just . . . went out. I haven't seen the Blinker and the Firestarter in a while, either — pretty sure they'll be back, though. Anyone hurt there?

No, we're okay. Your Tribe?

We're good. I'm gonna try to find out what happened to the fire!

There was silence in my head, and I said to Daniel, "Jaz said the fires on the grasslands are gone, too."

"Good. Did they get the Firestarter?"

I shook my head.

"We should still go to the ledge, then. In case the fires start up again."

We hurried through the forest and up the rise of the ground to the big ledge and the deep pools that dotted the orange rock. Daniel began to organize the Tribe into groups, pairing up different abilities and getting them to keep watch on one another and on all the forest that we could see from here. The fires still didn't come back. Jaz's voice did.

Georgie, the Blinker took Ash! No one knows where she is — Connor's going crazy!

I'd never heard Jaz sound frightened before, not even a little bit. He sounded a lot frightened now. I was frightened, too. *We have to find her!*

I know! I'm getting the saurs to check the grasslands — watch out for the Blinker there!

"Georgie!"

Daniel was standing in front of me and holding my shoulders. "What is it? You're shivering!"

"The Blinker has A-a-a-ssss-hhh. . . ." I couldn't speak anymore because my teeth were chattering too much to make words. Daniel wrapped his arms around me, holding me tightly until the chattering stopped. I still wasn't warm all the way, and I knew I might never be again. The blizzard was here and it wanted to eat the world.

Someone tugged at my hand. I looked down, but there was nobody there. Then I realized it wasn't a person who wanted my attention. "The bean!"

I stepped back from Daniel, reaching into the

pocket of my pants and taking out the taffa bean that Starbeauty had given me. It was the time of the bean, and if it was the time of the bean when Ash was missing, maybe the bean could help her.

I put it under my tongue.

The world grew bigger and bigger and then it broke. Now it was many worlds, a thousand possibilities that were forever changing and being changed by one another. I could See more than I ever had before, and I knew that I would be able to until the bean dissolved in my mouth.

I Saw a future.

There was a broken barricade, and a camp, and Ash! She was sitting on a chair in a room with Neville Rose. He was hurting her.

He killed her.

But that was a future and not the now.

I called out to Jaz, *I know where she is!*

How — Actually, never mind how, where?

At the barricade, in a camp, with Neville Rose.

Got it!

I tried to See Ash some more, wanting to know if I had made a difference, but the bean took me away from her futures and to another what-would-be.

The Blinker appeared with the Firestarter near the

edge of the forest. The Firestarter raised her hands, and the grasslands burned, and the Firstwood burned.

Jaz? The Firestarter's going to be at the edge of the Firstwood where the Traveler leaves the trees. She's going to be there very soon.

Hatches-with-Stars and Tramples-My-Enemies and me are on our way!

Possibilities shifted. I had spoken a warning and changed what-was-to-be, and a different future came to pass.

The Blinker appeared with the Firestarter near the edge of the forest. The Blinker disappeared. The Firestarter raised her hands, and a fireball hurtled toward the forest. Then it swerved back over the Firestarter's head and into the hands of someone who was approaching from behind her.

The Firestarter swung around.

Jaz was perched on the back of Hatches-with-Stars, tossing the fireball from one hand to another.

"Think you're a pretty good Firestarter, huh?" Jaz bared his teeth. "Think again."

The Firestarter snarled and sent flames shooting toward Jaz. But Hatches let out a defiant trill and Jaz threw up his hands, drawing the flames into his body. The flames burned brighter and hotter, and Jaz began to tremble. Then a huge black shape flashed across the grasslands. Tramples-My-Enemies extended his neck, bit down on the Firestarter's middle, and hurled her through the air into the Traveler.

There was a sudden blazing inferno in the water. The Firestarter was dead.

I saw a new image.

I was looking at some of the Tribe, only they weren't the Tribe. They were wearing Tribe clothes, but they didn't have Tribe faces. Three of them came out of the forest near the center, stepping from the trees and onto the gravel between the center and the grasslands. They mingled with the Menders and enforcers and ex-detainees, moving toward the rubble at the front that had been the main gates. When they reached it, they joined hands.

Everything exploded. Everybody died.

I called out, *Boomers are going to blow up the center. Three of them—dressed like the Tribe—they'll come out of the forest and walk up to the main gates. You've got to warn everyone! Tell them they can't let them hold hands; it does something to their ability. Makes it bigger.*

I'll get Pepper to tell 'em. And however you're doing this, Georgie—keep it up!

391

A different future unfolded, and became what was.

I was looking at some of the Tribe, only they weren't the Tribe. Three of them came out of the forests near the center, stepping from the trees and onto the gravel between the center and the grasslands.

Enforcers raised their streakers, and one of the enforcers spoke, demanding their surrender.

The minions reached for one another's hands.

The enforcers fired.

The Boomers were dead, and the center did not explode.

I had made new futures. But I hadn't seen whether I had helped Ash, and the bean was almost gone. There was only a tiny piece left under my tongue, and it was dissolving into nothing. I could hardly look ahead at all; what I was seeing was moving closer and closer to the now. The last piece of bean was almost gone when I glimpsed one final future.

The Blinker blinked. He had the Electrifier with him, and they Blinked in and out of the trees, searching for a target.

They found the Tribe gathered together on top of the rock ledge with no shelter around us. The Blinker left the Electrifier on the rock. Electricity sparked, hissing out in vicious waves, and there were screams from the Tribe as some of them died.

Except it wasn't a future. It was a now.

I had no time to warn the Tribe. I had no time to do anything other than turn and hurl my body toward where the Electrifier hadn't been a second ago but was now. Her eyes widened, and she sent a stream of electricity shooting at me. In the same moment Helper leaped from my hair, his gray body soaring through the air onto her neck. He bit, and the Electrifier collapsed.

The electricity was still in the air, arcing toward me, and I knew I hadn't Seen this in time. But it never struck me.

It never struck me because someone moving very fast materialized in front of me, and it struck him instead.

Daniel collapsed onto the rock, twitching and shaking. I fell down beside him. *Jaz! We need a Mender! Where's Stella?*

Mending Jasmine—I'll send her. Where are you?

On the rock ledge above the Overhang.

She's about half an hour away.

Daniel was still now and he seemed to be hardly breathing at all.

"Stella's coming," I said. "Everything's going to be okay."

He stared up at me out of green eyes that were hazy with pain. "Georgie . . . it's all right, you know. Starbeauty told me I might die."

"She never told me!"

"Asked her not to. She said . . . you couldn't See it . . . too close. She said . . . I could have been the sixth person whose choices mattered."

I didn't see how he could have been the sixth. Hoffman was the sixth. But I wasn't going to argue with him about who was sixth and who was not.

Daniel coughed a horrible cough that made his whole body shudder.

Jaz, Stella has to come really fast!

She is. Gnaws-the-Bones is bringing her, and she's coming as fast as she can, I promise.

Daniel's hair was falling over his face. I smoothed it back. "Stella will be here soon."

"No, Georgie . . . listen. I told Starbeauty . . . I wouldn't be the sixth. She let me choose because . . . because I am of cat. She said you would be in danger, too, and . . . if I had been the sixth that would have meant being near Ash. Not you."

He tried to reach up to me, but his arm was too

394

weak. I took his hand in mine, and Daniel said, "I chose you, Georgie." His voice was getting softer and softer, as if he were walking into the distance.

"You have to stay with me," I said. "You have to stay."

"So sorry. I don't think I can. Love you. Always . . . always with you . . ."

I kissed his hand. "I love you always and forever and in all the futures I can See and the ones I can't."

Daniel smiled. Daniel smiled at me a lot. Then his face went still and his eyes didn't see me anymore.

Georgie? Stella's about twenty—

It doesn't matter. Daniel's dead.

Oh. Georgie. I'm sorry, Georgie.

It was the Electrifier. She's dead, too.

Is anyone with you?

Daniel's with me.

Um . . . anyone else?

I don't know. I heard a chittering, and Helper scurried over, crawling up my arm and into my hair. He kept on chittering. *Look, look . . .*

I looked around. The ledge was filled with people.

The Tribe is here.

That's good, Georgie. I think you should let them take care of you now.

Jaz?

Yeah?

Daniel's dead.

I know. Georgie, I know. But Daniel would want you to let the Tribe look after you, so that's what you should do, okay?

Okay.

The Tribe did take care of me. They stroked my hair and spoke softly, and when I began to cry they all gathered around and held me tight.

I Saw no more futures.

I saw nothing.

THE SIXTH

ASHALA

The Blinker had taken all the minions now, and I couldn't bear to think of what they were doing to the center, and the grasslands, and the Firstwood, and the Tribe. I couldn't bear to think of Wentworth, or Ember, either, even though Em was only sleeping.

So I didn't. Instead I thought that the Blinker had been taking longer and longer to return, and was looking increasingly pale and exhausted. He was obviously straining his ability to well beyond its limits. Also . . . *no explosion.* It had been a while since he'd left with the Boomers, and there'd been no explosion. Maybe we were too far away to hear it? But an explosion big enough to take down the center would have to be huge. Surely I'd hear something.

Neville was sitting behind his desk, shuffling through papers like he wasn't worried. But I didn't think that was true. Leaning back in my chair, I said, "Awfully *quiet,* isn't it?"

His mouth tightened in anger, just for an instant. *Ha.* He *was* worried. *Yay, the Tribe — the Saur Tribe — the ex-detainees — whoever is interfering with Neville's plans.* Then something ripped through me, something that made me gasp for air and left me feeling like there was a giant hole in the middle of my chest. *Grief.* I'd lost someone else. *We'd* lost someone, because I must have been feeling what Connor was feeling.

"Is that arm bothering you?" Neville asked with false sympathy. "I will get you a Mender. Eventually."

I didn't care about my hurt arm and I didn't care about Neville right now, either. I tried to think a question at Connor. *Who? Connor, who?* The only answer I had was that the awful hollow feeling eased, as if Connor had sensed my response and was now shielding me from it. Someone important to me had died, and I didn't know who. Someone had died because of Neville.

Neville wasn't looking at me right now — he'd gone back to his papers — but I looked at him, or, more particularly, at the streaker that was resting beside him on the desk. I'd been thinking a lot about that streaker in the time that I'd been sitting here. I just needed Neville to move a bit farther away from it to make a grab for the thing. So far he'd kept it close.

The Blinker suddenly appeared just inside the tent entrance, swaying on his feet.

"Report!" Neville snapped. "What's happened to the center?"

"It . . . didn't blow up," the Blinker answered, staring woozily at him. "All of the others . . . captured or dead, I think."

"How?" Neville demanded.

"They knew where we were! When I Blinked in, it's impossible, but — somehow they knew."

My mouth turned up into a smile. *Georgie.* Because if anyone could have predicted where the Blinker was going to be, it had to be her. And if she'd been able to do that, it meant she was alive.

Neville's gaze flicked to me, and he saw the smile. Rage twisted his features, and he didn't take his eyes off me as he snarled at the Blinker, "Get out."

The Blinker lurched out of the tent, leaving me alone with Neville. I was in trouble. I knew that look on Neville's face, the sudden flash of fury. I'd seen it once before, when I'd spat in his face back in Detention Center 3. He had a temper, and it was vicious. *He won't kill me. Not when he wants me to tell him where Terence is.* But that didn't mean he wouldn't hurt me, and I wasn't in much of a shape to put up a fight.

Neville got up and walked around the desk to stand in front of me. "How did you do it?" he asked. "How did they know where the Blinker would be?"

There was no way in this or any other world I was giving him Georgie's name. I had to deflect him, and it wasn't going to be hard; he was already angry. I straightened, did my best to imitate an annoying Jules grin, and drawled, "Guess you're just not quite as bright as you think you are. Bet you wish you had enforcers in all those trucks now, huh?"

He backhanded me across the face, once, then again, two quick, shocking blows in succession. Pain exploded across my jaw, and I fell out of the chair, landing awkwardly as I twisted to avoid hurting my injured arm. I staggered up, ears ringing, only to be floored again by a kick to my gut. I gasped, curling up into a ball.

Neville was standing over me, breathing heavily, and there was a crazed look in his eyes that reminded me disturbingly of Terence. I'd underestimated his temper. He hadn't expected to fail here. Now he wanted someone to hurt. He *needed* someone to hurt, because that was who he was, and I was the most obvious and convenient target. I didn't think he intended to kill me. That was going to be no comfort at all if he lost control and did it by accident.

He shifted his weight, and I knew he was going to kick me again. Then there was the sound of streaker fire from outside, and the tent flap stirred. Something blurred through the air and slammed straight into Neville, knocking him to the ground. I seized my chance, scrambled up, and lunged for the streaker on the desk. I grabbed it and swiveled back to Neville — only to find that he was still on the floor.

Next to him was Alexander Hoffman, hovering on a flyer. He eyed me up and down and said, "Dear me, Ashala. You've looked better."

I gaped stupidly at him. His clothes were stained with blood, but he didn't seem to be hurt. No, he wasn't hurt *anymore*. He must have healed from whatever injuries he'd taken from being buried under a wall. He stepped down off the flyer and strode over to take the streaker from my trembling hand. "I think you'd better give that to me."

I wasn't going to argue; he was in better condition than I was. Instead I sank back down into the chair, shaking. There were still streakers being fired outside the tent—some kind of fight was going on out there. I hoped my side was winning.

Hoffman hauled Neville to his feet and pushed him over to the desk. "Sit down, if you please. Hands flat on the desk in front of you."

Neville obeyed, and Hoffman said, "I'd like the code to that collar she's wearing. Now."

"And what will you do if I don't give it to you?" Neville asked. "Kill me? I hardly think so. I'm quite sure the Pretender Prime wants to see me brought to justice."

"I don't have to kill you," Hoffman replied. "I'll just hurt you very badly. You'd be *astonished* how much pain a human being can live through." He jabbed the streaker against Neville's temple. "But I'm sure I don't have to tell a man like you that. The code. Now."

Neville spat the numbers out: "847561928."

I entered the code with clumsy fingers, feeling at the keypad. I had to get Hoffman to repeat the numbers a couple of times before I got it, but the collar finally came free. I threw it to the ground, looked up at Hoffman—and shouted a warning as the Blinker appeared behind him with a streaker in his hand.

The Blinker fired at Hoffman's back, then collapsed into a heap on the floor. Hoffman gasped, and the weapon he was holding against Neville's head slipped. It was only for a moment, but Neville took advantage of it. He twisted, knocking the streaker from Hoffman's hand and running for the entrance. I dived for the weapon. My hand closed around it and I swung it up and around, pointing it at Neville, who was halfway to the opening to the tent. "Stop or I'll shoot you!"

He stopped and turned slowly to face me. Hoffman was standing, although he looked a bit gray. "Check the Blinker," I said to him.

He went over to the boy on the floor. "He's dead."

This was the second time today I'd seen a person exhaust their ability into death. But Wentworth had done it to save a life. The Blinker had done it for, what? Neville? *No. Salvation.* Because he'd believed that having an ability or not having an ability were the categories that separated the bad from the good, the Imbalanced from the Balanced. He'd attacked us for a difference that didn't matter, and Wentworth had died, and I was uselessly angry at the sheer waste of it all.

I motioned Neville to the chair. "Sit. Try to run again and you'd better believe I'll shoot you."

"Or I will," Hoffman said. I glanced over to see he'd retrieved the streaker the Blinker had been carrying and had it pointed at Neville, too.

The tent flap opened. I spun and just about fired before I saw that it was Connor. I dropped my hand to my side, and Connor strode up to me, his gaze running over the arm I was holding against my chest to the bruises on my face. He cast a flat, furious glance at Neville before saying, "Shona's outside. She's Mending Laurie, but she'll be done soon. I'll go get her."

I shook my head. "Connor. Who?"

He didn't answer. He didn't want to answer. I glared at him. "You tell me who and you tell me who right now!"

He let out a sigh. "Daniel."

There was no name he could have said that would have been okay. No name that wouldn't have resulted in this raw grief that made me want to throw back my head and howl. But *Daniel* . . . Daniel, who could always be relied upon absolutely, and who Georgie loved so much. Daniel, the person around whom nothing ever seemed quite so difficult or so desperate. I hadn't even realized how much Daniel had been part

404

of the bedrock of the Tribe until now, when I felt as if I were standing on shifting sands that dipped and sank beneath my feet. My whole world was tilting.

Then Hoffman said, in a tone of mild curiosity, "Are you going to shoot him, Ashala?"

What was he—*Oh.* I was pointing the streaker at Neville Rose. I'd moved closer to him, too, close enough to see the sheen of sweat on his skin. For once, he was afraid of me. And he should have been. Because now *I* wanted to hurt *him.* I wanted it so powerfully I could taste it.

"Ashala." Connor moved to stand behind Neville so that he was in my line of sight. His gaze met mine, and I knew he was as heartsick as I was, and not only for Daniel, but for Ember and Penelope and everything and everyone we'd lost. It had all been too hard and too much, and today—when we'd lost Daniel and maybe Ember, too—we were both capable of doing things that we might not have done yesterday.

"Kill him if you like," Connor said. "Just be sure you can live with it afterward."

Neville opened his mouth to speak, and I growled, "Shut *up.*"

He did. He wasn't stupid; he could see I was on the edge of doing something that I'd never thought I'd do,

405

and being something that I never thought I'd be. The world would be a better place without Neville in it. Like Terence, he wouldn't stop hurting people until he was stopped. Only . . . Neville himself had said it, when he'd told Hoffman that Willis wanted him brought to justice. I wanted justice, too, and this wasn't it. Justice was everyone Neville had ever hurt getting the chance to tell their story and see him answer for what he'd done. Besides, I couldn't take Neville's life on the same day we'd lost Daniel. Because it was no way to respect who Daniel had been.

I stared into the grandfatherly face of the most evil person I knew, and lowered the streaker.

Hoffman said quietly, "I didn't think you'd do it."

And he pointed his own streaker at Neville and fired.

Neville slumped, and I staggered back, reeling from not being able to keep up with what was happening. Connor rushed across to me, throwing an arm around my waist. I leaned into him for support, staring at Hoffman as he bent over Neville to check for a pulse. He straightened and gave a satisfied nod. "He's quite dead."

For a stunned moment I just stared at him. Then I yelled, "What did you *do*?"

He sighed. "You are a child of the new world, Ashala. A hero of it, even. But I . . ." His face grew hard and grim. "I am of the old." He nodded at Neville. "And so was this man. There were thousands like him in my time. People who could wrap foul deeds in righteous words. Men and women who made it acceptable for others to give voice to their hate and their petty desire to hurt or humiliate or exclude." His face grew grimmer still. "You have no idea—*none*—of the true scale of the evil of which people like Neville Rose are capable. Nor should you. His time has passed." He looked over at me and added, "So you see, he had to die."

"I don't see that," I snapped. "Because we're better than him, and we're better than killing him, and *you* . . ." I glared at Hoffman, sick with disappointment in him even now. "You're the one who told everyone we had to be better! You said . . . about the Balance and, and caring for one another and the earth—and I *believed* in you!"

It was a ridiculous thing to say. I knew it was a ridiculous thing to say, and I expected him to laugh at me.

He didn't, although his lips did quirk into a smile. Except he seemed to be laughing at himself. "How very strange. Because in the end, Ashala, I believed in you. I might have written of the ideals that would make this earth a better place. You, however—you are the one who can live by them." His gaze returned to Neville, and his smile vanished. "You are better than killing him. But not I."

The tent suddenly seemed too small and too closed in. I pushed away from Connor, needing space and air. "It's too small . . . too close . . ." Something was building in me, a pressure that needed to be let out. I had a sudden, deep sense of the wrongness of everything, a world gone twisted with hate that was supposed to be better than the old one but wasn't in so many ways. Even Alexander Hoffman, the person who'd actually written the "Instructions for a Better World," couldn't live by his own words.

I flat-out screamed my anger and frustration, "It isn't supposed to be like this!"

And I heard Nicky bark. "Woof!"

The tent disappeared. Then it came back, but only for a moment before vanishing again. Everything kept flashing in and out. Here, and not. Here, and not.

Someone shouted, "Ashala!" *Connor.*

I opened my mouth to say, "I'm here."

But I was not.

THE AWAKENING

ASHALA

I was in the Firstwood. There was movement in the trees ahead, and laughter. It sounded like two little girls, giggling together.

"Hey!" I called. "Who's there? Wait up!"

They took off running. I could hear their footsteps pelting along the ground, moving away from me. I ran after them. But no matter how fast I went, I always seemed to be just a bit behind, and I couldn't catch up. Then I broke out of the trees and onto the grasslands — and there they were. A smiling girl with ribbons in her hair, holding the hand of a chubby brown-skinned kid. Penelope, and Cassie, my long-lost baby sister.

Someone else said, "Hey, Ash." I turned to see that Daniel was there, too. I hugged them one by one, so happy to see them all I just about burst into tears. "You're here! You're okay! I thought . . . I thought you were . . ." I stopped. "You're not really here, are you? You're dead." The weight of grief came crashing back down on me. "I'm asleep and this is a dream." Then I brightened. "I can do anything I want in my dreams! Maybe I can bring you back!"

Cassie shook her head. "This isn't your dream, silly! It's ours."

I didn't understand. "How can it be yours?"

Cassie went twirling around in a circle. "You remember, Ash. I dreamed about running away somewhere where you and me and Georgie could live together forever and ever."

"And," Pen said, "I dreamed about a place where no one took dogs away from kids who loved them *very much*."

Daniel said, "I dreamed of a magical place where I could Run as much as I wanted." His lips curved into a smile that was a mixture of sweetness and sadness. "And of a magical girl."

Cassie said, "So you see, Ash, it's our dream. And you don't want to take it away from us, do you?"

"Of course not, but—"

"The thing is," Daniel interrupted, "lots of people have a dream like ours. Only it doesn't come true for everyone."

Cassie stopped twirling. "That's why you're here, Ash. You have to make it come true. Like you did for us." She frowned. "Except some people aren't very nice."

"Like the Blinker," Pen said. "He wasn't nice."

That was true, only it wasn't the whole truth. "Yeah, but—he didn't start out not nice. I don't think anyone starts out not nice. They just start out as people."

"So what changes?" Daniel asked.

"The world changes people," I said. "Or people change the world—and everyone is supposed to know that what matters is that they *are* nice. To one another, and the earth."

"So show them, Ash!" Pen said.

"I don't know how!"

"Yes, you do," Daniel said. "You've always known."

I did. This was my dream, and I could do anything I wanted, and what I wanted was to bring the whole world into it. But I hesitated. To dream this dream I was going to have to go somewhere else.

"Will you all still be here when I get back?"

They laughed, like I'd said something hilarious. "We're always here, Ash," Penelope said. "We're just a little way ahead, for now."

That was okay, then. I turned and walked back into the Firstwood, wandering through the trees until I found one in particular. The first tuart I'd ever met on the day I'd come to the forest. This was when I'd known that I belonged. That I was part of the Balance, and I mattered as much as anybody else.

I turned, leaning my back against the tree. Then I closed my eyes and imagined a world. A world of connections, where everyone understood that the difference between good and bad was the difference between the people who valued those connections and the ones who didn't. Only it wasn't just a world for organic humans or synthetic ones. It was for trees and saurs and rivers and flowers and rocks. It was for wolves and yellowcrests and spiders and hawks and crows, and for all life everywhere. All of us or none of us. *All life matters or none does. All people matter or none do.*

This was the world that was meant. I imagined it,

holding it in my mind. Then I looked at the world that was.

Everything connects, Grandpa had told me once, *but not everyone sees those connections.* I could sense the fragmentation, the disconnection from others and from the earth. I knew every variety of it. The twisted viciousness of Neville and Terence. The indifference of Citizens who never spoke out about the accords because they didn't think our suffering was theirs. The minions, who'd hated themselves so much they'd been willing to do anything to anybody to be part of the world that rejected them.

I couldn't force anyone to be any different than what they were. It had to be their choice. All I could do was show them how things could be. So I reached out to place my hands on the web of connections that made up the world, the ones that people sometimes didn't see. They linked everyone together whether they knew it or not, which meant this was how I could reach everybody. I gave the world a dream of a better one, the one that was meant. *Feel what I feel.*

The dream traveled, flowing along the links that tied everyone to one another. Except my reach didn't extend far enough. I wasn't getting to everybody. But the ones I had reached responded. Not everyone liked the dream. Some people ran from it, and some turned away, and some thought it was a nightmare. But some reached out and grasped it, and I suddenly found I was stronger and could reach farther. They became part of me and I became part of them, and now we shared the dream and expanded together. *Feel what we feel. See what we see.*

More dreamers joined us, and more, until we were thousands. Except I knew we still weren't enough. We couldn't quite encompass the world. Then another set of dreamers came, and while I didn't recognize all of them, I knew some. Grandpa. Starbeauty. *Feel what we feel. See what we see.*

I was starting to shake. My legs went out from under me and I fell, crashing to the ground. *I can't dream anymore.* Except I knew I had to. I had to dream until there was nothing left in me to give. That was what dreams demanded. So I poured out everything I saw, everything I felt, and everything I was. I gave myself to the world and the hope of a better one.

Something left me. It flew out of my chest and became energy, scattering to become part of all that was. That was okay, because it was where it had come from to begin with. And I knew I'd finally given enough.

I drifted into peaceful darkness, and sleep.

Someone said, "Ashala!"

I opened my eyes, annoyed—and found to my surprise that I was floating among stars. Something shining coiled around me, twisting and dipping until I was staring into a familiar Serpent face. **Hello, Granddaughter.**

"Hi, Grandpa!"

You have become as you were meant and dreamed of what was meant. And it has taken something from you, as all great dreams must.

"Oh, yeah? What?" But I knew. "My ability. It's gone, isn't it?"

Yes.

I had a dim idea that it was important, but it was difficult to gather up the energy to care. "Can I sleep now?"

No. His eyes swirled. **I gave him back to you once. Now I am giving you back to him.** He flicked out his big tongue, licking the whole of my face.

"Eww, Grandpa, that's disgu—"

He was gone. There were no stars, only darkness. I could hear a voice, the same one that had been speaking before. "Ashala!"

I blinked, and everything came back. I was lying

on the ground, looking up at trees and at the people looking down at me. Hoffman. Shona. Laurie. And Connor, pale and shaking. I reached up to put my hand against his cheek.

"Are you all right?"

"Am I—" He broke off, shaking his head. "Yes, I am all right. Now."

He put an arm under my shoulders, helping me to sit up. I was surrounded by trees, but they weren't tuarts; I must be in the forest around Neville's camp. "Wasn't I in the tent before?"

"I carried you out," Connor answered. "You kept saying it was too small . . . then I realized your ability had kicked in. . . ." He sighed and drew me against him.

Shona reached across to wrap her fingers around my wrist. My arm didn't hurt anymore. "Shona, you Mended my arm?"

"Your arm was the least of your problems," she told me. After a second she let me go. "Well, despite everything, you're okay." She rose to her feet. "I'd better go help Bran with the enforcers."

Laurie beamed at me. "I'm glad you're alive and not dead like Neville Rose, Ashala Wolf!" Then he turned and trotted off after Shona.

Everyone seemed to be very concerned with my

health. I cast a questioning glance up at Connor, who said, "You stopped breathing."

Oh. "I was dreaming."

"We know," Hoffman replied. "We saw it."

"You did?"

"Versions of it, anyway. As far as we can work out, everyone experienced something different." He stood and added, "You may just have saved humankind, Ashala—and you should be careful about that, you know. When you've done it once, people expect you to do it *all* the time."

He strode off into the trees, leaving me alone with Connor.

"I don't understand," I said.

"You . . . showed everyone. What it was to belong. How we're all connected. Everyone saw it differently, but, well—if you can walk, we can go to the clearing and you'll see."

I lurched up to find that my legs were weak. Connor put his arm around me, and we made our way through the forest together. As we went, I asked, "How'd you even all get here?"

"Laurie carried Shona and Ran. Bran and I balanced on the flyer with Hoffman. As to how we knew where to come—Georgie Saw it, in a future."

"How is she?"

"I don't know," he answered. "Last I heard from Jaz he said the Tribe was with her."

I needed to get back to her, only it seemed like there was trouble here. Now that we were closer to the clearing, I could hear a lot of sniffling sounds. "Is that crying?"

"Wait and see." I could hear the smile in his voice; whatever was ahead was nothing bad.

We emerged through the last of the trees. The enforcers who worked for Neville were sitting on the ground, confined by shrubs that had snaked up to bind their hands and feet. Some of the enforcers were staring straight ahead, looking numb and shocked. A few seemed angry. Many were crying. And the rest kept trying to catch Shona's attention, or Laurie's, or Bran's, babbling, "I'm sorry! I'm sorry!"

"Yes, yes, we know you're sorry," Shona told them, sounding harassed. "There's really no need to keep saying it!"

I'd dreamed a dream for the world, and the world had dreamed it back. But all I wanted to do right now was return to my world, my trees and my Tribe.

"Connor? Let's go home."

THE BEGINNING

ASHALA

Darkness, and me.

I was floating, as I had been before the memories started. Before I'd lived it all again, this time seeing it through Georgie's eyes as well as my own. I liked the darkness; I needed the peace after having experienced everything for the second time around. Except that a lot of it had been for the first time around. Maybe all of it had been, because putting Georgie's memories together with my own changed the way I saw things.

The darkness began to fade. I tried to hold on to it, but it slipped away, delivering me back into the world.

My eyes blinked open, and I found myself staring up at the flat ceiling of the room where we'd revived Alexander Hoffman. Then Hoffman himself came into view, leaning over me.

"How do you feel?" he asked.

Exhausted. Heartsick. "Thirsty."

Someone else moved across to me. Connor, bringing a bottle of water. I sat up so I could drink, guzzling the cool liquid. Between swallows, I asked, "How long?"

"You've been unconscious for about a day," Connor said.

One day? It seemed a lot longer than that. But it *had* been a lot longer than that, because the events I'd lived through, and that Georgie had lived through, had happened over the course of a couple of months. Apparently remembering it all didn't take anywhere near as long as actually experiencing it.

Hoffman reached across to disconnect the nanomite drip from my arm, and then started on the wires on my head. It had been a month now since the Awakening, during which time Hoffman had gone to visit his children in Spinifex City and returned again. He was due back there in another week; Leo had him on a visitation schedule to make sure he didn't lose contact with the aingls. I had no idea if Hoffman would keep to it, only . . . he might. Seeing Georgie's memories had shifted my perception of him again.

"You didn't have to kill Neville to save me," I told him. "But I know you were trying to help my Tribe help me, so — thanks."

"I didn't do it to save you," he replied. "I did it to save the world — as I said before, Rose had to die." He pulled the last wire off my head. "There. You should suffer no ill effects from the memories, but let me know if you do. And try not to take things so to heart, Ashala. Not everything is about you. In fact, for the most part" — he winked — "everything is about me."

Hoffman strolled out, and Connor said, "Tell me what you saw."

"You're not going to like it."

He climbed up onto the table and sat with his legs swinging over the side. "Tell me anyway."

So I did, starting at the beginning — at Georgie's beginning, with the Foretelling — and moving all the way through to the end. When I'd finished, Connor said in a stunned voice, "They were trying to save us?"

"They did save us."

"Penelope . . . Starbeauty . . . Nicky . . . Ember . . .

Jules . . . Daniel . . . Hoffman?" He drew in a sharp breath and shook his head. "Did they really think we'd let them?"

"They knew we wouldn't. That's why they didn't tell us."

He fell silent. I knew he'd be absorbing this for days, and so would I. Right now there was something I absolutely had to do. I climbed off the table. "I need to talk to Georgie."

"No."

"No?"

"She came in while you were unconscious and said when you wake up you go see Ember."

"Oh. Well, I guess I have to go see Ember."

We walked back through the tunnels and into the caves. The world had changed in the month since Daniel's death. It hadn't taken Willis long to get her city back with Terence and Neville gone, plus the effect I'd had on everyone with the dream I'd shared. Not everyone believed in that dream, but enough people did to cause a shift in the way people with abilities were treated. The Primes had held an emergency Council meeting, and they'd all voted to continue with the repeal of the accords. Detention centers everywhere were in the process of being closed. And Detention Center 3 — which had been a center, and then a museum, and then the home of the government — was going to become a school. But not just any school. It would be the first-ever school for children to learn how to use their abilities, and Shona and Laurie would be among the first teachers.

We wound our way through the passages until we came to the cave where Ember was sleeping. She was lying on a bedroll near the opening onto the forest, surrounded by the things the Tribe had brought her — shells, and feathers, and drawings, and so many flowers that this place was starting to look like a garden. Nicky was lying across her feet, and Jules was sitting at her side, speaking softly. He never did run out of things to say to her.

He looked up as we came in, tired hazel eyes focusing on me. "Guess you know it all now, huh?"

"Yeah." I tried to think of everything I needed to tell him, how I felt about what he'd done and why. In the end I found I could sum up my acceptance of it, and him, in a single word. "Yellowcrest."

He smiled something approaching his normal crooked smile. "Guess so." Then his gaze shifted back to Em and the smile faded. "Did you . . . was there anything that might help her? In the memories?"

"I don't know yet. I think it's going to take me some time to process it all."

He nodded, his attention drifting back to Em. He seemed to have lost a little more weight in the space of the day since I'd last seen him, and gotten paler, too. I flicked my gaze toward Connor, then at Jules, and Connor understood.

"Come and get some food, Jules," he said. "Ashala will sit with Em for a while." When Jules didn't move, Connor strode over and bent to grip his arm. "You have to maintain your strength. For her."

Jules rose reluctantly and followed Connor out of the cave. Nicky rolled to his feet and trotted over, nuzzling at my hand. I petted his ears, my dog who'd preserved my chance to save the world. He'd activated my ability in the moment when I could dream a dream for everybody, and now enough of the world was trying to live the dream that there wouldn't be a blizzard of disconnection. People wouldn't become blind to other people's existences, or deaf to their voices, or cold and indifferent to their pain.

"Thank you," I told him. Nicky licked my fingers and bounded out after Jules. He'd been spending a lot of time with Jules; he knew Jules needed a guardian of his own right now.

I went and sat by Em, staring down into her still face.

"I know everything now," I told her. "I know you did this to save me. But you can't be sure it was necessary, or you would have come back." I sighed. "And I think the reason you can't be sure is because you blame yourself for Terence. You think that if you'd done something differently somewhere along the way, he would've been different. That's why you can't be sure — you think you could have kept it from coming to this. But there was something wrong with him, Em, and I don't think you could ever have put it right. So please — you have to wake up!"

Nothing. Then someone spoke from the entrance. "Ash?"

I shot to my feet. "Georgie!"

She took a few uncertain steps into the cave. "Are you mad at me, Ash? Now that you know what I was doing?"

"No. Georgie, no." I strode forward to hug her, holding her tight. "Of course I'm not mad."

"Are you sure?"

I stepped back so that I could look into her face

and she could look into mine. "Georgie, I wish none of you had made the choices you did. Because I'm not worth . . ." My voice cracked. I stopped, drew in a breath, and began again. "I'm not worth the sacrifice. But I'm not mad and I'm not going to say those choices were wrong now. Not after everything that's happened and after everything everyone gave up for me. Otherwise it'd be like you all worked really hard to give this gift, and I just threw it away. So I won't do that." I wiped at my eyes and added, "All I can do now is value the gift, and be grateful for it, and you. Even though I don't deserve it. And I don't deserve you, either."

"You do, Ash! We all deserve one another. That's why we're Tribe." She took hold of my arm and drew me out of the cave into the passageway, saying in a whisper, "I heard what you were saying to Em."

She'd been in the doorway longer than I'd realized, and I wasn't sure why we needed to be out here whispering about it, but that was okay. She'd have a reason, and she'd explain it me when it was right to explain. "She won't wake up, Georgie."

"No, except, Ash, I asked Daniel something once." She paused, her lips curving into the smile she always smiled when she said his name now, a mixture of sweetness and sadness. "I asked him how you were always so sure of which world was real. And he said it was because you knew I needed you to be sure. And you see, now Em needs someone to be sure."

"You think that's all I have to do? Be sure? Just . . . sound certain?"

Georgie shook her head. "No. I did think that, but then I had another thought, and my other thought was, maybe it isn't you Ember needs to be sure."

She moved past me into the cave and settled on the ground next to Ember. I followed to sit on Ember's other side. Then Georgie reached for Em's hand, and when she spoke it was in a tone I'd never heard from her before—crisp and clear and totally confident. "It's Georgie, Em. I want you to know that I made a map. A Terence map, and I looked at all the things your brother could have been. And he was never any different. You couldn't have changed him, and in every single future that *would* have been after the Conclave, he killed Ash. Sometimes he sent other people, and sometimes he did it himself, but he always killed her. You took his life to save her life, Em."

I gaped at her, realizing why she'd been whispering

outside. She hadn't wanted Ember to overhear us and have exactly the same doubt I was having right now. Because Georgie could have Seen all those things. She could have made a Terence map and Seen everything she'd described.

Or she could just know that Ember needed her to be sure.

"Ash? Did she just move?"

I looked at Ember, hoping so hard it hurt. "I don't know!"

We searched for any sign of life. But Ember was as still as she'd been before, and — no. Wait. "I think . . . Georgie, are her eyelids fluttering?"

"Her hand! Ash, her hand just twitched!"

I started to shake Em, gently but firmly. "Ember? Wake up! Wake up, wake up, wake up!"

Her eyes blinked open. "Ash?"

"Yes! It's us, Em, it's me and Georgie! Um — you should sit up! Sit up so you don't fall back asleep."

Between us, Georgie and I helped her into a sitting position, the both of us grinning like idiots at each other and at Em. Ember gazed around the cave in bewilderment. "I'm in the caves? I — I was on the Steeps."

428

"That was a month ago, Em!"

"A month?" She clutched at my arm. "My family . . . Neville . . ."

"Your family is in Spinifex City, and Neville is dead. It's over, Em. It's all over."

"Over? You mean . . . Ash, did we win? Is everyone okay?"

"We won," I answered quietly. "But everyone isn't okay." I looked across at Georgie, who was staring down at the ground and not smiling anymore. Then I looked back at Em and said the words I knew Georgie didn't want to have to say, that she should never have to say. "Daniel's dead, Em. Everyone else is okay, Jules is okay, but . . . Daniel's dead."

Ember drew in a breath that had a whimper at the edges of it, and then another. She turned to Georgie, reaching out to lay a hand very gently on hers. "I'm so sorry."

Georgie threw her arms around Em and buried her face against her hair, and I hugged them both. The three of us sat there like that for a while, saying nothing and grieving together. Eventually we broke apart, and I began to tell Ember the story of everything that had happened since the Steeps. Sometimes Georgie interrupted and sometimes she was quiet. At the end of it she stood up, holding out her hands to me and Ember both, and said, "You have to come."

She took us through the tunnels and into a cave, this one with a massive opening onto the trees that flooded the space with air and light. There was a map against one wall, and a pug dozing in the sunshine. The day after Daniel had died, Mr. Snuffles had come back, and he'd come back to take care of Georgie. She didn't miss meals anymore, not when Mr. Snuffles would bring her dead animals if she forgot to eat. She didn't map for too long, either, because if he thought she was getting tired, he'd tear her spare vines into pieces. Georgie had helped Mr. Snuffles when he'd been sad, and now he was helping her.

Georgie pulled Ember and me over to the map and said, "This is our futures. Look!"

Em and I both looked. Helper darted across the map. I didn't yell and leap backward like I would have done before. I wasn't so scared of spiders now that I'd seen them through Georgie's eyes. Helper stopped, then scurried somewhere else, then stopped, then scurried—he was trying to show us something. In all the places where he was pausing there were three river stones with connections clustered around them. In fact, the entire map was more like a bunch of mini maps joined together, of the stones and their connections, and then another map of the stones and their connections, and then another . . .

"Georgie? Are those stones meant to be me and you and Ember?"

"Yes, and all the links around us are the Tribe. Cassie is here, too, Ash because she's Tribe as well, even though she died before there was a Tribe, in this life. But that doesn't mean she always will."

My jaw dropped. *Our futures.* "Are you saying — in different lifetimes? The Tribe is always together?"

Georgie nodded, and Ember reached out to run trembling fingers over the stones. I knew what this meant to her. Like Leo, she'd once doubted she had a spirit that could take her to the Balance and lives beyond this one. "How many lifetimes?" she breathed.

Georgie smiled a sad, sweet smile. "All the ones I can See."

Daniel would be back again. And Penelope, and Cassie. We would all be back again. That didn't keep us from missing them in the now. But they weren't gone for always. I reached for Ember's hand, and Georgie's — and for a while, the three of us looked ahead.

Then Jaz's voice sounded in my mind. **Ash! Connor says, Where are you? And Jules says, WHERE ARE YOU AND WHAT HAVE YOU DONE WITH EMBER? He's kind of freaking out.**

Tell Connor we're in the cave where Georgie's been making her latest map. And tell Jules—Ember's awake.

Oh, yeah? 'Bout time!

Jaz's voice vanished. Before long there were pounding steps in the passage outside and Jules burst in, followed by Connor and Nicky. Em pulled her hand free of mine to run to Jules, and the two of them collided, clinging to each other as if they'd never let go. Nicky circled around them both before settling at Em's side, pressing against her leg with his tail thumping against the floor.

She reached down to pat his ears, and Jules asked anxiously, "Do you need anything, Red? Is there anything I can get you? Water, or food, or—your dad's in the forest if you want to see him."

Ember glanced at the map and smiled a bright, open smile. I'd never seen her look so . . . young. "I want to see the Tribe, Jules. Dad, too, but first take me to the Tribe!"

Then Em caught sight of Connor. She ran over to hug him, and he hugged her in return before she darted back to Jules, throwing her arms around his waist. He put his arm across her shoulders, and the two of them walked out together with Nicky trotting along behind them.

There was a snorting sound below me. Mr. Snuffles was sitting at Georgie's feet. He snorted again before waddling off in the direction of the entrance. Georgie let go of me and went after him.

"Wait!" I said, hurrying across to her. "Are you going somewhere?"

"Mr. Snuffles doesn't like it when I never go outside," Georgie answered. "So I'm going outside."

"I could come outside as well! If you want me to, that is."

She sighed. "You keep doing this, Ash."

"Doing what?"

"Worrying, and asking over and over again if I'm all right, and following me everywhere."

Okay, when she put it like that it sounded really annoying.

"You have to let me be sad, Ash," she said. "You have to let me be sad in my own way, and happy in my own way, too."

In other words, *Back off.* And if Georgie's memories had shown me anything, it was how much it mattered to give her the space to be herself. I stepped away, physically giving her room to breathe, and said quietly, "I understand you."

Her eyes lit up, and she turned to follow Mr. Snuffles out of the cave with a skip to her step.

I let out a breath I hadn't even realized I'd been holding. "She's going to be all right."

"Yes," Connor agreed. "Will you?"

"I didn't lose you."

"You lost your ability."

"That's nothing!"

He walked over until he was standing in front of me. "Just because other losses are bigger doesn't make losing your ability nothing. You're allowed to miss Sleepwalking."

"I do miss it," I admitted. "It's like—a piece of me is gone and I don't quite know who I am yet without it there."

He reached out to clasp my hands in his and moved even closer, bending to speak against my ear. "Close your eyes, Ashala."

I did, and he said, "Feel what I feel."

Air. I could sense the air. Connor was sharing his ability, or at least the way it felt to him. My senses

434

seemed to expand outward, traveling along currents, and I knew I wanted to *fly*. The air responded, catching us up and sending us spiraling out of the cave and through the trees to the sky above. We turned in a slow spin above everything, and my eyes were still closed, but I didn't need them to see. The air showed me the Firstwood in a way I'd never seen it before. It swirled through the trees and around the Tribe, here and alive and safe. It shivered over rippling water, swept through the caves, and made the leaves dance. And it traveled beyond the trees to the grasslands, where the saurs and the Saur Tribe were teaching the new hatchlings to hunt. Air was in everything, and everything was in air, and to hold it was to encompass the world.

I opened my eyes to look up at Connor, grinning in sheer delight, and he grinned back at me. Then he bent his head to mine, and we breathed each other in.

When the kiss ended I rested my head against his shoulder, and we continued our gentle spinning across the skies. This and every other moment was Penelope's gift to me, and Daniel's — and I knew I'd been stupidly wrong about something. The story told by Georgie's memories and mine hadn't been the one I'd thought it was going to be, because it hadn't been a tale about what the world had done to extraordinary people. It had been a tale of how extraordinary people had turned the world with their choices and changed it for the better.

I gazed out over the tuarts, and thought, *This is the story of how they lived.*

AUTHOR'S NOTE

So we come to the end. Anyone following this series
from the beginning knows it was originally intended
to be four books. But when I came to write this book,
I realized it was a trilogy, and as the story developed
I understood why I'd initially thought this last book
was two instead of one. This final story is told in two
voices, and that is only the beginning of its dualities,
which readers can discover as they like. To me, one of
the most interesting parallels is that between Hoffman
and Ashala, the heroes of the old world and the new.

This book is also the story of the three girls — one
to look behind, one to look into the now, and one to
look ahead. And here at the end, I thought I would

say a little about past, present, and future in the Tribe series.

The Citizenship Accords are not really an invention. They are based on legislation that applied to Aboriginal people here in Australia, and particularly on the Western Australian Natives (Citizenship Rights) Act 1944 (which was finally repealed in 1971). This legislation offered a strange kind of citizenship, if it could be called that, because what it did was exempt Aboriginal people who obtained a citizenship certificate from the discriminatory restrictions that only applied to them in the first place because they were Aboriginal. These restrictions included being unable to marry without the government's permission or even to move around the state. Citizenship could be easily lost, for example, by associating with Aboriginal friends or relatives who did not have citizenship. Many Aboriginal people referred to citizenship papers as dog licenses or dog tags — a license to be Australian in the land that Aboriginal people had occupied for more than sixty thousand years.

What about the present? The Tribe series tells of a world in which the young are in danger, and for far too many of the young across our planet, this is not a tale of fiction. It is their every day. So in many ways these books reflect the truth known to every child and teenager who has ever been in real trouble: adults will fail you. I do think that we, the collective adults of this earth, are letting down the next generation to a truly spectacular degree—which is why in the Tribe series it is a teenager who saves the world. The hope for the future rests, as perhaps it always has, with those who come after us.

What then of the future itself? In *The Disappearance of Ember Crow*, Ashala speaks of a fight bigger than any that has gone before, but it is not a conflict between the privileged of her society and those who are not. It is a fight between those who want to stop the hating and those who don't. I believe humanity is in that fight now, and it might well define what is to come for our species. In *The Foretelling of Georgie Spider*, a better future is ultimately created by the global interconnection of those who choose compassion over intolerance, courage over fear, and love over hate.

Perhaps this could be the real world.